ESSENCE
OF FEAR
BOYKOV BRATVA

BETHANY-KRIS

Published by Bethany-Kris

www.bethanykris.com

ISBN: 978-1-989658-23-9

Editor: Nina S. Gooden

Cover Design © London Miller

This is a work of fiction. Names, characters, places, organizations, corporations, locales and so forth are a product of the author's imagination, or if real, used fictitiously. Any resemblance to a person, living or dead, is entirely coincidental.

CONTENTS

PROLOGUE

"NOW, WHAT are you going to do for me, Pavel? Tell me, yes?"

Pav kept a tight hold on the comic book in his twelve-year-old hands as he glanced up from the glossy cover featuring a man in a red cape to see his father staring at him from the driver's seat. He'd been too distracted by the fact he had a comic book to even realize his father was speaking to him.

He didn't get comics often.

Rarely, actually.

It wasn't that his father, Dimitri, didn't want to give him things, Pav knew. Dimitri gave Pav as much as he possibly could, but only *when* they were having a good month. Or, that's how his father always put it whenever he came home with a little toy or a bag of sugary sweetness for Pav.

A good month, son. It's been a good month for the boss.

Pav never thought his father meant *he* was the boss, though. Dimitri was always careful to make that clear. *Kotovs aren't anything but scum to use or wipe off around here, yeah? Remember that, Pav.*

And he did.

Remember it, that was.

"Well?" his father demanded.

Dimitri's dark eyes darted from where Pav was sitting in the passenger seat to the big building in front of them. Well, *one* building. It looked like one of many that was connected to other buildings. A few dark-colored cars were parked haphazardly throughout what might have been a parking lot, but there weren't exactly lines to designate spots for the vehicles.

Pav had never been here before. Anytime his father worked, Pav stayed with one of Dimitri's friends.

Looking at the dark, looming building, he wished he could have gone to his father's friend's home instead. One was a man they lived with; another was a nice lady with crinkly skin and white hair who always smelled like bread and reminded him of what he thought a grandmother would be like ... you know, if he had one.

He didn't, though.

1

He didn't have a grandmother, or even a mother, for that matter. He didn't even know his mother's name. Dimitri said the dead should stay dead, especially when the dead was *that* kind of dead. Pav wasn't sure what that meant.

But he had a bed that was clean, with sheets that had his favorite superhero printed on them. And he had a few toys that he took special care not to break because he knew to take care of his shit, as his father liked to say. And, of course, he had his dad, too.

His dad who kept him warm, fed, and clothed. His dad who never raised a hand to him and kept him out of trouble.

Pav didn't want much more.

"Pavel," his father said. "What did I tell you?"

Pav held tight to the comic and glanced down at the glossy cover again. "Stay here, don't get out of the car, and be quiet."

Dimitri's shoulders relaxed a bit, and his stare softened. Without a word, his father reached over, cupped his head in his large palm, and drew Pav close enough to hug him and press a kiss to the top of his forehead.

"That's it, my boy. That's it. I'll be out in a few."

He thought he heard the shake in his father's voice, but he couldn't be sure. That was the thing about Dimitri Kotov. Even when he was afraid of something, he didn't show it. He taught Pavel to be brave in that way.

"Don't you get out of this fucking car; I *will* be right back."

His father said it like Dimitri was the one who needed to hear it, and not Pav. He didn't get the chance to ask his father about it, though, because in the next second, Dimitri was out of the car and slamming the door to their shitty Corolla shut before Pav could even open his mouth.

He watched his father walk toward the building and waited for Dimitri to glance over his shoulder even once. He didn't.

That was the last time Pav ever saw his father. Walking into the Boykov Compound. Dimitri never came back out.

Not alive, anyway.

• • •

Pav was still clutching to that comic book hours later when he was dragged across the cement floor of the Boykov Compound and tossed at the feet of a man who, from the ground looking up, seemed bigger than a bull.

And the man looked about as irritated as a bull, too.

Sneering a bit at him, the man nudged at the comic book in Pav's hands with the tip of his shoe. "What is your name, child?"

Pav heard the shudder of papers, caused by the comic book's pages fluttering as his hands shook. He bet his eyes were peeled as wide as they could go as he struggled to find words to say to this large, domineering man waiting for an answer.

Around him, shoes shuffled on the floor, and a cough echoed. Other than that, it was all silence and fucking *dampness*.

He would remember that the most about this place, later in life when he relived these memories. The dampness and silence.

"*Your name.*"

"Pa-Pavel," he whispered.

The man above him grunted, and Pavel tried to ignore the stinging in his arms and legs from the many scratches and scuffs he'd received as he'd fought against the men who had dragged him out of his father's car.

Dimitri had told him to stay, after all.

They didn't listen, though.

"Could just … get rid of it," a man behind Pavel suggested. "I know the kid's father—there ain't a person to take him, boss. He's got no family. A mother who died from shooting poison in her veins, and everybody else is gone, too, or they want to stay gone because of what his father was involved with."

Again, the man above him grunted as cold, gray ices looked Pav's way once more. "Seems a shame, no? A child as a sacrifice because his father's a thief. But what else could be done with him? Look at him—small, and frightened. Like a puppy."

"Puppies can be trained and *kept*," someone else muttered.

The man's eyes lit up for a minute as he regarded Pav with a hint of a smile forming. "Yes, trained and kept. Just like a *puppy*."

Pav blinked.

What?

The large man kneeled down, but was careful to never let his dark, fitted suit touch the dirty cement floor as he came eye level with Pav. He pointed between Pav's wide-eyed gaze with two fingers, and then at his own narrowed eyes in the same way.

"I see you, Pavel Kotov," the man murmured, "and soon, you'll learn to see me, too. My name is Vadim Boykov, but like everyone else, you may call me *boss*. Learn it quickly, follow the rules, and unlike your father, you may someday see the outside of these walls again."

Vadim.

Pavel was never going to forget that name.

Then, Vadim used those two fingers of his to tap at the bottom of his throat. An action Pavel didn't understand, but the coldness that radiated from Vadim as he did it was enough to make him shiver on the ground.

"You belong to me now. To the *Boykovs*." Vadim tipped his head to the side and nodded to himself, adding, "Beware of those who show you mercy, young Pavel, for those are the people who know the essence of your fear."

• • •

Ten years later …

The screams down the hall were only muffled when a morbid crack echoed down the corridor. Pavel continued his work three chambers down, as though he hadn't heard anything at all and nothing was wrong. That was best. A decade working in the Boykov's Compound taught him there was nothing worse than sticking one's nose where it did not belong. Unless something directly involved him, Pavel was better off staying far away.

Filling the bucket with ice-cold water from the tap sticking out of the wall again, he headed to the man shackled in the corner. Other than the food Pavel brought him once a day—which wasn't much— water and bread, just enough to keep him alive in between daily beatings and whatever punishment he was delivered from Vadim— this was the man's hell.

Cold water splashed on him regularly. A beating whenever someone came in to deliver it, unless it was Pavel ordered to do it. Food when the time struck twelve in the afternoon. A hard, cracked cement floor that was always cold and wet. Shackles around his wrists and ankles, and occasionally one around his throat when he needed to be reminded that he was now a Boykov dog, and nothing else—an animal made to sit in his own waste, and be fed or taken care of when someone else deemed it appropriate.

He was no longer in control of his life.

Pavel didn't even know the man's name. He also didn't know why this man—or why any of the other people locked in the chambers of the Boykov Compound—had been brought to this place. All he was told was that quite simply, these people deserved to be here because perhaps they had broken the rules, or maybe they had stepped out of line and needed a reminder about who exactly was the boss.

It didn't matter.

He'd never asked for more details. His curiosity was not important enough to risk his own safety. He could be the next person shackled to a cement floor getting cold water poured over his head regularly with daily beatings in between.

Wasn't it bad enough he was *here*?

That he'd been here for ten fucking years?

It was easier this way.

Hauling the water across the floor, Pavel tipped the bucket over the sleeping man's head. How he was able to fall asleep while a man was killed just two chambers down—making sure he screamed the entire time, right up until his last few seconds on earth—was anyone's guess.

Maybe because they became numb.

This was life now.

It took the cold water splashing down over the man's shaking body—even in his sleep, he trembled, his bruises darker than normal and his one arm twisted at an awkward angle—for him to wake up. The man gasped and his eyes flew wide. Bloodshot and terrified. Like for the moment, he was somewhere else in his dreams. Now, he was awake again.

"Welcome back to hell," Pavel murmured.

Bending down to be at a similar height to the man, he used the rag he'd tucked into the pocket of his black jeans to wipe at the mess of the man's face. No one had ever told him not to be kind to these prisoners. No one had ever told him that while he often was made to deliver harsh punishments, and keep them alive until their next ride through hell, that he could not give them some sort of reprieve.

If anything, it helped him.

The man's trembling didn't let up, but he was far more relaxed to see Pavel standing in front of him and not someone else. Pavel knew that who woke this man up would determine how the remainder of his day would go.

Either pain, or ... well, less pain.

Sometimes.

"*Death*," the man croaked.

Pavel's hand slowed from wiping the rest of the dried vomit from the man's mouth. "What did you say?"

They were the first words he could ever remember saying to the man. He rarely spoke—if he didn't indulge conversation, it was highly unlikely that he would learn anything about them. Learning things about them might cause him to get attached. He could not afford to be attached to people who were only destined to die.

Possibly by his own hand.

"When I see you," the man whispered, "I see death."

Pavel stilled in place. "Why?"

"Doesn't death always offer a kind hand before he pulls you to the other side?" Swallowing hard, the man said, his voice tired and raspy, "Your kindness only hides what you're here to do. You will use that same kind hand that you use to feed me and help me, to kill me someday, won't you?"

"I—"

"You are the *Zhatka*—the Reaper."

Pavel hadn't realized it, then, but conversations always traveled in the chambers. This man hadn't been the only one to hear that nickname. He wouldn't be the last one to use it, either.

It was not a name Pavel wanted.

Not one he needed.

And yet, as the days melted into months, and then into years ... he found being Zhatka in the chambers was easier than being *Pavel*. He even started to forget who Pavel was.

1.

Present day ...

"YOU CANNOT stay here forever, Viktoria."

Truer words had never been spoken. Of that, Viktoria was most sure. Not that she needed to tell her father that—she was sure the man already knew, like he always did.

That was the thing about Vadim Boykov ... he was far too intuitive for his own good. He simply needed to look at her, the same way he had done time and time again during her life, to know she was struggling in her mind and heart. On the outside, she appeared cold and calm. Nothing new for her. Inside, she was a ball of blackening human, dying and disappearing.

Vadim only needed to look at her to know.

She wished, often, that wasn't the case.

"Are you pretending to be deaf now?" her father asked. "I've spent twenty-four years helping to raise you, I know you can hear me."

She sighed, and glanced away from the window overlooking the private property, which was surrounded by a rather large stone fence. Despite being Russian, she wasn't fond of the Russian countryside. Perhaps because she much preferred the cement and noise of a city. There, it was always cold and distant.

A lot like her.

Here, the countryside was none of those things.

She couldn't connect.

Vadim arched a brow at the same time she did, when their eyes met. That was probably the only thing that she took from her father—her expressions and her ability to seem indifferent to everything and everyone. Even if she was anything but ...

Everything else, she'd taken from her dead mother. From her platinum blonde hair, to the ice blue of her gaze. Her angular features, soft lips, and wide eyes all came from her mom, too. She wished she remembered the woman better, but she'd been a bit young when her mother passed. All she was left with were the stories

7

her brothers shared, and the occasional memory her father liked to tell when he was a little too drunk and free with his tongue.

Vadim, on the other hand, looked nothing like Viktoria. He was as big as a barrel in his chest, his face mean and weathered with age. Thin lips and a strong jaw that set off his roughened features.

The two of them didn't look alike at all, but they were more similar than she cared to admit.

"I know I can't stay here forever," she said.

Vadim smiled a bit, although it didn't quite reach his eyes. To be fair, the man *rarely* smiled, anyway, and when he did ... something bad was sure to follow. No one was exempt from that rule, not even his children. He had never hurt her. She wasn't stupid enough to think that he wasn't capable, though.

"Then, why are you still here?" Vadim asked, coming over to take a seat on the bench near the window with her. "You don't even like Russia, girl."

When she opened her mouth to lie and deny his statement, Vadim grinned and chuckled.

"Don't bother with lies, yes? I know how you feel about the country."

Of course, he did.

She wasn't quite sure what he wanted her to say, though. The truth about why she hadn't gone back to Chicago, where her brothers were waiting and reorganizing the Bratva that had once belonged to her father, was not as simple or as clean-cut as Vadim would like it to be. Or maybe it was Viktoria who didn't think her answer was easy to understand.

After all, it was wrapped up in her father.

Vadim had been exiled to Russia—for *good* reason—by her older brother, Konstantin, after he'd taken over the Bratva. And while, sure, Viktoria had her brothers and a handful of friends in Chicago, it didn't feel the same without her father.

Viktoria was the favorite.

The *favored*.

And still, she knew her father lied and hurt those she cared about, herself included. She was still struggling to connect the man who she knew had done terrible things to her brothers and the man she adored.

Because that was the thing about daughters and their fathers, wasn't it?

Daughters adored their dads. Daughters saw their fathers as kings on unmovable thrones; as men above other men; as Gods among mortals. They put their fathers on a pedestal, and when they crashed down, it was always the daughters breaking the fall at the bottom.

Or rather, their misguided hearts and beliefs.

Squashed and shattered.

She was not exempt to the rule. If anything, she had been willing to pretend the bad parts of her father and the things about him that scared her the most hadn't existed until she no longer had a choice but to face them head-on. By then ... it was already too late.

She hadn't been able to get out of the way when her father fell from his throne. So, she'd been crushed by the weight of his misdeeds, a lot like everyone else around her, too. Although ... Viktoria, more so than others, if the way she felt meant anything at all. She wasn't sure that it did.

Vadim gave her a look from the side, saying, "Chicago would be a far more comfortable place for you to be—especially with your brother taking over. I'm sure that extends you some grace and status. Why stay here longer than you have to?"

Maybe she wasn't ready.

Maybe she hadn't said the things she came to say quite yet.

She still wanted to love her father. She still wanted to adore him, even in his much-deserved exile from their family and life after all that he had done. He was her favorite, too.

"You know," she said, "you asked about Konstantin and Kolya ..."

"Mmm, my sons may hate me, but does that mean I have to hate them, Vik?"

Maybe.

Maybe not.

That wasn't what she meant to ask.

"But you've yet to ask about her," Viktoria said quieter. "Zoya Bennett, I mean."

Vadim stiffened, but his expression didn't flicker with even a hint of his emotion at her blatant, pointed statement. The other daughter he had—the one he'd hidden from them. The child she had never known about until the girl was practically grown, and even now ...

instead of embracing the young woman, Viktoria felt cold toward her. Like just her presence was enough to make Viktoria feel like her entire life with her father had been a lie.

My only girl. My printsessa. My favorite.

Maybe she was spoiled. Maybe she had an unhealthy adoration for her father, and that's why this stung her so badly. Maybe it wasn't Zoya or Vadim's fault at all for her feelings, but rather … her own.

Zoya, the half-sister her father had decided to keep hidden and lie about, was just another piece of the puzzle. Viktoria didn't see the girl—never said more than a couple of words to her when she did meet her. It wasn't like the young woman had a problem with that, or so it seemed. Viktoria didn't have room in her life for yet another person she was meant to care for, but didn't feel like she could trust.

So, she stayed away from her half-sister.

She was still pissed at her father for lying to her for all these years, though. Although, if she were being honest, Zoya was just one piece of many. And not a piece that Viktoria cared to think about very often.

Why was she still here again?

Viktoria really didn't know.

Vadim tucked one of her stray strands of straight, blonde hair behind her shoulder. A tender action for a man she knew had almost killed one of her brothers and tried again with her other. "I haven't asked because there is nothing I need or want to ask about her."

No, that really didn't help.

Viktoria still felt cold.

"Sir, your lunch is ready to be served. Will you take it in the enclave again?"

At the sound of a man's voice—unknown to her, despite her visit having lasted several days here at her father's Russian estate—she stiffened all over. It was like in a second, she couldn't breathe, her gaze tunneled and blackened at the edges, and her heart raced out of control. All it took was the voice of a man she didn't know coming from behind her, and Viktoria felt two seconds away from passing out or throwing up.

Either one, or both, was likely. That was the thing about fear. There really was no controlling it. She wasn't good at hiding it.

Vadim's gaze darted to her, and then to the man wherever he stood at her back behind the bench seat. "In a moment, Anatoly."

Footsteps receded.

Viktoria still wasn't okay.

Her father knew it.

"*Izvini,*" Vadim murmured, his gaze drifting down to her shaking hands she'd balled in her lap. "I never thought to explain to the men who work here about your … issue."

Issue.

Yeah.

That was a good way to put her absolute *terror* of unknown men. Which was funny because the man who had caused this hadn't been unknown to her at all.

"And I'm sorry it happened at all … this," her father added, nodding at her.

Viktoria forced herself to speak—if she didn't, she might not say a word for hours. "Can we just eat, yes?"

Vadim nodded. "We'll eat, but then you're going home."

Home.

Where even was that anymore?

• • •

From up above, Chicago seemed bright in the darkness, what with the clusters of lights from the city. And yet, Viktoria knew the second she stepped foot into the city, the wind would remind her just how cold the place was on its good days.

The pressure in the plane's cabin released just a fraction before it started building again. Viktoria focused on the sights down below, which were getting closer and closer as the plane dropped for its final descent. There was always a brief moment before the plane's wheels touched down to the tarmac that would have her heart leaping into her throat, but for the most part, she enjoyed flying.

What could happen twenty-thousand feet in the air?

Very little.

She shot the guy sitting next to her a look. *Well* … except when she had a chatty neighbor. It wasn't like she gave off the *let's talk* vibe, but God knew this asshole had tried again and again to engage her. He'd finally gotten the hint when Viktoria had literally stared him dead in the eyes, put her earbuds in slowly, and then cocked a brow as she turned the music on in her phone before turning to face the port window.

She was sure it'd hurt the guy's feelings a little bit. And if not that, then it certainly hurt his pride. She wasn't the chatty type, honestly. She certainly wasn't going to talk to some stranger on a plane just because she was sitting beside him, he was bored, and he figured she would be a good conversationalist.

Surprise.

She wasn't.

Did that make her a bitch?

Absolutely.

Did she care?

Absolutely not.

Bitch and *Viktoria* had become synonymous in her world. People threw that word at her like it was a knife. They said it with the intention to hurt her—to *cut*. It was funny, really, because instead of letting it affect her in a bad way, she just turned it around on them. They wanted to see a bitch? They didn't like that she was cold?

Okay.

Then she could be worse.

Nobody had ever thought to figure out the reason why Viktoria was the way she was, anyway. Other than her brothers, maybe. Not that they needed to figure it out—they already knew. Everyone else, though? It was easier for the people who didn't know her to just label her with a slur, and go on their way.

She just owned it.

The remainder of the flight passed by rather quickly. Before she knew it, the plane had taxied into the gate, and they were allowed to deplane. Slinging the messenger bag that she'd used as a carry-on over her shoulder as she came down the arrival's escalator, her gaze landed on the person waiting a few feet away from the bottom of the moving stairs.

She might have been surprised to see him, but she couldn't be, given he always seemed to know everything anyway. Even when he wasn't directly told something, her brother, Konstantin, just seemed to have … a way about him.

Kolya, her oldest brother, was the one who scared everyone because of his size, and ever-changing moods. His coldness could rival hers on his good days, but it was the sudden bursts of violence that he was very capable of that *really* lingered in the minds of those around him when he was long gone.

Konstantin, though?

He was a little different.

Konstantin was calculating—he was the king on the chess board, in a lot of ways. He thought several moves ahead, and he never let anyone know what those moves were before he made them. Some people might call that unpredictable, but she didn't know if that was the word she would use. The fear Konstantin invoked in others came from his ability to seem harmless until it was far too late, and he was never *obvious*.

Nothing he did was obvious.

Standing there in his three-piece suit, Konstantin looked almost out of place in the rest of the crowd. There was just an air about him—something that warned people from his aura alone to *stay back; don't engage*. His usual smirk was gone as he looked at something off to his left, giving her a good view of his profile and the hard lines of his face. It was his features, that strong jaw and the coldness in his gaze, that reminded her of their father. But it was the structure of his face that reminded her of their long-dead mother.

Kolya looked just like their dad.

Her and Konstantin, though?

They took more after their ma.

She wasn't sure how she felt about her brothers, but more importantly ... she didn't know how she felt about Konstantin. He'd been the one to send their father away, after all. He'd made Vadim leave Chicago and exiled him to Russia.

Viktoria wasn't stupid. She knew that the way her father treated and raised her was quite different from the way Vadim had behaved toward his sons over the decades. She'd always blamed that on the Bratva—on her father being the Pakhan, and her brothers being his soldiers. But she couldn't ignore that there had never been a time when Vadim acted like their *father*, either. It was always just the boss and his men. Even when they were young, Kolya and Konstantin had needed to be men and not boys.

She was always able to be Vadim's little girl—his daughter. Nothing more and nothing less. It was that reason why seeing Konstantin waiting for her because, apparently, he'd gotten news she was coming back home without her actually telling him, put her on edge. It left her feeling confused.

She loved her brother.

And her father.

Now, her father had been taken from her. Konstantin had done that. It left her with a complex that she wasn't exactly ready to deal with, not that she knew the first place to begin with it all.

All at once, Konstantin turned, and his gaze leveled on her. That was another thing about her brother. His stare was always penetrating—yeah, that was the best way to describe it, she supposed. *Penetrating.*

A person didn't need to say a thing when Konstantin was around. He didn't need words and explanations to know what someone was thinking or feeling. It was like he just stared at you and he knew it all, anyway.

Viktoria was not an exception to that rule.

"Your trip was good?" her brother asked.

Viktoria came to a stop a couple of feet away from him. It allowed her enough distance that he wouldn't assume she wanted to greet him with something like a hug. "Good enough."

Konstantin nodded. "And Vadim?"

"You don't care."

Her brother arched a brow. "Vik—"

"You sent him away. *You* wanted him to go and you took over his place here. You don't have to pretend that you care about how he's living in Russia, *brat.*"

Konstantin's jaw tightened before he relaxed and offered her a smile. "I wasn't asking for him, actually. More for *you*, hmm?"

Well ...

"He's making do," she replied.

That was about as much as she wanted to give her brother, regarding their father. She had no doubt that Konstantin had a whole handful of people to watch Vadim. Likely the same people who reported back to him on their father's behavior and actions while he lived out the rest of his life in exile, away from his family. He didn't need her filling him in on the details.

"Was the trip ... worth it, then?" Konstantin asked.

Viktoria sighed. "If you're asking if it helped me with anything, then the answer is no."

"I figured."

"Where is Kolya?"

"Busy with Maya. You know how he is about that wife of his. She comes first."

"You say that like it's a bad thing."

Konstantin smirked. "No, I don't. You simply hear it that way, *sestra*."

"You can't tell me what I hear. Unless, of course, my ears have suddenly become attached to your head. Let me know when that happened."

She didn't even try to tamper the coldness in her tone. She didn't particularly have a reason to be icy to her brother, but this was her life, now. It was easier to keep people at a distance, and let them know their place, than it was for her to keep fighting them when they tried to get too close. Better to make that line in the sand clear before they ever got started.

Konstantin nodded. "I take it you don't want to tell me the things you discussed with Vadim, then?"

"*Nyet.*"

"A hard no, huh?"

Viktoria smiled thinly. "Take it how you may."

"You seem like you're feeling ..."

"*What?*"

"Extra nasty."

Viktoria stared at the people passing them by instead of her brother. It was just easier. She didn't need him to see the war in her gaze—a battle of emotions that was ever-present, and always constant in her heart and mind.

Life was not nice to her.

Not lately.

"We have an upcoming party," Konstantin said when Viktoria kept quiet. This was typical for them. He'd try to engage her, and she just stayed silent until he gave up. "A baby shower for Maya and Kolya. I expect you to be there, be *pleasant*, and bring a proper gift."

"Fine."

"Oh, and since I know how Vadim always puts you in a headspace, perhaps you should go see your therapist while you're back in the city, yes?"

Her jaw ached from how hard she was clenching her teeth.

He wasn't wrong, though.

It wasn't just Vadim and her brothers who left her with a complex whenever she was in her father's presence. It was far more than just that. It was like every conversation with Vadim thrust her right back to a time when he had failed her the very most.

That made her feel *angry*.

Guilty.

So ashamed.

Dirty.

She didn't want to blame him for what had happened to her, but she still did. She loved him, and she hated him.

"I think I will visit her, actually," Viktoria said.

Konstantin smiled briefly as she looked back at him. "Good."

"But not because you told me to."

"Of course not."

2.

THERE WAS nothing comforting about the smell of musty cement. The putrid mixture of dampness having seeped and collected for far too long inside the walls of the chambers of the Compound was ever-present. It lingered on everything, too.

Dying bodies.

Clothes.

Skin.

It didn't matter which chamber Pavel entered to do his job, that same smell remained. And though he occasionally left the Compound at night when he was allowed, that scent followed him. He often kept clothes tucked away in a plastic storage box, just to keep the smell from remaining on the items, but he still smelled it.

He figured he always would.

After living and working in this Compound for fourteen years, the smell was as much a part of him as this place was. It was strange, in a way. He could walk these dank, dark halls with his eyes closed. He knew the scars on each prisoner's body and he could still hear their raspy, pained voices long after he'd closed his eyes to go to sleep. He could pinpoint each and every creak or moan from this old building.

But he couldn't remember his own birthday, although, from his occasional trips out of the Compound where he could find out the date and year, he knew he was twenty-six, now. A lot of the time, he didn't know what day of the week it was because that wasn't an important detail for him. Or that's what he'd always been told.

Pav had learned to find comfort in *discomfort*. In a way … Here, in the deepest part of the Compound where the light rarely touched, fresh air was rare, and the mold was beginning to grow in the corners, comfort was nonexistent. Even his living quarters felt a little too much like the cells where the Boykovs kept their prisoners.

Not that it mattered.

Here, he felt at home. Here, he did his best work. In the musty darkness. Alone, usually. With death all around …

Pav walked into one cell with a bucket of cold water ready, and a cloth hanging from his other hand. Most of the cells didn't even have doors to close—although there were a couple that did—not that they would need them, anyway. His gaze found the man who stayed in this cell huddled into a corner, and the reason Pav had brought the bucket and rag smeared on the wall beside him.

Shit and vomit.

The man, shackled to the wall by a thick rope of chain connected to his ankles, and one around his neck, too, looked Pav's way when he came into the cell. His eyes connected with Pav's, but he found no life staring back. Just a wild gleam and a rotted smile.

Pav *blinked*.

The man's teeth hadn't been rotted before.

Blyad.

Fucking hell.

Shit—that's what was covering the man's mouth. *Shit*. His feces. Pav had seen far worse things in the chambers, that was for sure. He'd seen bodies after they'd been beaten to a pulp. He'd seen a man skin and debone a human body. He knew what someone's insides looked like when they were on the fucking outside.

Bodily fluids came with the territory.

They made his stomach roll, sure, but he usually just put it out of his mind, and went about doing his job. He'd then spend a couple hours in the shower making sure he'd washed every bit of it off that he could.

But *this*?

Feces smeared on the wall?

In the guy's mouth?

The gleam in his eye?

The crazy smile?

The man didn't even say anything and he still seemed like, despite the fact he was staring right at Pav, he was actually looking past him. As though Pav were nothing more than a ghost standing there in the doorway, and he wasn't seeing him at all.

Add in the wild look in his eye and the madness in his smile … well, sometimes, a mind just couldn't take what happened in these chambers, day in and day out. Sometimes, a mind broke from it all.

Not that it changed anything. Pav still had a job to do. He headed farther into the cell and made quick work of washing what he could.

The wall, and the parts of the floor that had also taken a few smears of the waste. The man wouldn't let him touch him, and even hissed *Zhatka* at him when he tried to wash out his mouth.

Pav wished he could be surprised that even in his madness, the man remembered who he was, except he couldn't be shocked at all. The people he shared these chambers with—while he lived his life unshackled and with less punishment than them—they were still the same in a lot of ways. Owned by people they rarely saw. Their futures determined by men whose names they rarely whispered.

These prisoners ...

They respected Pav as much as they feared him. He was the man who often washed and fed them. And he was the same man who would beat them, or kill them.

They knew it.

Pav knew there wasn't much more he could do for the man in the cell. Not to mention, the fact that he would have to wait for someone higher up to come down to the chambers so that he could explain the situation before a decision could be made about what to do. Pav left the cell and the man behind.

He moved silently down the hallway, passing two more cells as he went and peeking in to check on the people inside—nothing out of the ordinary. One was sleeping. Another was sitting up, awake, and rubbing dirty fingers through his hair. He'd bring them their ration of food for the day around noon, and then leave them be unless other orders were given for him to do something different.

That was typically how it worked, anyway.

It was the silence at the end of the row of chambers that made Pav slow in his walk. The rest of the prisoners in the cells? They kept quiet. They knew that the more noise they made, the worse the pain that would come for them later. The man at the end of the row, though? He didn't *care*. At all. He was constantly causing problems, day in and day out. It was like he got off on pissing the rest of them off because he knew how this was going to end for him, one way or the fucking other.

As much as it annoyed the hell out of Pav on a regular basis, he also respected the man's tenacity. He didn't even know his name— the Boykovs rarely gave him that information about their prisoners. He was given orders, not details. He was to do what he was told to do, not make friends with the people in these cells.

Coming up to the cell at the end of the hall, one of the only ones with a door, Pav pushed the sliding cover over the small slot that acted as a window. He peered inside, his gaze sweeping the stained cement floor to find where the man should be huddled in a corner with his shackles and chains.

Oh, Pav found him, sure.

Dead.

He cursed under his breath and yanked the door open to get a better look at the dead body suspended away from the wall. It took him all of three seconds to figure out what the man had done. Standing straight, the prisoner had put his back to the wall, and then leaned forward. With the chain attached to a metal shackle around his throat, he hung there—still suspended, although dead now.

Pav sighed.

This wasn't a common occurrence. Suicide, that was. Sure, the prisoners threatened it occasionally, but very few actually figured out a way to make it happen during the hours that Pav was sleeping in his own living quarters.

He felt robotic as he crossed the chamber to check the man. Just to make sure, although he already knew the guy was *dead*. Once he'd confirmed it, Pav stepped out of the cell again and knew what he had to do.

When there was a body, it had to be disposed of. Sometimes, if there needed to be a message sent, then he would put the body in the freezer a floor higher until it was handled by whoever was going to do the job. He'd already been forewarned on this particular prisoner, though. If he died during his stay, Pav was simply expected to dispose of the body the regular way.

Which meant the furnace on the other side of the basement of the chambers. Simple, easy, and quick. As long as the furnace was burning at a hot enough level, of course, which meant Pav would need to make a trip to the other side and check before he could start the process of cleaning up.

It took him a good fifteen to twenty minutes to navigate the maze of hallways in the basement of the Compound before he finally stood in the doorway of the furnace and boiler room. He eyed the men standing in front of the furnace, as they tossed paper after paper into the flames licking out of the large door they'd thrown wide open while they did their work. He didn't care to ask the two what they were doing.

Dressed in black clothes and talking to one another in low, hushed Russian, they seemed intent on finishing their task of burning papers. So much so, that they didn't even notice he was standing in the doorway at first. He recognized them, of course. He'd seen their hawk-like faces around the Compound often, but he rarely spoke to them. The same way he often chose to keep quiet with anyone else who came around.

Boykov men—*soldiers*. No one particularly important, but at the same time, every man who worked for the Boykov family held some kind of importance.

It just depended on who liked them.

His time here taught him that.

"Zhatka, nice to see you this evening."

The taller of the two greeted him first when he finally noticed Pav standing there. The other man—rounder and shorter—looked up at his comrade's statement, and his gaze darted to where Pav was standing in the doorway. He didn't miss the fear that flickered in the second man's eyes while the first seemed entirely unconcerned.

That wasn't unusual, either.

Some of these men were terrified of Pav—maybe it was because they had been a witness to the things he was capable of one too many times, and they were worried they might be the next man to find himself in one of Pav's chambers.

Who knew?

"I need the furnace," Pav said, not bothering with a greeting for them. He didn't care to say hello, or make nice. That wasn't his job here—he only cared about that, not them. "Finish up your work by the time I get back here, will you?"

The first man—Anton, he believed was his name—lifted his head from the papers he was looking over in a folder. "What do you need the furnace for?"

"None of your business. Finish your work by the time I get back, or you can help me with *mine*."

That did it.

Both men were quick to nod.

Pav might laugh, if he were capable of it. No one wanted to be the Zhatka. No one wanted the job of *death*. That was just left for him, in the darkness and shadows. Maybe that was what he found comfort in.

Death.

It did feel like an old friend, now.

"Oh, Pav?" Anton asked as he turned to leave.

"*Da?*"

"Any reason why I heard the boss wants to talk to you?"

Pav's shoulders tensed, but not for the reason one might think. The boss was gone—Vadim, the man who decided to keep and train him like a puppy ... well, he was no longer running the Boykovs. He'd heard those whispers and rumors.

There was always a bit of truth to them, right?

Instead of answering the man's question, Pav simply asked, "Which boss?"

"Konstantin."

Ah.

The second Boykov son.

Well, what the fuck did he want with Pav? Couldn't they leave him to his musty, death-filled peace? Konstantin's father always did. It was easier this way.

• • •

There was something to be said for the familiarity of routine. It was one of the few things Pav chose to take comfort in because it was the one thing—other than the chambers—that he truly had control of when it came to his life and days. His days, and evenings, were often scheduled down to thirty-minute increments. From the time he woke up, until the point he laid his head back down on an old mattress covered with a black sheet to sleep.

He had one clock in the chambers. A digital clock that sat on the counter in the small kitchen section of his living quarters. One might call it an apartment, but he didn't know if he would call the total of two rooms that. It was set up like a bachelor's loft—the kitchen, dining, seating, and bedroom area was really one semi-large space, and the bathroom was offset in a separate room.

The place was made of cement walls, no windows, and bare bulbs for lights. Any and all things that decorated the place—which was basically nothing except for his clothes, the blankets on his bed, and the towels in the bathroom—came from a supply area in an upper section of the Compound. He didn't know who kept the supply room full of personal items and household things, not to mention, *food* … but someone did it. He was grateful because it was one less thing he had to worry about.

He'd come to the Compound a young boy—all of twelve. He'd known how to care for himself on a very basic level, but not much more. Occasionally, a man would show up to his living quarters when he was younger and show him this or that. The people who taught him things like how to shave, how to cook something that didn't come in a can … he didn't even know their names.

He supposed it was no different than someone training an animal. They came in, he was taught how to do a specific thing, and once he had mastered it, they'd pat him on the head like he was a good boy, and left him to his business.

Just like Vadim had said. He was an animal to be trained. *And kept.*

Those men didn't just come to teach him how to take care of himself, either. No, they also came to beat the hell out of him occasionally—*toughen you up, suka.* He quickly learned how to fight back, too. They'd come to make him watch as they dragged a begging, broken man into one of the many chambers.

At first, Pav tried to hide away in a corner, terrified, as they did their business. He learned to stop being scared.

It wouldn't help.

He needed to be the one who made others scared of *him.* That was the only way Pav could survive here. He couldn't be easy prey. He had to be the predator hiding in the dark, and he needed everyone to know it, too.

Pav passed a look at the clock, noting he had another ten minutes to finish washing the one plate, bowl, set of utensils, cup, and pan he'd used to cook that day. He'd finish out his evening by cleaning the rest of his living quarters by hand with hot, soapy water and a rag, like he did every night, do one last walk through the chambers, and depending on how he felt … he might read.

Books, or the ones he found lying around in the old, forgotten rooms upstairs in the Compound, kept him from becoming bored. And, where his education had officially stopped at age twelve, he at least continued *reading.* That spoke to something good for him, surely.

"Why haven't you run yet?"

Pav almost dropped the cup he was currently scrubbing at the new voice coming from behind him, but he didn't. Usually, he just left the door to enter his quarters open because no one came this far into the lower part of the Compound. He was mostly left alone, now. If someone had business down here, it was almost always in the furnace room or with one of the prisoners in the cells.

Never for him, though.

He recognized the voice and maybe that was the reason why he relaxed a little. Not enough that he felt safe, but safety was a fucking joke here. Nothing was ever safe.

"Konstantin," Pav greeted, not unkindly.

"You didn't answer my question."

"There's nothing to answer."

"I think there is, yes?" Konstantin's sigh echoed through the space, crawling to Pav's spot at the kitchen sink slowly. "My father is gone—and he's the one who put you here over a decade ago."

"Fourteen years ago."

"Hmm."

Pav finished washing the cup and set it on the cupboard with the other washed dishes sitting atop a drying towel. Turning slowly, he found Konstantin Boykov standing in the doorway of his quarters. The man hadn't even stepped beyond the threshold, and Pav wasn't sure if he appreciated that, or if that was a sign of something bad yet to come.

"He's gone," Konstantin said, "and so why aren't you? Nothing is keeping you here and no one would stop you."

"Wouldn't they?"

He'd tried to run once.

It hadn't ended well.

Konstantin arched a brow, and it made the man's hard features sharpen even more. He didn't look entirely like his exiled father—there were obvious differences—but his features were similar enough that it made Pav pause, and wonder ... *how alike are you to your father, Konstantin Boykov?*

The answer to that question would likely decide how this meeting ended, honestly. Pav still wasn't willing to ask the question out loud.

"I don't have any place to go," Pav replied, "the Compound is my home."

Konstantin said nothing, but Pav didn't miss the way the man's throat jumped like he was swallowing back those words and trying to digest them. "Is that really how you feel?"

"The outside ..." Pav cocked his head to the side, choosing his next words carefully. "I don't know it well."

"You've been allowed to leave."

"Occasionally. Usually with someone else. Always at night. I know *some* people beyond these walls—people I met through the people *here*. Should that make me feel safe enough to trust that I know what the rest of the world is like, too?"

Again, Konstantin said nothing.

Pav didn't blame the man.

He went back to his work at the sink, finishing up the last few dishes he had to wash, and setting them to dry on the rack. He found Konstantin was still standing in the doorway when he was done, and turned back around.

Pav frowned. "Why aren't you coming in?"

Konstantin's brow dipped. "This isn't my home. You've not invited me in."

That never mattered to anyone before.

This place wasn't *his*, either.

Or, that's what he'd always been told.

Konstantin cleared his throat, drawing Pav's attention back to him once more. "You've always been good to the Boykovs, haven't you?"

"I wasn't given a choice."

"And yet ..." Konstantin trailed off with a wave of his hand. "Here you are, Pavel."

"I'm surprise you even know my name."

"Do you prefer Zha—"

"*Nyet.*"

Konstantin nodded. "Settles that, then."

Did it?

Pav had no idea.

"It's time the Boykovs are good to you," the man murmured. "Beginning with protection and letting you have ... well, as much freedom as I can allow."

"What does that mean?"

"I'm sure your time spent here has afforded you some education on the Bratva and our life. The *rules* and so forth."

"Enough to get by," Pav returned.

Konstantin smiled coldly. "That's all you need. We'll start with the stars—two, on your clavicles. They'll give you rank and protection. As for your duties … they will vary, but you'll begin answering to me and my brother today and beyond, yes? You won't die in these chambers, Pavel. I think you've atoned for your father's actions long enough."

Pav blinked. "When?"

"For what?"

"The tattoos."

"Soon. I'll have a date and address for you, and that's where it'll happen."

Pav's cheek twitched and his hands balled into tight fists at his sides. Konstantin didn't miss the actions.

"What is it?" the man asked.

He wanted to swallow the words and keep his weakness to himself. Here, weakness was a target and the last thing he could afford to be around any of these men was *weak*. Even if it was something as innocent as words and his truth, saying them at all felt akin to stripping himself of the only things in his life that allowed him a sense of safety and comfort. His knives. He didn't hand those weapons to anyone in this godforsaken place; he didn't offer his true feelings or thoughts in the same manner.

Still, even with that in mind, Pav decided he had to offer Konstantin some semblance of trust, considering what the man was currently giving him. He kept that in mind as he replied, "Leaving here makes me uncomfortable when I'm—"

"We'll work on that, hmm? And for this … I could make an exception."

Well, what did that mean?

Pav didn't bother to ask.

3.

INSTEAD OF taking one of the three plush couches in the waiting area of the office, Viktoria opted to stand near the window. It was less awkward than pretending to read one of the many magazines on the coffee table while she waited for her appointment. Plus, with her back turned to the girl sitting at the modernly designed desk, she didn't have to act like she gave a fuck about talking, either.

All wins for her.

It wasn't her first time at this particular office—not even the tenth. Yet, it didn't get any easier. Her anxiety about the things that might be discussed behind the office walls hadn't lessened with time. She still felt like, more than anything, she wanted to shrink away and hide from the rest of the world.

The place was comforting, sure. Clean and modern. White walls and chrome accents. A few tasteful, scattered pieces of artwork hung from the waiting room's walls. Mostly abstracts of women's faces. They matched the whole modern theme of the rest of the area.

Viktoria couldn't remember which person in her life recommended this particular therapist to her, but after trying three others who'd either made her uncomfortable or immediately wanted to put her on some kind of drugs to deal with her issues … well, this had been her last stop. If this therapist hadn't worked out, then she wouldn't look for another.

This wasn't like trying *food*. She didn't have to *do* therapy to keep going day to day—she was going to be fine one way or another. She was going to survive, just like she had been surviving for the last couple of years.

Or, that was the lie she kept telling herself.

"Miss Boykov, Cindy will see you now."

Viktoria turned away from the window and gave the receptionist behind the desk a tight smile in silent thanks as she passed. Although, she wasn't even sure if the smile came out as true and honest, or not.

Did it even matter?

She was the bitch.

Ice queen.

It wasn't like anyone expected different.

Viktoria walked down the hallway that led to the door at the very end. She knocked once on the white wood and waited for the usual permission to enter.

"Come in," Cindy called from within the office.

She took one deep breath—just enough to settle the tightening of her chest and the racing of her heart. Truthfully, it didn't help at all. It was just yet another little white lie that Viktoria liked to tell herself, because if she could pretend she was fine, then that was all that mattered to her at the end of the day.

She knew she was a mess.

No one else needed to.

"How long has it been, Viktoria?" the therapist asked as she entered the room. "A few months, hmm?"

Viktoria nodded as she headed for the spot she usually sat in while they had their hour of time. A white chaise in the corner of the room facing the only large window in the office. She could sit on the chaise, turn to the window, and watch the people with their normal, unbroken minds walking to and from wherever they were going while she was once again forced to spill all her secrets and pain.

It was easier.

She was all for the easy things …

"About that long," Viktoria said.

She sat on the chaise and turned her back to Cindy, but she knew the woman wouldn't mind. The therapist was up for whatever made a patient feel comfortable. She would talk to Viktoria like the two were looking one another in the face, and not like she was speaking to her back. She appreciated that.

"I decided to take my brother's advice after I came back from my vacation, and come see you," Viktoria said.

Cindy made a noise under her breath. "And how is he—I'm assuming you're talking about Konstantin, because the other one … Kolya, correct?"

"Kolya is the oldest."

"Yes, Kolya. He doesn't discuss your personal business in the same way that Konstantin does, right?"

"Kolya is smart."

"Or he thinks it's better to leave you be."

Viktoria could hear the amusement in Cindy's voice and she didn't need to turn around to know that the woman was probably wearing a soft smile to match, too. She'd spent enough time sitting in this office to know exactly what Cindy looked, like depending on her mood or temperament that day.

The woman had never once changed her sharp, angular brown bob, and she always kept a pair of large, black-rimmed glasses on the top of her head because she needed them to read. She preferred pencil skirts and silk blouses to pant suits, and she kept her face clear of makeup for the most part, except the occasional lip balm. She was soft-featured, brown-eyed, and her round face was made to look slightly longer by the bob that she always kept pin-straight.

"Kolya is … easier not to talk to," Viktoria admitted.

"So you've said before." Cindy sighed, and then asked, "So, why did Konstantin think you should make an appointment with me after it's been so long? He's probably moved out of your house in Melrose by now, hasn't he? The last time we spoke, he was apparently getting married. I assume that panned out."

"He did get married, and he is out of my house."

Thankfully, she added silently.

She loved Konstantin, of course, and was grateful for the fact that he moved into her house with no questions asked after … everything had happened. He was there, just a room away, to wake her out of nightmares that seemed constant night after night. He was there to see her through the first few weeks of panic attack after panic attack when she'd seen strangers walk past her house.

And he also drove her crazy.

They were not the same people. Konstantin had his habits, and Viktoria had hers. Her brother, before his wife, had also greatly enjoyed the company of other women. He was a smartass, and with that came a sharp tongue.

Yes, she appreciated him being there.

She was also glad he'd left.

"Also," Cindy murmured, "do not think that I forgot about the fact you didn't answer my question. Why did your brother think you should make a trip to visit me?"

Viktoria frowned at the glare of her reflection in the window. She wasn't sure if Cindy could see it or not, and she didn't care either way. "I went to visit my dad in Russia, and that always … screws with my head."

"Is that all?"

"Before I went, the nightmares had started again."

"I see."

"Two or three a night," Viktoria added.

"What about flashbacks?"

"A few times a week."

The sound of a pen scratching against paper echoed throughout the room, but Viktoria still didn't turn around on the chaise to see what the woman was doing. She already knew, anyway. Listing all the symptoms of Viktoria's trauma—the shit that just wouldn't leave her alone no matter what she did.

"Depression?"

Viktoria cleared her throat. "Moderate."

"Anxiety?"

"Constant."

"Self-harm?" the therapist asked.

Viktoria frowned. "I don't do that."

"But do you *think* about it?"

Well, that wasn't an easy question to answer. Viktoria never actively thought about hurting herself to ease the pain, and she didn't think about killing herself on a daily basis, either. But she couldn't lie and say something like suicide had *never* passed her mind, either. She had, briefly, considered the fact that ending her life would take away *everything*. She didn't seriously entertain the idea, though.

"You don't have to answer," Cindy said, "I think your silence explains a lot."

"Oh, does it?"

She didn't even try to hide her sarcasm.

Cindy just ignored it.

"You know that with PTSD—"

"Could we not put labels on … all of this?" Viktoria said, gesturing with one hand at herself like that was going to explain it. "I don't like that."

"No labels, then, but I do think there are some medications that would help to ease some of your problems that are causing other issues to be made worse. Treating things like the anxiety and depression with meds could ease things elsewhere."

"I don't want to take medications."

"You do know mental illness isn't cured by a cold demeanor and shutting yourself away from the rest of the world, right? You can put on the mask for everyone at the beginning of each day, Viktoria, but when you take it off, you're still going to be the same woman underneath it all. And that woman needs help."

Viktoria continued staring out the window. "So be it."

"All right, since this is a dead-end and I know better than to keep pushing, let's talk about these nightmares."

Great.

• • •

"Nope, not strong enough," Viktoria muttered, passing the wine despite the fact their pretty labels and shiny bottles on the shelves all but beckoned her to come closer. She was going to need something with a far higher percentage of alcohol to get her through the night. "Vodka, vodka, vodka ..."

She was sure the woman at the other end of the aisle in the liquor store thought she was crazier than hell, and honestly, the woman wouldn't be entirely wrong. After spending an entire hour with Cindy to discuss her nightmares in great detail, the only thing Viktoria could currently feel was a deep, thumping fear in her chest. It echoed with every single beat of her heart and felt like it might be trying to crawl up her throat.

She didn't want meds to deal with this.

But she would drink it away.

Drink the fear away ...

Was it healthy?

Probably not.

Did she have a problem?

Not yet.

She only resorted to alcohol to help her get through a night like the one she knew would be coming that evening when nothing else would do. Before Konstantin moved out, she'd felt comfortable enough to try and push through it because she'd known he would be just one room over.

But after verbally reliving those nightmares with Cindy because the therapist was sure it would help to stop them on some level—it wouldn't—she had no doubt they would be doubling their appearances in her dreams tonight.

Best way to fix that was to drink so much she wouldn't dream. Yeah, that was a real thing. She'd drink until she blacked out, wake up with one hell of a fucking hangover, and move the hell on like nothing had happened.

Hopefully, it would be enough.

Viktoria wasn't sure it would be.

What else could she do?

The woman stocking shelves at the other end of the aisle passed Viktoria one more look. Viktoria didn't even bother to hide the glare that time. The woman's eyes widened and she quickly picked up the empty box on the floor and left.

Good. Now it's just me and my problems.

Viktoria turned her attention to the rows of vodka on the shelf. She was smart about this—she knew better than to *keep* liquor in her house, which was kind of fucked up in a way. She was all too aware that she would absolutely overdo it if she had easy access to liquor. She would quickly find herself with a problem, then.

Instead, she made it more difficult on herself by *forcing* herself to buy liquor. Which meant going out ... entering a store and being around *people*. She didn't like doing that—didn't like the idea that she might have to talk to a strange man who gave her a bad vibe. Although, all men she didn't know gave her that vibe.

She was quick to find the vodka she preferred—Grey Goose. It would probably kill her father a little inside to know she didn't like his favorite brand of vodka. Russians had their ways, after all, but she needed something a little smoother than the brand he liked. At least with her Grey Goose, she could mix it strongly with something else and drink it down fast. It wasn't like she actually liked the taste of liquor. She just liked the way it allowed her to sleep without—

The ring of her phone stopped Viktoria's inner monologue, which frankly, was probably for the better. She didn't need to keep trying to justify to herself why she was drinking or how it wasn't a problem.

One didn't need to drink all day, every day, to have an issue.

She didn't want to think about it.

"Viktoria, here," she said, answering her phone as she sat the bottle of Grey Goose on the counter for the cashier.

"*Sestra.*"

She scowled at Konstantin's greeting. "What do you want, Konstantin?"

"You've been to your therapist?"

"How do you know that?"

"Your attitude."

"Oh, *not* because you have me followed?"

"Well, that is for protection, and you never see the person, do you?"

Viktoria's face felt like it was going to permanently stay in some form of a scowl or frown for the rest of her life if she didn't get this shit under control. She also wasn't stupid enough to miss the fact that Konstantin purposely refrained from saying *he* when it came to the solider for the Boykovs who occasionally kept an eye on her. He'd made the mistake of telling her it was a man once, and that hadn't ended well when she'd realized a strange male followed her around pretty regularly. He tried not to make the same mistake a second time.

"What do you want?" she asked.

"Nineteen dollars, twenty-three cents," the girl behind the cash said.

Konstantin, on the phone, said calmly, "Have you picked out a gift for Kolya and Maya's baby shower yet?"

"Have you made that Italian wife of yours any more Russian?"

"There's no need to be purposefully hurtful."

"That depends on who you ask."

Konstantin grunted under his breath. "You really do make it a chore to be pleasant, Vik."

And ...?

"Did you just call me to remind me of the party?" Viktoria asked. "Because I will be there, and with a gift, *brat*."

"And with a kind attitude, hmm?"

"I'll try."

Konstantin sighed. "Best I can ask, I suppose. And no, that isn't why I called. It was just something I remembered when you picked up the phone."

Oh, good.

Something else ...

"I have a job for you to do," Konstantin said, "at the Compound."

Viktoria's brow dipped. "I rarely go there … and what kind of *job*?"

"The only thing we ever ask you to do for the Bratva."

Ah, yeah.

"A tattoo, then," she muttered.

"Stars, actually."

Viktoria's jaw felt like it was flexing harder with every second because now it was starting to ache. "On a *man*?"

"Details," her brother countered, "and we can deal with those tomorrow when you get here."

"Kon—"

"Tomorrow at twelve in the afternoon, yes? Be here."

He hung up.

She cursed him to hell and back while paying for her vodka.

• • •

Viktoria *hated* the Compound. No, that was too nice. She despised the place. It was huge, old, and smelled like it, too. In her memories from childhood, this place had never done anything good for her. The only time she remembered her father bringing her to the Boykov Compound was if something bad was going on, and he didn't have a choice but to have her tag along, too.

She purposefully tried to avoid the maze of warehouses—and one old factory—that made up the Compound because unlike her brothers who had their offices here, there was nothing about the place that comforted her.

Like now.

Because she was lost.

Fuck.

That was the thing about the Compound. It was far too easy for someone like her—who wasn't familiar with the many hallways, stairwells, and connected warehouses—to get lost by simply taking a wrong turn. She was sure her brothers could navigate this musty-smelling hellhole with their eyes closed. After all, they'd spent the majority of their life behind these walls, under the watchful eye of their father.

Her?

Ha.

She had no idea where she was.

Viktoria felt like she had now been walking around the Compound aimlessly for at least twenty minutes—a good estimation. She could absolutely call her brother, and have Konstantin come find her, but she didn't want to give him that satisfaction. Knowing him, he would likely take great enjoyment from the fact she had managed to get lost and needed *him* to come find her.

He probably already knew she was lost.

She glanced up and saw a camera pointed in her direction at the end of the hallway in the right corner. A blinking red light told her the thing was live and watching every movement that happened in the hallway. No doubt, her brother was watching those cameras, and just waiting for her to call him for help.

Nope.

She would figure this out on her own.

Viktoria stuck her middle finger up to the camera as she passed it by. Just in case her brother was watching her and getting a kick out of her predicament as she tried helplessly to find the floor where his office was situated. Then he could know how she was feeling before they finally came face to face.

She was starting to regret bringing her large kit instead of the smaller kit that she usually used to travel with when she was tattooing. She'd taken some time off just because her mind was everywhere *but* tattooing, but even when she was working regularly, she typically traveled with the smaller kit.

It was lighter and easier to unpack or clean up. The larger kit was making her arm tired as she navigated the maze of hallways.

She came around a corner at the end of the hallway and ran right into someone coming out of an opened door.

No, not *someone*.

Not just *anyone*.

A man.

A *strange* man.

Viktoria's kit fell from her hand and crashed to the floor. Her first instinct was to immediately step back from the man, and put as much distance as she could between him and her. In her mind, her thoughts raced. They screamed at her to *relax, calm down … don't let him see you're scared; don't panic, Vik.*

She hadn't even looked at his face yet. Not that she needed to—just the sight of his large form, fit, tall, and lean, and the smell of his musky, spicy scent was enough to make her nervous. Her gaze drifted a little higher, traveling over the expanse of the black T-shirt that stretched across a broad, muscular chest, and then over his lower throat dusted with dark hair.

"Hello," he greeted.

Viktoria's gaze snapped up all at once to find his face. His eyes—a dark ocher color, flecked with brown and gold—met hers, and she sucked in a sharp breath that ached in her lungs. He really did have a beautiful face, with his strong jaw and sharp cheekbones. The strong lines of his face were only accentuated by the intense coldness in his stare and the way his lips seemed to be pulled into a permanent line.

No smile.

No smirk.

Nothing.

His dark hair was a little long on the top, but messy, like he'd been running his fingers through it. A small scar through his left eyebrow only added to the straightness of his brow line, giving him an even more disinterested expression.

Yeah, *beautiful.*

And fucking terrifying.

"Do you not speak?" he asked.

She wasn't sure what to make of his tone—it was both flat, and yet dark. Like he was accustomed to speaking in low tones, but it was just husky enough to suggest he could get loud if he needed or wanted to.

Viktoria swallowed hard, determined not to show the fact that being alone with this strange man in a hallway put a fear into her very bones that she would never be able to get out. "I can talk, thank you."

Yeah, she meant for that to come out as sharp as it did.

He only arched a brow at her. "Are you lost?"

"*No.*"

His gaze drifted over her shoulder, and she swore the edges of his lips threatened to lift into some form of a smile, but he held back. She had the strangest thought, then—what would he looked like if he did smile?

Then, his dark eyes came back to her.

"You are lost."

Viktoria balled her fists at her sides, but if he noticed it, the man didn't say. "So, what if I am?"

"What are you looking for?"

"Who," she corrected. "Konstantin."

Immediately, and without questioning her further, the man nodded. "*Da*, this way."

He turned and gestured with one hand for her to follow. She didn't move, and he walked a bit down the hallway before he realized she wasn't following him. He stopped and glanced over his shoulder with another arched brow.

"I will take you to him, come on," he said.

Viktoria still didn't move.

Who was this man?

She didn't know.

That bothered her.

The look of him ... the unknown ... all of it was horrifying to her. Her worst fears and the nightmares that constantly plagued her sometimes started exactly like this, and that's what scared her the very most. Not that she could tell this man that. She didn't even tell her brothers these things, honestly.

She was terrified.

He was terrifying.

The world was playing a joke on her, surely.

"I don't know you," Viktoria managed to say.

Maybe then, he would understand her discomfort.

At that statement, the corner of his lips did lift into something akin to a crooked smile. It did nothing to soften his features, but rather, darkened them further.

"I don't know who I am either, woman, but most people just call me Pav."

"Pav," she echoed.

"Or Pavel."

That doesn't help, really.

It seemed like he could read her mind because he shrugged, adding quickly, "At the end of this hallway, you will find an elevator. It's loud and old, but it works. Press the button for the highest floor, and it will take you to Konstantin's office."

He didn't give her the chance to say anything before he turned around and passed her by in the hallway. He took extra care not to touch her as he passed, and he didn't even glance at the kit she had dropped on the ground. He disappeared around the corner of the hallway and never once looked back over his shoulder.

Viktoria was still frozen.

Fear was horrible like that.

4.

PAV WATCHED the second hand on the clock on the wall across from Konstantin's office tick past the two with a slowness that rivaled death. He felt like he could safely make that statement. After all, he'd watched enough death in his lifetime to know it could be incredibly slow when it wanted to be. Even when someone begged for it to be faster.

He leaned against the wall and stared down the empty hallway. He never really understood why there was a hallway in this portion of the Compound. There was only one elevator here, and in Konstantin's office, there was another elevator that brought someone directly *inside* the office, if that's what the man wanted to do.

Then again, Pav supposed that was probably meant to appease Konstantin's paranoia and need for safety. Kind of like the way he also had entire sections of his walls—inside them, of course—that were just slabs of metal, in case someone outside with an automatic assault rifle got any bright ideas.

Between the two Boykov brothers, Konstantin was the one a person needed to mind, where the man's thoughts were concerned. He was dangerous because he planned everything down to the slightest detail, never told a soul what he was thinking, and he was meticulous about it.

As for the other brother ... Kolya, well, he was just plain fucking dangerous. And violent. Pav had been on the other end of a room one too many times when Kolya had come in ready to kill someone, and it was never very easy for the person who was about to die.

The two were quite different in that way. One, entirely subtle and cunning. The other, obvious and vicious.

Glancing up again, the clock's second hand was moving past the six, now. Another thirty seconds and he could knock on the door. Konstantin had been clear—twelve, no earlier and no later. Pav was the type to be right on time.

The door to Konstantin's office was closed tight. He couldn't hear any noise coming from inside the space, but that wasn't unusual,

39

either. Not considering how thick the door was, and the effort Konstantin put into making sure his office was completely private.

Pav had only been inside the space a handful of times over the years, and that was usually to relay some message from someone else. He certainly didn't stay in the office long enough to get comfortable or look around. Not that he could get comfortable in another man's space. That wasn't how he worked.

The only place Pav felt truly comfortable was in the shadows—deep in the belly of the Compound where no one bothered him, and very few called on him for their business. He could move between the cells, take care of the broken down there until it was their time to go, and live out his days in relative peace. He didn't need a lot to get by because he had never been given a lot in the first place. He never asked for anything because no one ever cared to listen to what he wanted, anyway.

Except ... well, that was about to change, wasn't it? That's what Konstantin had said days earlier. It wasn't as though Pav had been able to forget.

Pav was still trying to decide how he felt about all of that. He wasn't sure, and he didn't like feeling like the ground he currently stood on was unstable for some reason. He found comfort in familiarity and routine, and he wasn't sure he wanted to find out what would happen when someone decided to change everything he was accustomed to.

The clock's second hand hit the twelve at the same time Pav looked up again to check. Despite the thoughts still running wild in his head and the shit he had yet to figure out about this whole plan of Konstantin's, he moved away from the wall and across the hall. He knocked on the door twice—fast and loud raps of his knuckles against metal that made his bones ache.

Not that he needed to.

Up above the door rested a camera trained on whoever was standing in front of the door, and probably capturing a large portion—if not all—of the hallway. He bet Konstantin had been watching him stand outside of the door for a while now, wondering what in the hell he was doing, or why he hadn't already knocked on the door to be allowed entry.

The answer was simple.

Twelve was *twelve*.

Pav was told twelve.

A humming buzz echoed throughout the hallway before Konstantin's voice came through a speaker next to the door. "You may come in, *Zhatka*."

Pav was already pushing open the door with a muttered, "It's *Pavel*."

He hadn't asked for that nickname.

He didn't want it at all.

Pav already laid eyes on the woman inside the office before the door shut behind him. She sat across from her brother at Konstantin's desk with wide eyes as she looked at Pav over her shoulder. He thought, like he had earlier when he'd run into her downstairs and realized she was lost, that she looked awfully *dainty* for such a cold woman.

How did he know she was cold?

She radiated it.

In her gaze ...

The hard set of her lips ...

The way she carried herself.

The woman was cold all over.

Not that it bothered Pav one way or another. If anything, he found her coldness comforting, seeing as how he felt the same way a lot of the time. But there was something else about the platinum blonde, blue-eyed woman that interested him more. Something beyond the high cheekbones and cream skin that showcased her very obvious beauty that made him take a second look at her. Oh, sure, she was something else to *look at*—bow-shaped lips, and round eyes; soft features, and a sharp gaze.

But it was her fear ...

He could practically smell it.

Was that because he constantly spent time with people who felt only fear when he was near, or something else? Pav didn't really know, but that changed nothing about what he felt first and foremost when in this woman's presence.

Her fear was *vast*.

Thick and real.

Visceral, even.

And he liked it.

That was probably wrong.

"Yes, Pavel," Konstantin said, "my apologies. Or Pav, Viktoria, he likes that, too."

"We met already," she muttered.

Pav didn't miss the way Konstantin's gaze drifted between the woman—who hadn't looked away from him since he walked into the room—and Pav standing near the doorway. "Is that so?"

"I was lost. He helped me."

"Hmm."

Konstantin didn't sound surprised. Pav didn't believe he was, either. Nothing happened in this place without one of the Boykov brothers knowing. If someone didn't tell them what went on, they were capable of watching it all happen as it played out on one of the many security cameras.

Konstantin drummed his fingertips to the desk, bringing Viktoria's attention back to him. "Pav, this is Viktoria. My sister. She'll be doing your tattoos today."

Pav didn't miss the way Viktoria's shoulders tensed at that statement. Just like earlier when she had run into him, her fear bloomed.

Visceral, again.

Thick, again.

If fear were a physical color someone could see on someone else, Pav swore Viktoria would have been covered in it in those moments. And yet, other than the tensing of her back and shoulders, one couldn't tell simply by looking at her. Her delicate features—still pretty, but cold—remained like stone. Unmovable and telling *nothing*. She didn't smile or scowl. The woman could be a doll.

Oh, a beautiful one, sure.

But a doll, nonetheless.

"Is this necessary?" Viktoria asked quietly.

"I don't exactly have another choice. Pav needs some standard of protection just like the rest of us. The only way I can do that is to allow him the stars, and since he's not exactly comfortable with leaving the Compound today, I figured it was better to bring someone to—"

"Then call someone else," she hissed.

Konstantin's gaze darted to his sister, fast and warning in a blink. "*Vik*."

"You didn't ask me if this was okay."

"I'm here," Konstantin replied at the same level. "What will happen with me here?"

If that helped to relax Viktoria, she didn't show it. Pav was still interested in why the woman was scared of him at all. It wasn't like she knew him, and hell, he hadn't even known who she was. It wasn't possible that she knew anything about him to *be* afraid of him, but he had a dozen reasons to give her if she really needed something to be scared of where he was concerned.

Was it just him, or everyone she was frightened of when alone with them?

"Can't you just get someone else?" Viktoria asked.

Pav didn't really care about the tattoos, or the protection they would give him. He'd gone this long without them on his chest, he was sure he would be fine to go a while more without them, too. But what he didn't want … well, suddenly, he didn't want this woman leaving here. He was more curious about her. He couldn't learn anything about her if she was gone, could he?

He didn't have a lot of experience with women—the few times he'd left the Compound with whatever companion had been designated to go with him for the night, he'd been taken to a handful of women who'd made it their missions to educate him. Those women had all been paid for their time, and although he was grateful, this woman was not the same.

She was not a whore.

She was not like them.

She was not even like him.

He brought fear.

She only felt it.

Pav's mouth decided to work before his brain had even properly thought the comment through. Yet another thing that was so unlike him, but it seemed this woman—this, *Viktoria*—was bringing that out of him a lot.

Did he like it?

That was yet to be determined.

"Would it help if he held a gun to my head while you did the tattoos?" Pav asked.

Viktoria's head swung around and her gaze landed on him. All wide, and cold again. Ice-blue, and deep like the sea. He bet she was as dangerous as the sea, too. Expansive and amazing, but just vicious and hazardous enough to kill him if he wasn't careful.

He didn't know what he expected her to say, then.

Her laugh shocked him. It was soft, sweet, and melodic. A complete contradiction to the carved-from-stone woman who had been staring at him only moments ago.

And, apparently, her brother was shocked, too, if Konstantin's blinking expression was any indication as he stared at his sister, confused.

A small smile graced Viktoria's mouth. If one could even call the ghost of a grin tilting up the edges of her lips a smile. He didn't know if he would, but he liked it. Pav very rarely made someone else smile. He usually had them sobbing, crying, or begging—one of those things, or a mixture of them.

Never a smile, though.

He liked hers.

"Okay, Pav," Viktoria said, "I'll do your tattoos."

Why did that feel like a battle won?

Whatever.

He'd take it.

• • •

Pav was hyperaware of Konstantin sitting in the corner of the office, surveying a newspaper he'd opened on his lap. Occasionally, the man would glance up from the paper and peek at what was happening across the room, but he never said anything to Pav or Viktoria, and he quickly went back to reading like he hadn't looked at them in the first place.

Viktoria, on the other hand, was zoned in on her work as she wiped an ink-stained paper towel across Pav's chest. She was almost done—he could tell not by the stars she was inking on his clavicles, because he hadn't actually looked at them when he was too busy watching her—

but because of how long they had been sitting there now.

Three hours.

He was accustomed to doing nothing for long periods of time. Or rather, being told to shut up and stay still in a certain spot until someone was ready for him to step in and finish whatever business they wanted him to complete. He was, however, not used to staring at something as interesting as Viktoria Boykov while he had to do it.

"Why do you keep staring at me?" she asked suddenly.

She hadn't even been looking at him.

"How do you know—"

"I can feel your eyes."

Pav might have smiled, but he couldn't be sure. "I was thinking," he lied, "that you don't look like the typical tattoo artist, no? I don't see any obvious tattoos."

The tight tank top she'd exposed after pulling off her leather jacket had suddenly made the room a lot hotter for Pav, although he'd managed not to acknowledge it. How, he wasn't sure. Great fucking control, maybe.

She flipped up her hand, and for the first time, he noticed the cursive *B* tattooed on her middle finger. "For Boykov, obviously."

He chuckled a bit, realizing when she flipped someone off, it was like she was silently saying *fuck off from the Boykovs*. "I didn't see that one earlier. My mistake."

He had been too busy staring at her face ... the delicate, sexy line of her shoulders under that tank top, and the way her collarbones peeked out around the collar, asking to be bitten. *Fuck*, he had a serious problem right now.

"No others?" he asked.

Viktoria glanced up from her world, and those ice-blue eyes of hers found his instantly. "None that you can see."

"And none that I want to see," Konstantin murmured from across the room. "Save that for another time and place; we are here to work, not to talk."

Pav had the strangest urge to see if he could throw something and hit Konstantin in the head from his position, but nothing was really close enough, and he didn't think it would help his case. Not with the man across the room or with the woman currently working on his chest. He had to consider those things—they were important, he supposed.

Viktoria rolled her eyes, but quickly went back to her work. "This last bit of shading is going to hurt. Fair warning, yes?"

Pav smirked a bit. "I have felt far more pain than your little gun is going to do to me."

"Machine."

"What?"

"It is a *machine*, Pav. It is not a gun. It does not shoot anything from the needles, yeah? It is a tattoo machine."

"Fascinating."

It really wasn't.

He thought the way she said it was, though.

Viktoria looked up at him again, all ice-blue eyes wide and fear still lingering around her aura. Yeah, he could still taste it, too. As strange as that was. He could feel it, and he wanted to soak it all in. Because despite the fact she was clearly terrified of him, she was trying to suppress it. She pushed it down, and he wanted to know why.

Why for him?

"Almost done," she whispered.

Pav nodded. "*Spasibo.*"

Viktoria said nothing and went back to her work.

He went back to staring at her again.

Seemed like a fair trade, no?

• • •

"Do not remove the wrappings for at least six hours," Viktoria said as she finished packing up the kit she'd brought along. She didn't look up at him as she worked, but he didn't mind. "Make sure of it."

Pav nodded as his fingertips drifted over the cellophane that had been taped over his tattoos. "Understood."

"No scratching."

"I won't."

"And that's it," Viktoria said, standing straight and turning to face him. Although, instead of looking his way, she looked at her brother standing beside him. "Is that all for me?"

Pav didn't miss how Viktoria had easily reverted to the woman who had been sitting in the chair when he'd first entered the office. Cold and made from stone. Unfeeling and distant. She didn't want to be there, she just *was.*

He wondered why.

Konstantin nodded. "That is all. I'm grateful."

She nodded and then glanced Pav's way, finally. "I probably won't see you again, but it was … interesting to meet you, Pavel."

He didn't miss how she purposely didn't use the words *good* or *nice* to describe meeting him. Not that he blamed her. He wouldn't use those descriptors about himself, either.

"And you, Viktoria," he returned quietly.

She didn't wait to be dismissed by her brother like every other person who came into Konstantin's presence would do. Pav watched her go and didn't turn back to Konstantin until she was entirely gone from the office, and the door closed loudly behind her.

"She's broken," Pav said.

Konstantin blinked, but quickly fixed his expression. "Pardon you?"

"That woman. She is *broken*. In her mind ... something is wrong."

"I—"

"I can tell," he interjected before the man could interrupt him. "Mine is the same way."

Konstantin cleared his throat and shifted on his feet as his gaze darted to the door where his sister had disappeared. "Viktoria has reason to be a little different from everyone else. I won't lie and say she doesn't have issues—she clearly does. This was ... different, though."

Pav reached for the shirt and jacket he had thrown over a chair earlier before sitting down to let Viktoria work. Slipping the shirt on, and then the jacket, too, he asked, "What was different?"

The man's curious gaze—no longer sharp and calculating—drifted to Pav again. "She smiled ... laughed for you."

"And?"

"Well, nothing," Konstantin murmured. "Not if it was left up to her."

Pavel didn't understand what in the hell Konstantin was talking about, and he really didn't have the time to figure it out, either. He had other things to do now. The chambers had been left alone for a good portion of the afternoon, and that made him anxious. He wasn't used to leaving the cells and men inside them alone for so long. He needed to get back down there and make sure everything was as it needed to be.

He couldn't sit here and discuss a woman he would probably never see again. Even if that was the last thing he currently wanted—he felt a great urge to follow Viktoria; to ask more about her ... to know anything about her at all.

Konstantin made a noise under his breath and drew Pav's attention to him again. "Over the next week, I expect you to leave the Compound occasionally. The stock room where you gather the things you need for downstairs will slowly be left empty—you'll need to handle it, now. I will provide you with accounts to use. *Money*."

Pav scowled. "Hmm."

"These are normal things, Pav."

Maybe.

Not to him, though.

"And then next week," Konstantin continued, "there is a party for my brother and his wife. A baby shower. I expect you to be there. You don't have to engage, but I want you seen. Bring a gift."

Pav's brow dipped. "A gift?"

"For the baby."

"What do babies need?"

Konstantin looked his way again—amusement and sadness danced in the man's eyes. "I'm sure you'll figure something out."

That was debatable.

And not one he wanted to have.

"All right," he muttered.

"Good. This is a new start for you, Pav. Do not waste it."

5.

STEPPING OUT of the white Camaro, Viktoria eyed the bustling parking lot of the grocery store, and tried to convince herself this was, in fact, a good idea. She had practically hidden herself away in her house for a week, and she was starting to run out of food.

So was her life lately.

She would force herself to hide away from the rest of the world until she no longer had a choice and was forced to go out into the real world. You know, where there was *things, people,* and other uncomfortable situations that she really didn't want to deal with. Things that caused her anxiety to spike high, and her fear to be a constant buzz in the back of her mind.

She didn't want to be here, but she also needed to eat. So, it didn't seem like she had a choice but to go out and get food. Oh, sure, she could order whatever she needed online, and have it shipped direct to her doorstep, but that seemed like a problem waiting to happen, too.

That meant some stranger was going to come *to her house,* when she was likely going to be alone, and she was going to at least have to let them into her entrance hallway to get the bags. Which meant she would be alone in her house with a stranger, unable to really do anything, and …

Oh, God.

Just the idea was enough to make her puke. Already, her hands were shaking, and she could taste the bile on the back of her tongue. Her throat tightened; the slice of cold fear slipped down her spine, and she found it all too hard to drag in a proper breath.

Anxiety was a bitch.

Fear?

That was even worse.

Enough of that, she told herself. She wasn't stupid, and she knew exactly how her anxiety worked. It was a fucking monster. If she allowed herself to feed into the panic and fear, it would only grow until it was out of control and she was back in her car, sobbing behind the wheel because she couldn't get the thoughts of out of her head.

Viktoria was a mess.

No doubt about it.

She didn't think she needed to purposely make it worse, right? No, she would much rather pretend like she was just fine. When faced with something that challenged her in that respect, she didn't mind putting the bitch face back on to scare it away.

Simple enough.

Viktoria had made an art out of pretending her mind wasn't a constant warzone of flashbacks, memories, and pain. It had become almost a game for her to figure out different ways to hide the fact she was terrified of almost everything now. So, it really didn't feel like a big deal for her to cross the parking lot after dragging herself from the prospective panic attack that teased the edge of her mind instead of just giving into the hell that was waiting for her.

Oh, it would come.

The panic *would* come.

The attack would be horrible.

But for now, she had suppressed it. For now, it would fall to the back of her mind and taunt her from there. She was sure that once she was at home, and alone, it would come rushing back. Then she wouldn't be able to keep it at bay. That was usually how it worked for her, anyway.

Yeah, a constant war.

That felt appropriate.

Inside the grocery store, Viktoria ignored the way the people near the entrance and exit doors felt slightly *too close* to her as she grabbed a cart. A guy in jogging pants and a hoodie brushed against her arm as he picked up a basket from the pile, and she did all she could do not to shudder and turn away from him.

Instead, she turned and gave him a glare that burned, snapping, "Do you fucking *mind?*"

The guy's eyes widened, and he put up a hand as if in surrender. "Sorry, pardon me."

There was always a part of Viktoria's mind that reminded her in these moments that not all people were automatically out to get her, so to speak. That accidents were actually just mistakes, and it didn't mean something horrible was going to happen to her, just because someone got closer to her than she was comfortable.

But it didn't matter, either.

Already, the man had backed off. With his shopping basket in hand, he walked away shaking his head the whole time. Yet another person that would recognize Viktoria's face the next time they came face to face. The first thing they would remember about her was the fact that she was a bitch, and they would keep their distance.

In some ways, she liked that.

In others, it irritated her.

Bitch was meant to be a slur—she just fucking owned it now. She would rather be seen as a bitch by people than easy prey. If being a bitch meant people stayed far away from her at all times, then that was perfectly fine with her.

Viktoria made quick work of going through the aisles and grabbing enough items to keep her fed for at least a month. That meant less time she would have to spend coming back here over the next thirty days.

Winning.

Other than a worker who asked if she needed any help—a guy, actually—while she'd surveyed boxes of cereal, no one else tried to approach her. No one got close enough to make her anxiety pick up a notch.

She was just heading for the checkout, a feat that would probably mean she would need to have chitchat with the idiot running the register, when something off to her left caught her eye. She came to a stop in the middle of the aisle and stared at the man twenty feet away as he surveyed a whole row of Hallmark cards.

The first thing she thought?

He looks like he has no idea what he's doing.

It kind of shocked her that her initial reaction was not to keep walking; to pretend like she hadn't seen Pavel at all, and go about her day. It wasn't like on any other day she would stop to admire some strange man alone in a grocery aisle.

Oh, the nerves were present. The anxiety thrummed deep and the fear teased at her senses. Still, she watched him.

He put one card back, and then picked another out from the top row. Flipping it over, he read something on the back, and his brow dipped in the cutest way. The week before, when she had done his tattoos, he'd been wearing black jeans that molded to his ass and thighs, a plain black tee, and a leather jacket. He had the same wardrobe today, except the tee was white.

She wondered why in the hell he was here—she knew about the elusive *Zhatka*. Reaper, they called him. Sure, she hadn't known his face, and that *he* was the one they talked about when the name Zhatka passed their lips. But she'd heard about him. She'd heard the whispers; the ones that said he was owned by the Boykovs and hadn't left the Compound's property in years.

She knew he was dangerous.

She heard those whispers, too.

Was it all true?

If it was, the last thing she should want to do was head down the aisle and ask him if he needed help because he looked like he had never seen a greeting card before in his life. Another war started in her head—leave or go, basically. She had just decided to keep going when all at once, Pav lifted his head and looked her way. His gaze landed on her, and she swore there wasn't even a *hint* of surprise when he looked at her.

Like he knew.

She'd been there the whole time.

Well, there goes leaving.

She could leave, actually. She could go without saying hello. She never cared before if someone thought she was a bitch because she looked them right in the face one second, and then walked away from them without any kind of acknowledgment in the next.

Still, her legs worked on their own accord. Before she knew what was happening, she had turned her cart and headed down the aisle toward Pav. Something akin to a smile curved the edges of his lips, but she couldn't be sure if that's truly what it was. It looked slightly darker, and far sexier than *just* a smile. She didn't know if he meant for it to come across like that, but it did.

That was even more problematic for her.

This man terrified her.

She didn't need him turning her on, too.

Yep, she was a *mess*.

"Viktoria," he greeted quietly.

Now that she thought about it, his voice was kind of like his smile, too. Dark and husky. Yet, quiet and low at the same time. In all their conversations so far, she hadn't once heard him raise his tone and he spoke just below a normal level when he did talk.

Strange ...

And she liked it.

"Pavel," she returned, "you look a little lost."

He frowned and turned back to the card in his hand. "This is not suitable for a ... generic congratulations, is it?"

Pav held out the card for her to look at, and she did all she could do not to grin or God forbid, laugh at him. He seemed dead serious, and that just proved to her in a way that some of the whispers about him were probably true.

He hadn't been out of the Compound very much.

How sad was that?

"Unless you're congratulating them for the death of a pet, then no," she replied.

Pav blinked, and quickly put the card back to the row. "Oh. I just picked ones that looked nice. I didn't read the insides."

"Did you read the words on the outside?"

He shrugged. "They're platitudes. They don't actually *say anything*, do they? Generic. Boring. Meaningless. They'll be tossed in the garbage before the night is out, I assume. That's what I would do with them if someone ever thought to buy me a card to congratulate me on something that was obvious."

She had no idea what to say to that.

He wasn't wrong, though.

"What is the card for?" she asked.

Pav hummed under his breath and eyed her from the side. "A party to celebrate something beautiful."

"So, you really do need a generic card?"

"I suppose."

It took her all of three seconds to find a generic card with the usual congratulations stamped on the front, and the usual platitudes on the inside. She grabbed the matching envelop, and handed it over to Pav, too. He took them with the same smile as before.

"There you are."

She turned to walk away, but it was his hand quickly curving around her wrist that stopped her. She froze all over, and a small tremor worked its way through her sinew. Air sucked fast and sharp into her lungs.

At the same time, she enjoyed the warmth of his palm against his skin. She liked the way his fingers tightened against her skin, and the pressure of his fingertips pressing into her racing pulse point. There was no way to hide the way his touch both terrified her and confused her.

Excited her.

Viktoria looked back at Pav but said nothing.

He quirked a brow. "I was going to say thank you."

She nodded. "You don't have to."

Now, let me go.

The words came out in her mind, but not out of her mouth. She wanted to say them, and she didn't want to say them at the same time.

How strange …

"*Da.* I was going to say it, but now I want to say something else."

Viktoria wet her bottom lip, muttering, "So, say whatever it is, then."

"You're still scared of me?"

She blinked.

Her mouth worked, though.

"Yes," she whispered.

"Why?"

"The same reason that everyone else scares me, Pav."

He tipped his head to the side. "But do you approach them like you do me?"

"No."

He nodded, and then let her go.

Viktoria swallowed hard, pushing back her fear. "You know, you should get out of the Compound more often."

Pav's gaze darted back to hers. "Why?"

"You look good out in the light like everyone else."

Pretending to be normal. Acting like you fit in. Just like me.

He did smile that time.

Wide and beautiful.

Sinful, even.

She wondered if he could read her mind.

Was that possible?

"Except I'm not like everyone else, Viktoria."

She shrugged. "Yeah, me either."

• • •

"You look terrified."

Viktoria didn't even bother to hide her smirk when her oldest brother, Kolya, spun on his heel to face her. His gaze, colder than even hers on his good days, warmed momentarily as his stare landed on her. She grinned and held up the baby shower gift that she had brought along to add to the other three dozen gifts that were already piled high on a table and now spilling onto the floor. She was trying to ignore how full Kolya and Maya's house was with guests for their party—it was hard.

She would try for her brother, though.

Maya, too.

Viktoria liked her.

"Do I?" Kolya asked.

"Hmm?"

"Look terrified?"

Viktoria laughed. "A little. I watched you stare at Maya for a minute or two. You looked … out of your element."

Kolya passed a look over his shoulder at where his wife was currently engaging a whole room full of people. Viktoria didn't miss the young woman who stood close to Maya, either.

Zoya Bennett.

Her half-sister seemed slightly uncomfortable from all the attention, and she supposed that was normal, all things considered. Zoya hadn't really been a part of their world—Vadim kept her and her mother well-hidden from the rest of them.

"Who invited her?" Viktoria asked, referring to Zoya.

Kolya cleared his throat. "Be nice."

"I never see her to be mean, Kolya."

"Be that as it may, Maya invited her. *Be nice.*"

Her brothers assumed she just hated Zoya because she was the second daughter—the secret Vadim had kept. Frankly, Viktoria felt very little for Zoya in that regard. It wasn't her fault that Vadim was a goddamn dog, or that he'd lied to his children for their whole lives. She was just a byproduct of their father, the same way the rest of them were.

She was fine with letting her brothers believe whatever they wanted to about her feelings regarding their half-sister. She didn't plan to make an effort there—Zoya had never been a part of their world, and Viktoria figured it would be better if the girl stayed out of it altogether. Maybe then, she could be free.

God knew they weren't.

They never would be.

Viktoria wouldn't drag her in—not even to be *friends*.

She wasn't surprised that Maya had invited the young woman, though. Unlike the two of them, Maya was a social butterfly. She could make friends with the Devil, and then proceed to make everyone else like him, too. How her brother—being a man like he was, with very little desire to be around other people—had found a wife like Maya ... Viktoria would never understand.

But here they were.

"I just realized ..."

Viktoria raised a brow when her brother didn't finish his statement. "Realized what?"

"That I'm going to be a father."

"She's like six and a half months pregnant."

He scowled as he looked back at her. "Quite aware, yeah? I go to the appointments and keep up to date on it all."

Viktoria pressed her lips together to keep from laughing. Kolya sounded so fucking defensive that someone might question his involvement or level of dedication to his wife and unborn child that it was amusing. Anyone who spent more than two minutes with her brother when he was around his wife knew very damn well that Kolya cared about *nothing* and *no one* the way he cared about Maya Boykov.

He shook his head and sighed as he crossed his arms over his broad chest. His gaze came back to her, and she offered him a small smile. "I think I didn't have an ... example of how to be a good father. And seeing all the blue things made me realize some people here expect one thing from a boy of mine."

"Different than what you expect from him, you mean?"

Kolya shrugged. "Take it that way, if you want."

She would because she wasn't stupid. That was exactly what her brother meant, whether he wanted to say it or not. She could read between the lines. She and Kolya were too alike for their own good, even if it was for entirely different reasons.

A topic for a different day.

Today was supposed to be beautiful.

"I think the fact that you know you expect different things from your son than what was expected of you means your first concern is not an issue, Kolya."

Her brother's brow dipped as he muttered, "I don't understand."

"Our father would have never worried about whether he was going to be a good father to begin with. All he cared about was the fact that his boys became what his boys needed to be—other versions of himself."

A quick understanding dawned in her brother's eyes, but in true Kolya fashion, he didn't acknowledge her words. Still, she could see the gratefulness in her brother's soft smile. Another unusual thing for him—Kolya was soft in *nothing*, except for maybe with his wife, but Viktoria knew better than to tell him that.

"You came!"

Viktoria didn't even get the chance to ready for the oncoming attack from her sister-in-law before Maya pushed past Kolya's large form and came for her. Maya was a sprite-like thing. Tiny as a fairy compared to her very large and intimidating husband. Her smile was blinding, whereas his scowl was terrifying.

And yet, when she hugged Viktoria, it felt like little bars had come to wrap around her body and were squeezing her tight. Someone else, and Viktoria would have been quick to tell them to back the fuck off. She might even tell Maya that on one of her bad days, but she knew she would get a comment from Kolya for doing it, too.

Not today, though.

Today, she hugged her sister-in-law back.

"Of course, I came," Viktoria said.

Maya pulled back with one of her big smiles. "I know, but Konstantin said you were … not having good days lately, so I didn't want to assume. It would have been okay if you weren't feeling up to it, yes?"

Okay, so maybe she loved her sister-in-law for more reasons than just the fact she was Kolya's wife. Maya was one of the few people in Viktoria's inner circle and family who didn't push her for more than she was willing to give. The woman always seemed to understand that sometimes, people just had to deal with their own shit on their own time. It wasn't something that could be forced.

And Maya expected *nothing* from Vik. She was there if she needed her. That was exactly what she needed a lot of the time. She wished the rest of the people around her could understand that, too. Easier said than done ...

"Also, Konstantin should learn to keep his mouth shut," Maya added, winking.

Viktoria laughed. "I tell him that all the time."

"And he never learns, does he?"

"He's a fixer," Kolya muttered behind them. "He must fix all the things."

"Don't tell him that."

"Never," her brother agreed.

"Here, I'll take that," Maya said, reaching to grab the gift Viktoria had been holding. "I'll put it with the others, but in the family pile. We'll open those first."

"Sure."

By the time Maya had put the gift in the pile with the rest of them, someone else had come up to distract Viktoria's brother and his wife. She was left alone in the entryway of their living room, where she was again reminded of just how crowded this house was at the moment. All the guests moving from room to room and chatting had her anxiety picking up all over again. As much as she tried to ignore it and push it back down to deal with it later, it continued pressing up in her throat like vomit that wanted to spill from her lips.

Fuck.

Viktoria swung around, ready to slip out the back for a breather on the porch, when she nearly ran headfirst into Konstantin. He arched a brow at her sharp glare and scowl at having her quick exit interrupted by him.

"Thank you for showing up," he told her.

Viktoria didn't even swallow back the cutting retort that was at the ready—her standard to use when she needed to get the hell out of a situation in a hurry. "Thank you for reminding me daily like a child that I needed to be here, Konstantin."

He sighed.

She pushed past him.

It was easier this way.

• • •

"You know, to some people in that house," Viktoria said as she scratched a spot behind Kolya's dog's ear, "you are the most terrifying thing here, I think."

Sumerki's stubby tail wagged fast. He was as black as night, and in the dark backyard, he could probably blend in enough that someone might miss him if they weren't looking for him. But then when he opened those eyes of his—big, yellow, and bright—a person couldn't miss him at all. He was massive. Probably well over a hundred pounds of solid, pit bull muscle. She had seen this dog go after a poor, wild rabbit once.

It had stood no chance.

He could be vicious.

Nasty as fuck.

But with her, Sumerki had always been a giant baby. She knew people gave the dog a wide berth of space whenever he was out with Kolya. He could, and usually did, act as her brother's protection a lot of the time.

It was amusing.

She was so distracted with Sumerki that she didn't notice the form coming up to her side until he sat right down beside her on the steps. The shriek that came out of Viktoria when she realized it was Pav was inhumane, she was sure of it.

Her heart thundered.

He just grinned.

"Are you trying to give me a heart attack?" she asked him, glaring.

Pav cocked his head to the side. "You're ... interesting when you're scared. Do you realize that?"

Viktoria shivered. "And what, you like that?"

"Yes and no."

He glanced at Sumerki and held out his hand. The dog didn't hesitate to come forward, bump his forehead against Pav's palm, and then he licked the man's fingertips like the two of them were friends or something.

They probably were.

Kolya often brought the dog with him when he worked, and since he spent a lot of time at the Compound, it would make sense that Sumerki would go there, too.

It was no wonder the dog didn't alert her to the fact someone else was already outside and watching her play with him. He considered Pav a *friend*.

"You were invited to this too?" she asked quietly.

Pav shrugged. "Seems so."

"That's what the card was for, then?"

"It was."

"What did you get them for a gift?"

Pav smiled. "Different things; whatever the girl at the store said was good for a baby boy."

Huh.

"I could have helped you to pick out—"

"You were uncomfortable enough. I figured it was better to let you go."

All over again, she was left confused by this man. He seemed to enjoy her fear of him in some ways, and yet, he was also hyperaware of it and made deliberate choices that would make sure her fear wasn't made worse by anything he did.

He was a mess, too.

Just in a different way than her.

"These people ..." He grunted under his breath and shot a look over his shoulder. "I don't know what to do with them. I don't feel like I belong here, yeah? They *know* me, and that's what I feel when they look at me."

"Reaper, you mean. *Zhatka.*"

His throat jumped at the name coming from her lips, but he didn't tell her not to use it. "They know what I do—what I can do. I feel like I can hear what they're thinking. *Stay in your place, Pavel. Stay downstairs with the rest of the things that shouldn't be seen.*"

Why did that hurt her for him?

"You're human, too," she said softly.

"And so are the people who they've put in the cells for me to keep," he returned. "Should they be allowed off their leashes, too?"

"Do you feel like that when you see their victims, day in and day out?"

Pav let out a dark laugh at that. "They're not victims down in the cells. They've all earned their places, trust in that. I know they're human, but that doesn't change the fact that they've earned their punishments. Or, that's what I have always been told."

Then, Pav glanced over at her. Those dark eyes of his seemed even more shadowed in the dim lighting of the backyard. He leaned closer to her, until there were just a couple of inches between the two of them. She felt like a deer in headlights. Partly entranced by his scent and closeness, in the beauty of his features, and the way his lips curved sexily and dangerously. And yet, terrified at the same time because she had no idea what this man wanted with her, but she had no doubt he was capable of horrible things.

She wanted to move.

She also wanted to remain.

"Can I tell you something?" he murmured.

She nodded. "Yeah, sure."

"That fear of yours ... it's a powerful thing, Viktoria. For yourself and for others. It can be used, manipulated, or wielded. Do you understand?"

"I only know that it holds me back."

"Because you let it, girl."

She almost laughed at that. "Do I look like a *girl* to you?"

Pav flashed his teeth in his grin. "No, you look very much like a woman I would enjoy ruining, but I have to remind myself that won't work for you."

Viktoria sucked in a shaky breath.

He added quieter, "The allure of fear is learning to love it ... you'll find power in being able to do that because then no one but you can use it."

All at once, he moved away from her. He gave her space and room to breathe once more. But that didn't matter. Her body was still hot. Her lungs still felt tight. She could still taste sin and fear on the back of her tongue like she always had.

That's what he did to her, though.

He made her hot on the outside.

He stoked her fear on the inside.

It was quite a combination.

Viktoria couldn't remember the last time she had actually felt *attraction* for another human being, let alone a man. She noticed someone was good-looking, sure, but it never stirred anything in her. She didn't get a visceral need anymore. She never felt *lust* like it was a tangible thing she could reach out and grab.

Except she did.

Right now.

With Pav.

It terrified her, too.

Like him.

Wasn't that appropriate?

Before she even understood her actions, Viktoria whispered, "Pav?"

"Yes?"

He looked her way again.

She leaned in and kissed him.

Hard.

6.

PAV FOUND people rarely did things they didn't want to do. Even if the desire was something buried deep, and hidden from view, it didn't matter. When a person got what they wanted, *finally*, they didn't shy from it.

So, despite the fact that Pav could feel the slight tremor that worked its way through Viktoria's body when her lips pressed against his, he knew that fear of hers was an undercurrent. It was secondary to the thing she wanted—*him*.

Her kiss lingered for longer than a second.

And then two ... *three.*

Pav's next choice was purely brought on from his own wants. She wasn't nearly close enough to him on the steps, and he needed her far closer. Sliding an arm around her waist, he pulled Viktoria right into his lap, never once breaking their kiss.

A shudder ran over her shoulders and down her spine when his tongue struck out against the seam of her lips. He followed her shivers with his hands, driving them over the flimsy material of her dress and feeling the warmth of her soft body through the thin fabric. He heard the hard hitch in her breath when his hands gripped tightly to her hips, and those silky lips of hers finally parted to let him in.

That first taste of her wasn't nearly enough. A tease, really. The lust in her blown-wide pupils mixed heavily with the taste of her fear, but he couldn't fucking get enough. Neither could she, it seemed.

She didn't shy away from the kiss. She didn't turn away from letting her tongue tangle with his. It felt like war, in a way. How she fought him with her kiss, but her hands fisted into his T-shirt, and she pulled him impossibly closer.

Everything else was a background noise to *her*. The buzz of the backyard, and the flickering light on the porch that should probably be changed. The slight breeze whispered over his skin, but he didn't really feel the coolness at all. He couldn't, not when Viktoria started to grind her hips against his, and her exhale came out shaky when his teeth found her lower lip.

"*God*," she whined.

"You taste like cherries," he murmured against her mouth. "Cherries and *vodka*."

She really did.

It was addicting.

Like drugs shot straight into his veins.

She tipped her head to the side, and he let his lips trail over her cheek, and across the line of her soft jaw. Her lips trembled, and the quietest whine fell from her mouth when his hands slid around to slip under the skirt of her dress. The cotton of her panties met his fingertips, and her hips rolled faster in his lap. The sensation made him groan, and just as fast, her mouth found his again for another burning, deep kiss.

Fuck.

He couldn't get enough of her. If he was starved, then she was the feast laid out in front of him. A part of him wanted to see just how far he could push this woman—how much would she take? Could he get all those broken parts of her mind to show for him? Could it possibly be as beautiful as he thought it would be?

There was no hiding the growing erection straining against his jeans—not that he cared to hide it. Viktoria's fingers twisted tighter into his shirt the more he let his hands roam over her body under her dress.

Soft curves and warm skin.

She was perfect.

Perfectly broken.

"Pavel, we have a prob—*oh*."

Viktoria practically jumped off Pav's lap at the sound of her brother's voice coming from somewhere behind them. Pav had the sudden and striking urge to grab the woman and drag her right back where she was. He didn't give a fuck if the whole world wanted to watch him as he peeled back all the layers keeping her hidden. He just *wanted her.*

And even feeling that, the haze of lust that had taken over his mind for those couple of minutes quickly began to clear. He was fine with acting as though he hadn't had his tongue stuck in her mouth and his hands under her dress as they dry humped one another on the back porch. He stood from the step and brushed his hands down his pants.

Viktoria, on the other hand, seemed to turn into a statue of ice two feet away. Her cold, blue gaze drifted to the side and wouldn't turn to meet his, or the man standing on the back porch just beyond the door.

Konstantin, to his benefit, simply cleared his throat and went with Pav's way of thinking. He acted like he hadn't just interrupted anything, and that he saw absolutely nothing. Pav might thank the man for that, if he wasn't so irritated and his cock wasn't still hard.

Although, that was going away.

Shame.

"We have a problem," Konstantin said.

Pav glanced over at Viktoria, but quickly went back to her brother. "What kind of a problem?"

"At the Compound. There's been an ... issue." Konstantin's stare drifted to his sister as he said that, like maybe that problem had something to do with her and he didn't want to give details. Or, that was the impression Pav got, anyway. "We're going to have to head out of here and go there to take care of it. If you're not busy, I mean."

Pav almost scoffed.

He didn't get a choice.

Busy, or not.

Konstantin didn't need to pretend differently.

"We're leaving in two minutes," Konstantin said, already turning to head back inside the house. "I will give you a moment."

Pav wasn't given the chance to respond before Konstantin took his leave. The backdoor slamming shut was the only sound that echoed over the backyard after the man disappeared. He swore he couldn't even hear Viktoria *breathing.*

"Have a good night," she said beside him.

He didn't miss the iciness in her tone.

Or the way she wouldn't look at him.

Still.

Was it embarrassment?

Shame?

Or something else entirely?

Had that fear of hers come back to the forefront of her mind, and reminded her of exactly what she had been doing with him?

Pav was fine to let this woman do whatever she needed to do to keep herself in check. He knew that all too well. He understood what it was like to put the mask on for those who were watching to see something that made them more comfortable.

Yes, he understood.

He didn't like it, though.

Not with her.

"Viktoria," he said quietly.

Her next step froze before she could climb the stairs. He didn't miss the way her shoulders tensed at his call of her name, either, or the way a shiver crawled over her spine again. *God.* He'd love to get his hands on her when she was wearing nothing but skin and fighting that fear. There was something enthralling about that—he was a stupid moth dancing far too close to her flickering flame.

"What?" she whispered.

Her back stayed facing him.

He didn't mind.

Pav didn't actually know what he wanted to say to her. It was more like he just wanted two more seconds with her. Another moment to breathe her in and drink every drop that she was willing to give him.

"Make sure someone gets you home safely. And sleep well."

She let out a quiet laugh. One he didn't understand, but it still felt loaded. She didn't reply before she climbed the rest of the steps and headed into the house. He gave it twenty seconds, more than long enough for her to rejoin the party without it looking like he was following behind, and then he went inside, too.

He assumed she would find her family in the crowd and join them for the remainder of the party. Instead, he noticed her standing alone in the entryway of the living room, away from the guests. She said nothing to him. He said nothing to her as he passed.

Pav couldn't help but reach out to touch her as he headed for the hallway that would lead to the front door. It was nothing big, really, just the brush of his fingertips along the soft skin of her inner wrist.

But it was enough.

Enough to make her relax. Enough to make her shiver again. Enough to drive him *crazy.*

Pav was not done.

Not with her.

He tended to like broken things. She was certainly *that.*

And more …

• • •

Pav hadn't known what the issue was that needed their immediate attention at the Compound. For the entire drive, Konstantin drove in silence. Pav wasn't the type to talk anyway, so he hadn't bothered to press the man for details. Not that Konstantin owed him anything, if he had tried to ask.

But now, as he stood in front of the empty cell that had once housed a man for almost two years, Pav was beginning to think Konstantin was concerned over more than just the fact that one of the Boykov prisoners had escaped.

"He killed the man watching the Compound," Konstantin said from behind Pav.

Pav didn't turn away from the cell. His gaze swept the shackles at the other end of the cell—this was one of the few rooms beneath the Compound that actually had a door. He'd never known the name of the man housed in this particular cell, but the man refused to be broken. He was beaten more often than the rest, and for the first couple of months after he had been brought in, Pav remembered specifically that Kolya Boykov had made a few trips down to visit the man.

And the *screams* …

He wouldn't soon forget those.

"Someone let him out of the shackles," Pav said, cocking his head to the side as he eyed the chains and metal cuffs resting forgotten on the cement floor. They didn't look broken or ruined at all. They simply looked as though someone had undone them. "The man watching him and the rest of them, yes?"

Konstantin cleared his throat. "Likely. Would you have released him from his confines for any reason?"

"No."

"Why not?"

"I know better. Abused dogs never forget where they come from. They can pretend, and act like they're broken and incapable, but once they're free …" Pav trailed off with a quiet noise and shook his head. "You turn your back once, give them that chance, and I promise, they will take it every time."

"This was only the man's second time watching the cells."

Pav was aware. The man was intended to watch the lower part of the Compound—Pav's duty, normally—when Pav took his leave from the grounds. It was all a part of Konstantin's great plan to get Pav away from these four walls and back into some semblance of a normal life. This was also why it was pointless. No one was Pav. No one but him could possibly understand how dangerous it was to watch the people being held in these cells.

"Where's the body of the man killed?"

"Being taken to the furnace."

"Where was he found?"

"Just outside the cell, along with a cell phone that had been used to make a call."

Pav's brow furrowed. "Whose phone?"

"The dead man's."

"Do you think he made a call—"

"I think unless he choked himself out, and then laid the phone on the back of his head after it had been said and done, then it's probably safe to say it was the one that escaped who used the phone."

"Do you know the number—"

"As far as we know, the call went through to a burner. We have no other information."

Pav took a moment then to look over the cell again, and with new eyes this time. A little bit of information could go a long way. It could change one's perspective, and the way they approached a situation.

The shackles …

The dead man just outside the cell …

A phone call …

"He planned this," Pav said. "This was something he was waiting for, and when he finally got his chance, he took it."

"Looks like it."

"But why?"

That was the better question.

Konstantin shifted on his feet. Pav couldn't see him do it, being that the man was behind him, but he could hear it. He heard everything. One's senses were their best defense against something that might attack when a person wasn't expecting it. Pav had become accustomed to using all his senses to protect himself, and not just one or two.

"You're either uncomfortable, or thinking about lying," Pav said when the silence continued on from Konstantin. "Which tells me you know something about the man I was keeping in this cell, and why he might do this. I would like to know what those things are."

"It's not as simple as—"

"Words are *very* simple, Konstantin."

Pav knew his place, and he knew it well. He preferred to stay in his place because then, no one could say a thing to him one way or another about the things he did. He was quite aware that Konstantin's place was not like his at all. The man sat far higher on the totem pole than Pav, and he didn't owe him anything. He didn't get to make demands of a Bratva boss, and just expect to get an answer simply because he asked for it.

That's not how it worked.

Still, he risked it.

Something was wrong here.

Pav needed to know *what*.

"His name is Boris," Konstantin said. "Boris Antipov."

"First I've heard his name."

"Yes, I understand you were never told their names."

"It wasn't required for me to do my job."

"No, it wouldn't be." Konstantin sighed heavily and cleared his throat again. Turning just enough to look at the man, Pav watched as Konstantin waved a hand quickly, and the other men in the darkened, musty hallway scattered. It was only once it was just the two of them, alone in the doorway of the cell, that he started speaking again. "Boris was close to my father ... almost a right hand, if you will. His position was never very clear, but he'd earned his stars, Vadim found him likable ... perhaps because of his nature and the way he handled business, who knows? He often treated him better than he did us— his sons."

Pav's gaze narrowed, and he turned back to look at the cell again. "How does that relate to *this*?"

"Boris is volatile. I imagine you've noticed that during his time here, he still remained violent, and unpredictable. Now, imagine that when he was free, and allowed to do whatever he pleased because he answered only to Vadim."

"Hmm."

"As I said, he didn't have a proper position, but the rest of us considered him a bull of sorts for the boss ... if there was an issue, or someone needed to have a lesson beat into them, Boris was often the one who showed up. He had more run-ins with Kolya and myself than I care to admit, but that wasn't what brought him here to you."

"What was?"

"Viktoria, actually."

Pav couldn't hide the very visceral way that admission affected him. Ice had been poured into his spine while pure heat—*rage*— danced in his heart. He'd thought that organ was long dead. Somedays, it didn't even feel like it beat. But there it was, and he could feel it now.

"And what did he do to her?" Pav asked.

"He was picked by our father for her," Konstantin said. "An approved man, basically handed to her. Vadim might as well have spoon-fed Viktoria to a wolf, but he was never willing to admit that was what he'd done. Either he trusted Boris too much, knowing what he was like and the things he had done to others, or he simply didn't care because he figured the man would stay in line because of who Viktoria was."

"But what did he do to her?"

Because nothing Konstantin said answered his question, and Pav *greatly* needed to know and understand. He had a feeling he did know—Viktoria's constant fear was a good indication that trauma was ever-present in her mind. Terror followed her around like an old friend, and she used her cold demeanor and disinterested attitude as a way to hide it. Better for her to build those walls up than to dare let someone over them, he supposed.

"It was an ... arranged agreement for them to be married," Konstantin muttered, "and my sister was willing to go along with it. Perhaps she liked Boris at first, and maybe a part of her simply wanted to please our father. She always did see Vadim as a ... *god*."

"You're not telling me what I want to—"

"A month before they were to be married ... I don't know the details of what led into it, just what happened, and what came after." Konstantin's voice roughened, thick with emotion. Anger, guilt, and more. Pav heard it all. "He held her for several days—we didn't think anything of her being silent because she did that sometimes. But this time, it was because he had locked her in the bedroom of the house Vadim had bought for them. He raped her often ... every hour on the hour, as my sister once told me. He beat her when she fought back and he taunted her."

Pav's jaw ached. How hard was he clenching his teeth? His fingernails broke the skin of his palms when he clenched his hands into tight fists. The rage simmered into a slow boil.

"How did he taunt her?" Pav asked.

"He made calls to us ... to my father, and to me. One to Kolya, although he always hung up on Boris—he never cared to listen to the man talk. She would be at his feet, gagged and unable to ask for help while he talked to us like there was nothing wrong. As though it was just another day, and we had business to discuss. Other times, he would be actively assaulting her when he made the calls."

Now, Konstantin's voice was faint—oh, the anger was present, but something else was far clearer. *Pain*. The guilt. The regret. Pav understood, but what was done was now done. It had happened, and it couldn't be taken away because someone wished it was so. The event was already over, and it left scars that couldn't be ignored or hidden.

Guilt fixed nothing.

The regret came too late.

"How many days?" Pav asked.

"Five."

Fuck.

"And that was his punishment once she had gotten free, and we went after him. Ten years for every day he held her," Konstantin muttered. "Fifty years total in these cells, being kept alive only to make sure he wished he was dead for every single one of them."

"Seems appropriate."

"We thought so. There's a problem, yes?"

"And what is that?"

He turned to look at Konstantin when the man kept quiet.

"The problem is that Viktoria thought he was dead. That's what we told her. It was better for her to believe we'd killed him, when eventually, that's what would happen to him once he'd served his time. She puts on a good front, doesn't she?"

"She does," Pav agreed.

"She's so cold that you almost don't want to be near her at times. The things that come out of her mouth? They *cut you*. And they're not paper cuts, they're deep, and they're meant to kill. She does it to everyone else because it's how she protects herself. Better to keep people away than let someone close and be hurt again. But she does it to us … she does it to us because she blames us. She doesn't want to say it, she never has, but I know it. She blames us, and she should. We let it happen. And now he's free."

Yes.

That was … quite a problem.

"Someone is posted to watch her, right?"

"Yes," Konstantin replied.

Pav nodded. "I would like to help."

"I thought you might." Konstantin made a noise under his breath, adding, "I didn't acknowledge what I saw on the steps earlier tonight because I didn't know what to say. A couple of years ago, she was an entirely different young woman. I don't recognize who she is today, except when she's near you … she reminds me of who she used to be. Tonight was a lot like how I didn't want to point out the way you talked to her when she was here that day to do your tattoos, or how she reacted to you."

"She's terrified of me."

"And she doesn't want to be, either," the man murmured. "I thought … this—you—might be a changing point for her, if given the chance. That's why I invited you tonight. Another way to put you in her path. *What would it hurt*, I thought?"

Pav gave the man a look over his shoulder. "You shouldn't meddle, Konstantin."

"Sometimes, you have to."

"Yes, but *should* you? That is a different thing."

"I'm going to meddle again, but for different reasons this time," Konstantin said, shrugging. "Starting tonight, actually. I'll add you to her post—she's comfortable enough with you that even if she is scared, she'll allow you in. Someone should be inside the house with her, but I need the night before I can upset her entire life again with the truth."

Pav blinked. "You want me with her tonight?"

"I don't care what happens after the front door closes, as long as it's what she wants to do, Pavel. I only care that she doesn't know the truth about what's happening outside her door until I'm ready to tell her. I should be the one who does it. She already hates the rest of us … I'd like to give her someone who she won't hate when she finally knows everything. She doesn't hate you."

Yet.

7.

HOW TIGHT did I put the cap on this damn thing?

Viktoria glared at the bottle of vodka as she twisted on the cover harder in an attempt to get it off. She didn't think she was strong enough when drunk to put a cap on so tightly that she couldn't get it off when sober, but here she was, once again proving herself wrong.

Finally, she got the cap to twist when she used a dishcloth to aid her efforts. The promise of a full night's sleep, helped out by liquor, was on the horizon. After a night like tonight, being crammed into a space full of too many other people, she was going to need that.

It wasn't that she dreamt of other people attacking her—it rarely worked out like that in her dreams. Instead, she dreamt of Boris in the crowd, watching her. Even in her dreams, she could feel his jealousy like it was thick hands closing around her throat. She could practically taste his possessiveness the same way she could still taste blood in her mouth when he'd hold her head still so that he could shove his co—

The knock on the front door interrupted her thoughts from going any further. She wasn't sure whether she should be thankful for that or not. Especially considering she had started to close her eyes as the flashback came on because she still hadn't learned.

She had yet to figure out that closing her eyes and willing the memories away didn't actually *take them away*. If anything, it made it them sharper and clearer. She'd open her eyes, and still see him. She'd look around, find her place was empty but for her, and still taste blood and cum in her mouth.

Viktoria set the bottle on the counter and put the cap beside it, even as the knocking on her front door continued on. She had a good mind to shout at whoever it was to quit it, but she couldn't even talk like this.

Her throat was too tight, and she couldn't drag in enough air to satisfy her lungs despite the fact she was sucking it back faster than ever. Her hands trembled against the countertops, just like the rest of her body, too.

Five days of her life seemed to be what would define the rest of it. Five days of hell at the hands of a monster followed her day in and day out. Oh, sure, people didn't see it when they looked at her. She put on a good front and kept people at a distance with her cold demeanor and harsh attitude, but *she knew*. She couldn't ever fucking forget.

It was constant.

She ached in her bones.

The pain wasn't something anyone else could see because it was invisible and tailored just for her. Like a thousand little papercuts just under the surface of her skin. She didn't want to feel them, but she didn't get any choice.

She was a leaf in the wind.

Twisting.

Falling.

Dying.

In the cupboard, just above her head, two bottles of medications taunted her. She didn't even have to see them to know they were there. Despite being adamant on the fact that she didn't want to take medications to get this under control, her therapist went ahead and wrote the prescriptions anyway.

Viktoria didn't know why she decided to fill them when she knew there was no way she was going to take the anti-depressant and Xanax. Still, she'd done it, and now every single time she had another one of these moments—usually a couple of times a day on a good one—she felt like the medications there fucked with her head.

She was reminded that someone was still at her door when another knock echoed throughout the bottom level of her house. She didn't know who in the hell would be at her door at this time of night, and she had a good mind just to ignore it altogether. It wasn't like she planned on letting whoever it was come *inside*.

No way.

Then, she remembered that it could be one of her brothers. Occasionally, Konstantin did make his way by her place to check on her before he went home to his wife. He always tried to act like he was in the neighborhood, but she knew better. And Kolya, well, he didn't try to pretend anything. He outright told her when Maya would send her husband over to check on Viktoria.

If it was one of her brothers, she would be able to tell by peeking out the window on the other side of the kitchen and looking toward the stoop. She crossed the kitchen to do just that, expecting to see either her brothers, or someone else she wouldn't bother to go and answer the door for. Instead, she found someone else entirely waiting on her front stoop.

Pavel.

Viktoria blinked.

Surely, she wasn't seeing what she was seeing.

Right?

She'd had a moment with him earlier at the baby shower—a weak moment, perhaps. It certainly felt like that when after it was done, the only thing her mind could really focus on was all the ways it could have gone bad for her. Although, a part of her was still humming hours later, too, unable to forget the way his warm, calloused hands felt exploring her curves, or the way his mouth tasted as it devoured hers.

Viktoria had too many issues to name.

Sex was a *big one.*

How could she be both terrified of a man, and also want to fuck him? That didn't make sense to her. Sure, her therapist had explained that was something that would likely happen once she was ready to be intimate again, but she had laughed that off. At the time, she'd never thought there would be a time when she wanted to jump into bed with a man again.

Except now she did.

Because of *him.*

Why did it have to scare her, too?

Had that been another man waiting at her front door, Viktoria probably would have turned off all the lights, and headed upstairs where she had a gun hidden under her pillow. Not to mention ... all the other weapons she had stashed throughout her house. For whatever reason—likely a few she didn't want to face—she headed out of the kitchen and down the main hallway to answer the door.

Pavel didn't look the least bit surprised when Viktoria opened the door just a foot and peeked out to look him right in the face. He also didn't seem like he was getting ready to leave, either. Like he'd known she was inside, and he wasn't leaving until she answered.

"What are you doing here?" she asked him.

He shrugged. "In the neighborhood."

"I don't believe that for a second."

To his benefit, Pavel's neutral expression didn't change. "Someone dropped me off, actually. I thought ..."

"What?"

"That you might like to finish what we started earlier, Viktoria."

She blinked.

That was forward.

She hadn't been ready.

"Have you not noticed that I am a complete fucking mess?"

Pavel's gaze drifted to the side, and he watched the quiet, dark street as he replied, "I'm more concerned with *why* you feel that way than the fact that you have a few issues."

She scoffed.

His gaze came back to her.

"What was that for—that *noise?*"

Viktoria sighed, and shook her head. "A *few issues?* I am certifiable. I know because my therapist has told me so."

Pavel didn't look like that bothered him, and maybe Viktoria liked that a little too much. She wasn't the only strange and broken person standing at her door. She felt something familiar in this man, like maybe he understood her fractured mind a little too well. It drew her in—it was the same thing that made her curious about him time and time again, even if every single one of her instincts screamed at her to run far, far away.

"Are you going to let me in?" he asked.

"What happens if I say no?"

Pavel's brow dipped. "Then, I'll leave."

"But *will you?*"

He could lie, she wasn't stupid. He could tell her whatever she wanted to hear, and that would be the end of it. People lied all the fucking time. The thing was ... Pavel just didn't seem like the type. He was honest to a fault and his intentions always seemed clear to her.

Seemed being the keyword there. A person could change in a blink. Viktoria knew that better than anyone.

"If you tell me to leave tonight, then that's exactly what I will do," Pavel said, his dark gaze coming back to meet hers. It was the intensity she found there that practically pinned her in place. It had her heart racing, and her lungs aching … but for the first time in too long, it wasn't a bad thing. It didn't feel like a panic attack or a flashback was on the horizon, but rather, she felt a strong need to get closer to this dangerous man. "And if you ask me to stay …"

"Then you'll do that, too?" she asked.

He nodded.

"Even if I freak out?"

"*Da.*"

"Even if I—"

"If you ask me to stay, then I will stay," he said quietly.

There were far too many parts of Viktoria that were screaming at her to listen to her instincts. The parts of her that were just scared because she was always fucking terrified of something or someone. And then the parts of her that had so many questions to ask … Something had to be wrong, right? Hadn't he just gotten called away from a party with her brother because something happened at the Compound? Why was he *here*? And who had brought him here, anyway?

It was the other part of her …

The part that felt dead, but she'd learned was just sleeping. The part that was very much a young, sexual woman who'd thought she would never feel something like attraction or lust again, who had suddenly been woken up, who stepped back from the doorway and opened it wider.

Pavel nodded, and stepped inside after her.

Viktoria still didn't turn her back to him.

He didn't miss it.

"I have three knives on me," he said, "would you like to take them?"

She stilled in the hallway and hesitated to close the door. Once she did that, he was in here. No one would hear her cry for help or see that something was happening. It would be just her and him, and way too much blind faith and trust.

"You don't need a knife to hurt me," she muttered.

Pavel lifted one shoulder. "But do you still want them?"

Why lie?

"Yes, I would."

Unquestioningly, Pavel emptied his pockets of the three knives he'd been hiding. Viktoria took each of them, and while it didn't make her feel safer to have the weapons in her hands, that wasn't the point.

It might not make her *feel* safer.

It didn't have to.

It was the fact that he did it at all that meant something. She felt a lot of things in those moments—the usual war of emotions that kept her head barely above water while she still felt like she was drowning at the same time.

The one thing she didn't feel?

Regret.

Not about him.

"Why three?" she asked.

"Hmm?"

"Three knives. You only have two hands."

"Backup."

He glanced her way and *winked.*

If Pav noticed that Viktoria made a conscious choice to trust him enough to walk ahead of him, then he didn't say anything. It was unusual for her to let anyone walk at her back, but especially a man. He followed behind her silently as she headed for the kitchen to finish what she had been doing before he showed up.

Except now …

Well, now she didn't have very much interest in the liquor she'd left sitting open on the counter. That's where she went first, closing the bottle and opening the freezer to put the bottle back in its place. No doubt, there would be another night when she needed to pull it out and drink herself to sleep.

"Do you often drink alone?"

Viktoria spun around quickly, a sharp reply at the ready on the tip of her tongue. She ended up swallowing the reply when she found Pav was at the other side of the kitchen, looking over the items on her table.

Or rather, the sketch she had been working on since she'd come home. She thought it might settle her mind to sit down and draw with charcoal—it always used to, anyway. It had been far longer than she wanted to admit since she'd felt the desire to draw literally anything. But tonight, after being with him on that back porch, she'd wanted to do just that.

"Well?" Pav asked, his head tipping up when she stayed silent. His gaze landed on her and he arched a brow high. "Do you often drink alone?"

"Sometimes."

He nodded. "You shouldn't."

Had that been someone else standing there telling her what she should and shouldn't do with her body and time, she would have told them to shut their fucking mouth. Her business was her business, and it wasn't up for discussion. Her sharp nature was the best and first defense she had to keep people in line and at a distance.

For some reason, she bit her tongue.

She said nothing to Pav.

Nothing except, "Yeah, I know."

Pav went back to the sketch on the table and Viktoria was hyperaware of how hard her heart had started to beat in her chest. The sketch was unmistakable—there was no way he could look at it and not recognize his own image staring back at him.

She wasn't wrong.

"It's me," he said, half amused and half curious.

Viktoria wet her lips, trying to settle her nerves. "It is."

"It's very good. You even got the detail of the scar on my eyebrow right."

"Details are important."

Something akin to a smile curved the edge of his mouth, but he didn't look away from the sketch. "They are very important."

A part of her wanted to hide the sketch away from view and keep it safe from scrutiny. It wasn't that she thought he would criticize her art, but rather, she didn't want *anyone* seeing what she was drawing at the moment. Her art had always been a peek inside her mind, and maybe that's why she'd stopped drawing for so long. Because no one wanted to see the constant hell that was her mind.

The urge to take the sketch away from Pav's view was too strong to ignore, so she crossed the kitchen floor, and snatched it up from the table without a word. Quickly, she tucked it under the pad of paper where it couldn't be seen. All the while, Pav said nothing, simply watched her clean up the table and other items she had left sitting out.

"Do you draw every day?" he asked.

"I used to," she mumbled.

"Yet, you tattoo."

"Not as often as I used to. It's not that I did it for money; my father made sure I had more than enough of that to last me several lifetimes."

She didn't miss his nod from the corner of her eye, but he didn't touch on her words with his next question. "Do you not want to draw anymore?"

She swallowed hard. "I haven't wanted to in a long time."

"That's a shame. Look how beautiful your work is."

Her fingers trembled as she picked up the last couple of pieces of charcoal and put them back inside their box. Who knew when she would take them out again and draw? The thought both pissed her off and made her sad. Neither of which she wanted to deal with right then.

"I haven't wanted anything in a long time," she added after a moment.

It was easier to say that and keep staring at the pile of things she'd cleaned up on the table. If she looked at him when she said it, then she was going to see pity in his eyes. Or something worse … and she didn't want to deal with those things, either.

"But you want me," he murmured.

There he went again.

Being *forward*.

And not entirely wrong.

Viktoria lifted her head, and found he was staring at her just like she thought. Except she could feel his gaze, anyway. Heavy and pointed, it felt like it could nail her to the wall with the intensity she found staring back at her.

She didn't find pity there, either.

"Don't you?" he asked again.

Viktoria laughed under her breath. "Maybe I sometimes want some things."

"Try me."

"This isn't a therapy session, okay?"

"Your attitude doesn't scare me off like it does everyone else. I find it amusing, like a challenge to work through. I like challenges."

Damn him.

"You wouldn't understand what was happening in my head, even if I tried to explain it," Viktoria muttered. "Half the time, I don't understand it."

"You don't know that if you don't tell me."

She dragged in a shaky breath. "I don't want to be afraid of you, but I also don't want to trust you. I want to feel like I did on that back porch again, but I also want to drink myself to sleep because that'll be easier than what will happen after."

Viktoria was quick to look away from him, then. She focused on the things sitting on the table again, ready to pretend to reorganize them because she had nothing better to do. It was only his hand lifting up from his side and reaching for her that stopped her from doing anything at all. His palm was soft, yet rough from the callouses on his fingertips, as it came up to cup her cheek. His thumb stroked the line of her cheekbone, and sparks followed the same path. A chill raced down her spine, and heat flooded her veins at the same time.

Fear.

And lust.

How?

"What did I tell you about fear?" he asked quietly.

"To learn to love it."

"And what did I say about me being here?"

"That you'll leave, if I tell you to go."

"Do you care to hear what I want, Viktoria?"

She swallowed the knot in her throat, unsteady but still grasping to find stability in the war that was her mind and body. She looked up to find he was still staring at her. He was still there, and she was still a fucking mess.

"Yes," she whispered, "I think I would like to hear that."

Pav grinned, then, and she swore the world stopped spinning for a split second as she focused in on his smile. How he managed to look dangerous and sinful at the same time, she couldn't understand. She dragged in a quick breath when he leaned in closer, enough that there was only a very small breath of space between them, and she could see the tiny scar that split the right side of his upper lip.

"What I want, yeah, is to hear the different sounds you'll make when I'm learning what your body will do for me," he told her, his gaze slipping down her throat as he spoke. "I want to know what your skin tastes like when you're hot and begging for me. I want to know what your cunt tastes like when my fingers are buried in your ass and you're *high on it*. I want to find out how hard your pussy will squeeze my dick when I'm soaked with you and I've got you on your knees."

She blinked, her mouth feeling dry but her thighs aching. She was quite sure the spot between her legs was anything but dry, and that shocked her a bit. It had been far too long since she'd willingly laid down with a man.

And this man?

He terrified her.

"I don't think you understand how much that—"

"Scares you a bit," he returned, his grin deepening a bit. "I know; I can tell."

"You like that, I think."

Pav arched a brow. "I like that you fight it for what you want. You *want* more than you fear, and that gets me *off*."

Jesus Christ.

She swallowed the knot in her throat, because he wasn't wrong. She was all too willing to fight the constant war of her fear for the chance at feeling something—a taste of the kind of freedom only sex could provide.

Far more than willing.

"If you tell me no, or it feels like too much; if you need to *stop*, then you say so, and it's done."

"Not all of my cues are *verbal*."

Pav nodded. "I can tell."

"Can you?"

"Better than you know, Viktoria."

That was the thing, wasn't it?

She needed to trust him.

Yeah, terrifying.

And yet, she still wanted to try. She wanted to let him learn all those things he told her, and *more*. So much fucking more.

Pav lifted a brow high. "And if you tell me yes—"

"Yes," she breathed instantly.

That was all he needed.

In a blink, he was up from that chair, and closing the space between them. She heard the chair legs scrape loudly against the tile, which was enough to make her jump in her own seat. Her attention quickly went back to the man looming over her. Yet another thing that made her tense and hesitate.

But he saw that.

The flash in her eyes.

The draw back when he leaned down.

He saw it all.

Viktoria watched the recognition in his eyes when he cupped her jaw in his hands and lowered down in front of her chair so that he wasn't *above her* like that. So that he didn't loom over her like that. He didn't ask for a kiss, but she didn't mind. Instead, he pulled her in for one that she swore lit up fireworks inside her stomach.

His lips worked hard against hers, and she answered him back with the same. At first, she just wanted to feel the kiss, but then, she wanted to taste him, too. It was her tongue that struck out against the seam of his lips first—*her* that asked for more without saying a thing. She was quite aware of that, and she didn't miss how he let her do it, too.

The second his mouth opened for her, and their tongues met, a dance began. That kiss turned into something far hotter, a lot like the way her body felt in those seconds. She knew that she needed air—*needed* to breathe, but she didn't care.

In his eyes, she found anticipation.

Lust.

Appreciation.

She worried she might find something else, something that looked like her greatest fears staring back at her. But she didn't find that at all. She realized, too, that she'd never wanted a man—or rather, *this* man—to look at her more.

And all for what?

A *kiss?*

What would she feel when he had her naked and flying high?

"Breathe," he murmured, his lips trailing over her cheek, and then down to her jaw. She did as he asked, but only because it was slightly easier to do so. His dark words continued to dance along her skin, following the same path as his hot mouth over her throat, her racing pulse point, and then down to her collarbones. "Vanilla and *pears.* That's what you smell like, and it makes you taste like candy and *sex.*"

"Does it?"

"Here, it does," he said, his tongue striking out against her collarbone. And then, he bit her on the same spot. Not hard enough to hurt, but just enough to make her suck in a sharp breath. "And then it tastes like sex when I do that."

"*God.*"

"More?"

She wanted to use words. They were best, and *most* clear. Her words were definitive, but she didn't think she could speak. Instead, she nodded. He caught it when he glanced up at her and grinned like that's what he was expecting.

"Pick a room," Pav said quietly. "Any room."

She barely thought about it. "My bedroom."

"Do you have something there that makes you feel safe?"

She didn't say yes.

But she also didn't say no.

Because *yes*, she did.

"My bedroom," Viktoria repeated.

"Lead the way."

He stood, then, but she came with him because he grabbed her hand and tugged her up, too. He didn't walk behind her as she led him through the main floor, and then to the stairs. No, he walked beside her as to not be at her back. One of his hands stayed at her lower back, grazing the sliver of bare skin where her shirt had ridden up a bit. His thumb stroked her skin slowly—*gently*. A rhythm that lulled her into a warm place.

His touch was *good*.

It was only once they were inside her bedroom, and she was standing near the foot of the bed, that he moved away from her. Not far, just enough to give her space while he tugged his jacket and shirt off, only to toss them to a chair near the dresser.

She stared at him, then, unashamed that he knew she was watching. There was something to be said for a male body—all the hard lines and filled-in muscle. And Pav really was a beautiful man, she thought. Life may have been rough on him in some ways, but it treated him well in others. From the expanse of his shoulders, to the hard ridges of abs down his stomach, and then the deep cut V where his pants hung low on his waist.

Yeah, a beautiful man.

His skin was unmarked by tattoos but for the stars on his clavicles. And a part of her greatly enjoyed seeing those stars—*she* had put them there, and despite the fact they weren't hers, they still kind of felt like it. His skin wasn't unmarked by scars, though. Her gaze trailed over the number of faded and new scars that marked his torso and arms. Some larger than others, and some barely visible to her eye in the dimness of the bedroom.

"Ask about them," he said, clearly seeing what she was doing. "Ask, and I will tell."

"How?"

That seemed appropriate.

"Various ways. Fighting. Punishment. The chambers."

"Oh."

Pav turned a bit as he unbuttoned his pants and pulled down the zipper while he kicked off his shoes. On another day, that sound alone would have been enough to throw Viktoria back in time to an attack that almost killed her several times over, but right then, all she cared about was the shape of his ass as he shuffled those pants down his legs, and the way the muscles in his back moved as he did.

Damn.

Over his shoulder, his gaze locked on hers before trailing lower, taking in the shape of her hips and the length of her legs covered by the jeans she'd pulled on earlier.

"Undress," he said.

Viktoria bit her lip. "You don't want to help?"

"I want to *watch*. Just like you did."

Oh.

She was all too aware that he watched her undress, one piece of clothing at a time just like she had gawked at him. She understood, too, why he wanted to because the sensation that drove through her body the longer he stared was … intoxicating. She caught the way his jaw tightened when her jeans dropped, and how his gaze darkened when she tugged her blouse over her shoulders and tossed it to the floor.

Like he couldn't get *enough*.

Viktoria said nothing until she was naked at the foot of her bed, and he had turned to face her entirely, closing the distance between them one slow step at a time. A shiver raced through her entire body as he lifted one finger to trace the only other tattoos she had, other than the cursive B on her finger.

Two eight-pointed stars.

Bratva stars.

Right under her breasts.

That was what he touched first—not her pussy, her breasts, or any other part of her body that he'd stared at so intently as she undressed. No, he went for those *stars*.

"Why?" he asked.

She swallowed hard. "Someone thought I needed protection after … something happened."

Yes, that was as good of a way to explain it as any, she supposed. That was easier to say than explaining that after a man attacked her, Vadim forced the tattoos on her. Like those stars were somehow going to magically stop a man from sticking his cock in her body when she didn't want it.

Thankfully, Pavel didn't ask for more information because that *really* wasn't the conversation she wanted to have. He dropped his attention on the tattoos and his gaze came back up to her face as that finger of his drifted down her clenching, toned stomach.

"Do you care to find out what I can do with just my hand?"

Right then, her body was screaming for it.

"Show me."

Pav smiled. "*Good.*"

His finger trailed lower, over her navel, then her pubic bone, and came to a stop just above the junction of her thighs. She hadn't opened her legs for him yet, after all. His gaze lifted to hers as a war raged on in her mind—it was silent, and he couldn't hear the warnings screaming at her to stop before she found herself in a world of trouble with this man, or spent the night lost in nightmares she couldn't escape.

She battled it.

Warred the fear.

It didn't own her.

She had to stop letting it rule her.

"Viktoria?" he asked gently.

That finger of his didn't move. It didn't lift or try to lower more. He simply stayed still, and she was grateful. It took a moment, but when she opened her legs for him, he shot her a grin that had her stomach doing summersaults from the silent promise that smile alone offered.

First, it was just a graze of his knuckles against her clit as his hand brushed between her thighs. Then, it was the way his hand cupped her sex, covering it entirely with his palm, and squeezing hot, sensitive flesh in such a way that her thighs clenched, and she let out a whimper.

"I like that sound," he told her.

"You're teasing me."

"*Testing.*"

Oh, was that what it was?

He didn't test her much longer. One of his calloused fingers drifted between her folds, and already, she could hear the way her wetness answered his touch. She couldn't remember the last time her pussy got wet for a *man.* And yet here she was, already soaked and ready to ruin the sheets on her bed.

It felt like every single one of her inner muscles decided to clamp down around his finger when he slipped it inside her pussy. A visceral reaction of her body—the natural instinct of fear that something was happening that had hurt time and time again before.

But this time it didn't.

This time, it felt *fucking wonderful.*

Her pussy stayed tight as he added a second finger, and his thumb came up to rub against her clit at the second time. But now, it was tight because *more.* She wanted more.

Pav cupped the side of her throat with his other hand, and she tipped her head into the touch, lost in the sensations between her thighs that felt like they were crawling through her whole body. At the same time, she watched him.

That darkness in his eyes.

That *grin.*

How he watched her.

She was hyperaware of the feeling of his cock pressing against the thin cotton of his boxer-briefs as she pushed against his body. That cock of his—thick and hard—rested against her stomach, and she let her fingers drift over the ridges of his length just because she wanted to touch him somehow.

He didn't seem to mind.

Pav went on her cues. The louder her sounds became, the more he touched her in the same way. The harder her hips rocked into his hand, the deeper his fingers went inside her pussy. She realized then that when he talked about *cues*, it wasn't just the bad ones. He watched for the good cues, too, and because of that, knew exactly how to play her body until she was shaking and gasping for breath.

How long had it been since she'd orgasmed?

Too long.

Viktoria almost forgot how an orgasm felt until there it was, crashing over her body like a wave she couldn't possibly escape from. It was intense, and she almost couldn't take it. She almost lost her balance standing there, his name falling from her lips like a prayer. She'd worried that orgasm might taste like fear, or maybe … it would hurt somehow.

It did none of those things.

Instead, it reminded her that intimacy was in fact *good* when it was right. It reminded her that she was absolutely a woman with a body that craved pleasure and affection. It reminded her that she was human, and sometimes, humans just needed to be *touched*.

"Oh, my God," she mumbled into his palm.

Soft chuckles colored up the room as she felt his hand slip from between her thighs. "What do you want now, hmm?"

Her eyes flew open to find him still staring at her. Her answer came easily—too easy. "More. I want more."

"I need—"

"I have condoms in my bedside drawer."

A brand-new box. Bought *months* ago. Just in case, although at the time, she figured there was no chance in hell that she would ever use them.

Life was laughing at her now.

Or cheering her on.

Pav left her side, then, heading for the bedside stand, and she felt the loss of him in a way she hadn't expected. A coolness washed over her body, threatening to take away the high she'd been riding, but Viktoria refused to let it take over. By the time he came back to her, she was already sitting on the edge of the bed and looking up at him.

She didn't mind that he loomed.

Not now.

"Can I?" she asked when he readied to open the foil packet.

Pav hesitated. "If you want to, of course."

"I do."

Mostly because it let her touch him and *see* him. She liked being able to do that—to be the one to choose to free his erection from his boxer-briefs; to let her fingers trail over the length of his cock, drifting over the thick veins and grazing the head where his precum had started to gather on the blunt tip. She smoothed her fingers around his length and stroked once, then twice. His hips jerked forward from the motion, and a harsh grunt fell from his lips. She looked up to see his teeth were clenched while he watched her.

But he let her touch.

He let her play.

She needed that, too.

It was only once she'd slid the condom down his length and pushed his boxer-briefs down enough that he could step out of them did he finally push her back to the bed. Her legs fell open far easier than she expected. She welcomed him more willingly than she thought she would.

His lips connected with hers as the blunt head of his cock came to rest against her slit. His tongue clashed with hers as his hips jerked forward, and he took her. She was wet enough for it, but it still took a second, and then two before her body adjusted to the length and width of his cock. But she liked that feeling, too. Liked the way her pussy had to stretch for him, and how his back shuddered under her hands when her nails dragged down his skin.

He waited just long enough for her to breathe, and then her back arched high from the bed. She wanted more—needed to feel him pounding into her until she came again, and was spent enough that the dreams weren't going to visit her this night.

"Fuck me," she whispered.

His teeth found her throat, then, and his hips snapped back before meeting hers again. His pace was fast and deep. It was just enough to hit all the right spots, and have her tightening her legs around his hips to get him even deeper.

He was right.

It was *too much*.

It also wasn't nearly enough.

"Fuck," he grunted against her lips.

Viktoria laughed, breathless and spun.

God, she'd missed sex.

"*More.*"

Kissing her chin, his looked up, and she met his gaze. "You only have to ask."

8.

PAV HAD not expected to wake up with his cock in Viktoria's mouth, but he really wasn't going to complain about it, either. If she wanted to get his dick in her mouth, then he was up for that. Whatever she wanted.

She'd been timid the night before—at *first*. And then it was like she remembered what sex could feel like when it was good, and the woman was fucking insatiable. He was all too happy to be the one feeding into that desire of hers.

He couldn't fuck her enough.

Couldn't get enough *of* her.

The feeling of her.

Her taste.

The way she smelled.

All of her.

It drove him crazy.

"Fuck," Pav growled into his hands, doing his very best to keep them to himself as her tongue teased the head of his dick. He was *positive* she wouldn't react well right then, if he grabbed onto her hair and worked her mouth against his dick. In fact, he knew she wouldn't. Another time maybe, but not today. "You're going to make me—"

She came up from his cock, then, her mouth releasing him from that wet, hot heaven. He didn't know whether to be annoyed or glad for it, as she crawled up his body like a cat that had gotten her bowl of milk. *Finally*, he felt like he could touch her, too. He let his hands drift over her naked sides, up to her breasts where he tweaked her hardened nipples with his forefingers and thumbs.

She sighed.

A happy, sweet sound.

Yeah, just like a pleased cat.

He knew she had claws, too, though.

Viktoria's eyes, hazy with lust and need, found his as she bent down for a kiss. It was slow and burning. It had his dick growing harder, until it was almost painful as she sat down in his lap. There was no shame in this woman as she grinded on his cock—her wet pussy gliding in the best way along his length as she moved her hips back and forth.

"Morning," she whispered against his lips.

Pav grinned, and his hands found her hips to grip tight. "A very *good* morning."

"It soon will be."

He let go of her hip just long enough to reach for the newly opened box of condoms in the bedside stand. Once he had that foil packet in his hands, he passed it over to her. She seemed to like putting the condom on him, or it could be that it gave her a little more control.

He didn't know.

Or care.

As long as she wanted it, he would give it.

Viktoria's movements were quick, then. She was fast to put that condom on him, shift higher so she could reach between her thighs, place his cock where she wanted him, and then she was lowering down. Her cunt hugged him tight going down—he swore he could feel her fucking heartbeat thrumming against the walls of her sex as she seated on his cock.

He had the greatest urge to thread his fingers into her hair, pull her down so he could kiss her, and let her ride him crazy. So, he did just that, testing the waters by tangling his fingers into the ends of her hair first, just to see what she might do.

A shift of her hips.

The parting of her lips.

The soft sound that came out of her mouth.

Those eyes of hers …

It all spelled good things to him.

He got her just the way he wanted her—hands tight in her hair, lips bruising against his with a hard kiss, and her body working fast against his to push them both over the edge. His hand slipped around her hip to her ass, and all it took was one of his fingers pushing into her ass to match the pace of her riding him to make her come.

She looked godly like that.

An angel.

High off him and breathless. Spun, her gaze wild, and her swollen lips still wet from sucking on his dick. It got him off just watching her come, and that was shocking to him in a way. Not that he minded. He spilled all too fast into latex, but he held her tight to his dick, getting as deep as he could go when he finally did come.

"Jesus Christ," he grunted against her lips.

Viktoria laughed lightly. "Told you the morning would get better, but now I feel sticky."

He didn't mind that, either.

He loved how wet she got.

That her arousal turned creamy the harder she was fucked, and the more turned on she became. She could coat him in that, and he'd be in fucking heaven.

Like right now.

"Let me get a cloth for you," he said.

She nodded and rolled off him. He didn't want to move at all, but especially not when he still felt a little too high from fucking her, but he still got up from the bed. In the attached bathroom, he found a pile of folded wash cloths on the counter, dampened one with warm water, and came back into the bedroom. She let him clean her thighs and sex, giving him a sweet smile all the while.

After discarding the damp cloth to the laundry basket in the bathroom, Pav came back into the room to find Viktoria resting against the headboard. She didn't attempt to hide her nakedness from him, leaving the soft beige sheet to pool around her waist while she toyed with an item in her hand.

One of his knives.

"What are you doing?" he asked, slightly amused.

She spun the tip of the blade against the pad of her finger. He might have warned her that it was a terribly sharp blade, and took very little pressure to actually slice through the skin, but she looked fine. She seemed like she knew what she was doing. Who was he to tell her to do *anything*?

"Thinking," she murmured.

"I'll get dressed, and you think, yes?"

She gave him a look from the side, but Pav only shrugged. Being naked was only good for him if he was going to be doing something about it. He made quick work of pulling on his jeans and shirt from the night before.

"You wear a lot of black, huh?"

Pav's head tipped up and he caught that sinfully beautiful woman in his line of vision. She grinned when he cocked his eyebrow at her. She was still playing with that damn knife, and for once, didn't have that glare of fire or fear in her eyes.

All good things.

"I do, yes," Pav replied.

"Why?"

"Easier to blend into the shadows, hmm? Blood is less noticeable. Many reasons."

Viktoria nodded and put her attention back on his knife. He wasn't even sure when she had gone to get one of the three blades that she'd taken from him the night before. Maybe when he was sleeping, who was he to say? Usually, a simple noise would wake him up out of a dead sleep, but he had slept hard last night.

"I thought for sure I was going to have nightmares last night," Viktoria said, more to herself than him. Still, Pav looked her way as he slipped on his socks and shoes, waiting for her to say more if she wanted to. "I was so sure of it that I was going to drink myself to sleep to prevent it from happening. And then you showed up."

He couldn't help but wonder if she'd been scared that having him here, or rather, letting him have her, would bring on those nightmares, too. The thing was … this woman didn't give herself nearly enough credit about her own strength. She clearly lived within a war of someone else's making—they put the battle in her head, and she had to fight it every single day. The fact she woke up each and every morning proved her triumph.

Did she even realize that?

Probably not.

"Are we sharing secrets?" Pav asked.

Viktoria smiled a little. "I don't know, are we? Do you have something you want to share with the rest of the class?"

She was so sarcastic that he wanted to laugh. It was amusing. She was usually so cutting, but even now, softened and sweet, there was still a hint of that fire and bite in her. It wasn't that her persona or the front she put forth was entirely a mask, he realized. She'd just sharpened and honed it enough to use it as a weapon against those who became too close to her.

Viktoria was naturally quick-witted. She was always going to be a sharp-tongued woman with a bark far worse than her bite. It was all in how she chose to use that against someone else that determined whether or not her barbed-wire-covered heart was going to cut when a person came too close.

Well, if they were sharing secrets ...

"This is the longest I've been away from the Compound in a while," he admitted. "A couple of years, anyway. The last time, I was taken out for the weekend. But it's been a while since I was away for this long."

Viktoria glanced up. "Is it?"

"Yes."

"What else?"

Did she really want to know?

"Are we making pillow talk?" he asked.

Viktoria's brow lifted into a perfect arch. "Not used to that, or ...?"

"Usually, women I spent the night with were paid for their time, and then I would hope the next man treated them better than they typically get treated."

That made her swallow hard. "Oh."

Pav straightened to his full height, done with tying his shoes. He closed the bit of space between them, coming to stand at the side of the bed. She peered up at him, and he liked it entirely too much that she didn't shy away from his touch when he reached for her. No, she let her cheek lay against his palm, and her long lashes fluttered against her skin when he stroked her with his thumb.

"I am—*was*—as much a prisoner of the Boykovs as any other man down in those cells. The only difference, yes, was that they allowed me a bit more freedom than the rest at certain times ... and always with a companion to keep me in line."

"Sorry."

"Don't apologize."

"*Still*—"

Pav bent down, and pressed a quick kiss to the top of Viktoria's mussed hair. "*Then* doesn't matter. Now is what makes the difference."

"But does it really?"

"For me, yes."

Viktoria sighed, and he swore he could feel her shoulders deflate. "This must be … strange for you, then. Have you really spent all your time in the Compound?"

"The majority of the last fourteen years."

"So yeah, this is strange."

Pav chuckled, and stood straight again, letting his hand sift through the messy strands of her hair to comb it out the best he could. "I was handed documents that gave me a proper name, and cards with enough money on them to do me longer than I will need. *Repayment*, I was told, for the last decade and a half. I don't know how to drive. I can't remember my mother, or her name, and for a while, I almost forgot my own, too."

"What about your dad?"

He stiffened.

She didn't miss it.

"What?" Viktoria asked. "What was that for?"

"I just … he's not very important."

Lies.

He was.

Viktoria frowned up at him. "You sound like he is."

"Was," Pav corrected. "Your father killed mine. That's how I came to the Boykovs."

She quieted.

He understood why.

"The whole world is strange to me," he murmured. "I don't know anything about it."

"It used to be a nice place," she replied, "but not so much now."

• • •

Viktoria moved from one thing to the next in her kitchen, and while Pav thought to help as much as he could, he found it was far more interesting to watch her. There was something enthralling about this woman, and all the secrets she held tight to her chest.

She seemed innocent, in some ways, and sinfully wicked in others. He was caught by the way her hips moved as she slid from one end of the counter to the other. Her icy blonde hair was slightly more tamed than it had been earlier, now falling in soft waves halfway down her back. She'd pulled on an over-sized sweater to wear, but her legs were still bare, and he just now realized she walked on her *tiptoes.*

The woman had no idea about the things he knew. She wasn't aware that he knew her darkness and why it was there. He didn't feel it was right for him to know without her having been the one to tell him, but he didn't know what to do about the things he'd been told, either.

Did he tell her?

Let her tell him?

He knew one thing for sure … she was amazing, but he didn't think she knew it. She didn't have the slightest clue of her strength, or worth.

And wasn't that a shame?

"Are you satisfied with just watching me from over there?" Viktoria peeked over her shoulder at him, and he could tell by the glint in her gaze that she was teasing. "What do you plan to do, just eat my food and run?"

"Where would I run to, woman?"

"Well …"

Pav cocked a brow. "You'd know where to find me."

Viktoria laughed and went back to attending the eggs and bacon mess on the stove. "You're right, I do know where to find you."

"But would you come?"

He thought that was the better question to ask because he didn't know what her answer would be. He could guess a lot about Viktoria and the way she might react to something. However, she consistently had surprises when it came to him. And he had absolutely no idea what the two of them were doing with one another.

Was this a test for her?

Fun?

What was it?

Pav didn't know anything about women. Not on an emotional level, or how to deal with them in that sort of way. He was going to have to take his cues from her and go from there. Otherwise, he wouldn't have the first fucking clue of what to do here.

"Well?" Pav asked when Viktoria stayed quiet. "Would you come to find me, or no?"

He caught the sight of her grin, but she was quick to turn her head away to hide it. "We'll see."

"And until then?"

"Until then, you can come over here and help me cook instead of staring at my ass."

"That doesn't sound like a fair trade."

"I'm a Boykov, Pav. I never give when I've only been taught to *take*."

The two of them were halfway done with their breakfast, sitting side by side at the kitchen table, when the purr of an engine neared the house. Pav didn't look up from his plate, but Viktoria did. She didn't even get the chance to get up out of her seat to check the window before the front door of the house was unlocked and opened.

Her gaze narrowed. "Konstantin, I told you to give me back my keys!"

"I forgot," came the smooth reply before the man in question darkened the entryway to the kitchen. Just behind him stood another man—Kolya. Pav didn't miss the way Kolya's ice-blue eyes drifted to him sitting at the table. Or how his gaze narrowed as he considered how close Pav's position was to Viktoria.

This didn't take a fucking genius to figure out. It was incredibly early in the morning. Viktoria looked like she'd just rolled out of bed, and despite being dressed, Pav wasn't in a better situation. It wasn't like he walked over here from the Compound that morning, so the more obvious explanation was that he'd stayed the night.

With Viktoria.

"You could have let me know," Kolya said to Konstantin quietly.

"Let him know what?" Viktoria asked.

"Nothing, yes?" Konstantin waved a hand. "Kolya is just being … his normal self."

Viktoria gave the two of them a look, but picked up her fork to continue eating. "Since when do the two of you come to my house first thing in the morning? Don't you have *wives* now? Shouldn't you keep them company in the morning instead of annoying me?"

"My wife doesn't roll over before ten," Kolya replied. "I make sure of that."

Viktoria made a face. "Shame, that. Maya would be a great help right now—she's the only one who knows how to pull on your leash and keep you in line, Kolya."

Her words might have stung someone with thinner skin than Kolya, but the man in the entryway actually *cracked a smile*. Pav thought that was the first time he'd ever seen that happen in all the years he'd known the man.

And Viktoria?

She'd adopted that soft, teasing tone again.

She was *joking*.

Kolya chuckled and looked to Konstantin as he murmured, "And there she is, huh?"

Konstantin's gaze drifted to Pav, replying, "There she is—I told you."

"Hmm."

"What are you two—"

"Are you going to tell her now?" Pav asked quietly.

This moment was all great and good. He understood there was more at play for the siblings than he probably understood, but that mattered very little to him at the end of the day. If what he thought he knew about Viktoria was true, then she wouldn't want her brothers making a big deal out of her change in behavior and attitude. If anything, it would probably cause her to revert back to someone they didn't want to deal with at all.

He'd be fine with that. He liked her both ways.

The point remained ... "Are you going to tell her?"

Viktoria looked between Pav at the table and her brothers in the entryway. "Tell me what?"

The change in the room was palpable. Skyrocketing tension that slipped past each and every person like a breeze they could all feel. He didn't miss the way the two men shifted on their feet and passed looks to one another like they were waiting for the other to begin talking. Under the table, he felt Viktoria's suddenly shaking hand trembling against the side of his leg.

Did she know what they were going to say?

Was it possible she just felt it?

"Vik," Konstantin started.

"*What is it?*"

Konstantin flinched.

Kolya glanced down at the floor.

"I'll just say it, then? I won't preface it with excuses or explanations about why it was done, or *how* … if you want to know those things after, then I will tell you."

Pav slipped his hand over Viktoria's under the table and squeezed hard when she stayed silent. He could see the line of water filling her bottom lashes, but she didn't even blink. If she did, those tears would fall. People would *see*.

"Okay," Konstantin muttered, nodding as he continued on, "last night, during the party, I received a call from someone who needed to check in with the man at the Compound. He found the man dead and one of the cells in the basement empty. We have every reason to believe it was the person in the cell who killed the man before he escaped the Compound."

Viktoria's jaw hardened. "Who was in the cell?"

"Boris Antipov."

All that shaking stopped.

Like her breaths.

And maybe her heartbeat, too.

Pav swore he couldn't feel Viktoria's heartbeat for a split second as his fingers tightened around her wrist. "Hey—"

"He's supposed to be dead," she mumbled. "Daddy said … *you* said … Kolya said it. You all said it, Konstantin. He was dead."

"Vik—"

"He's supposed to be dead!"

Konstantin's gaze flicked to Pav, but quickly went back to his sister. He wasn't the same calm, cool man that handled any oncoming storm like it was nothing more than a breeze. He was hurting, he felt guilt, and he was showing it.

"The decision to tell you he was dead was made because he would be dead eventually. After we were all satisfied that he'd been punished for what he'd done. Death was too quick—it would have been a gift for him."

"You said he was dead."

Her voice ached.

The pain coloring her words hurt him.

Pav had never experienced that before.

It was shocking.

"Why would you tell me he was dead when he wasn't? Why would you lie to me, Konstantin?"

Konstantin shook his head. "The sins of the father ... the guilt of a man," her brother replied, sighing. "Vadim made the choice, and you act like the rest of us ever had any kind of say when he made a decision, Viktoria. You're asking the wrong man if you want answers. I know *why*, but it's not my place to say. Ask Vadim."

Viktoria went silent again.

Seconds ticked by.

Then, she *exploded*.

The rage was back.

The soft beauty was gone.

The tears started to fall, too.

"*Get the fuck out of my house!*" She stood fast from the table, toppling over the chair at the same time. "*Every single one of you—get the fuck out of here!*"

"Vik," Kolya started to say, "you have to understand—"

"Get out! All of you! Get the hell away from me!"

Pav was the first to move.

He was also the first to leave.

· · ·

Pav followed behind Konstantin and Kolya as they entered the front of the Compound. As they turned to go right, quietly discussing their plans in Russian, Pav turned to the left. That would lead him to a hallway, and then another, before taking him to a set of doors that would lead him to stairs for the downstairs.

Konstantin's voice stopped him as he turned. "What are you doing?"

Pav's brow dipped. "Going downstairs where I do my job."

"Your job is upstairs now."

He glanced between the two men, but they only stared at him, waiting. He wasn't sure what to say or do but he figured it wasn't the time or place to argue. Konstantin seemed to understand his inner struggle, though.

"I made it clear to you that your job here for us would be changing, no? Did you think I was speaking just to hear myself talk?"

"No," Pav replied, positive that was the correct response. "But—"

"The chambers will be handled. Your job is upstairs."

All right.

Without a word, he spun on his heel, waved a hand for them to continue, and then he followed behind the brothers as they headed down the main hallway of the Compound. Kolya and Konstantin continued their conversation like it hadn't been interrupted in the first place. All the while, Pav stayed tucked away in his mind, trying to figure out what exactly was happening here, and how he wanted to deal with it.

He'd never really been *free* before.

Sure, he'd heard Konstantin explain to him that it was going to happen. He would no longer be a Boykov dog on a leash, but he hadn't actually been listening. That had never been his reality, after all, and it didn't seem real.

Apparently, it was.

"And will you do that, then?" Konstantin asked.

Pav blinked out of his thoughts. "Do what?"

Konstantin arched a brow, annoyed. "Were you not listening to me?"

"Was I supposed to be?"

Kolya chuckled. "*Da*, Pav."

Oh.

Konstantin sighed. "We have a team ready to look for Boris. Viktoria, however, needs to be safe. I figure … sending her away for a time might be better than keeping her here. She's angry, and she won't want anyone too close. I suspect she'll be going through some things, too. Better for her to deal with it all where people aren't watching."

"She needs space," Pav replied. "From everyone."

He'd heard her shout that at Konstantin as he'd left her house.

"Maybe," Konstantin agreed, "but I thought she would also need someone to go with her. Someone she likes well enough, and perhaps even trusts."

Pav blinked, understanding. "You mean me."

"Yes."

"I don't think that's a good idea. She didn't want me there this morning, either."

Konstantin nodded. "*Smart*, hmm? Except I didn't ask what you thought—I asked if you would do it."

"You say that like I get a choice."

"You do."

Ah, yeah.

Freedom.

"Who else would keep an eye on her if I refused?" Pav asked.

"Any number of men—"

"Then, no, I will go," Pav interjected fast.

Fast like the heat in his gut, the swell of anger in his heart, and the burning jealousy on the back of his tongue.

It was *stupid.* Foolish, even.

There was no way Viktoria would even look at another man being the way she was, but that mattered very little to Pav. He didn't even want to consider it. And it wasn't her that he had to concern himself with, it was the man who watched her. Men could not be trusted, but especially not their kind of man.

Simple as that.

He would do the job.

Konstantin pressed his lips together like he was hiding a smirk. "All right. I will get you the information for where the two of you will be going."

"Fine by me," Pav returned.

After all, he didn't mind a nasty Viktoria. He liked her a little vicious, too. He suspected that's exactly what she was going to be like for this.

He welcomed the challenge.

9.

VIKTORIA WAS doing her *very best* to ignore the man in the row next to hers in first class who kept glancing her way. She'd barely spoken at all to the flight attendant when the woman asked if there was anything she wanted while they waited.

A Valium?

Vodka?

She had that bottle of Xanax in her carry-on bag, but she didn't want to actually take one. It wasn't that she was panicking because of the flight, or even the people on it. More like, the fact her rapist had actually been alive for the past couple of years when she'd thought he was dead, and now he was just out and about. Roaming somewhere, apparently. Probably looking for her … ready to come back for another round.

Holy fucking Christ.

Viktoria felt like her throat was closing. The panic came in like a wave. Small, at first, and then progressively rougher and rougher until it took a good portion of the shore away when the wave went back out. If she were a shore, then it was dragging her out to sea, too.

She was going to *drown.*

Her fingers curved tightly around the edges of the seat, and she dragged in a shaky breath that stung the whole way coming in. Fuck her brothers for doing this to her … for putting her on this plane today without an explanation because *they said so.* Fuck them for lying to her for all this time about Boris, and what really happened.

Yeah, fuck them.

The next time Viktoria opened her eyes, the first thing she saw was Pav making his way down the plane's aisle. She didn't even get the chance to make her mouth work to ask him what in the fuck he was doing there before he slid into the seat next to hers in first class.

There was no way that was coincidence.

Fucking Konstantin.

You know what, yeah, she wasn't even going to blame Kolya for this. All of this shit just *screamed* Konstantin's doing. He was the one who didn't seem to understand personal boundaries and had no problem with pushing Viktoria right to her goddamn limits every chance he could. Because he was an asshole.

"Apparently, I was almost late," Pav said, shrugging as he dropped a small messenger bag under the seat. "Do you know Uber drivers are very … *chatty*?"

Viktoria wanted to glare and snap at him. But knowing he was telling her some very important information, because the man had probably never needed to call himself a driver or something like an Uber before, made her just want to laugh for him.

And she did just that.

It was weak, sure, and still a little bitter.

But she laughed.

Pav shot her a look and smirked a bit. "I know you don't want me here. You want space, I get it."

"Yeah."

"But it's me or someone else. Maybe a stranger—whoever Konstantin felt like picking. It certainly wasn't going to be one of your brothers, when they are better doing work in Chicago. So this trip to Russia for you, yeah, will have to include me."

Viktoria nodded. "I hate them right now."

"I bet."

He offered nothing else, and she didn't bother to ask. When those tickets showed up taped to her door with a note from Konstantin saying she was to be on the plane to Russia whether she liked it or not, well … she'd known better than to fight her brother on it. Konstantin would simply show up at her house, force her into a car, and take her to the airport himself. There was only so much he would take before he just did what he wanted to do, anyway.

Pav had a point, too.

She would not have reacted well, had some random Boykov soldier come onto the plane, and sat down beside her because her brother said she needed a babysitter for this little trip. If anything, she probably would have thrown a fit so bad that she would have gotten kicked off the plane because *yeah* … she was not in a good place.

Not physically.

Not emotionally.

Not mentally.

Pav was a slightly better choice.

All things considered …

"Is that why you came the other night?" Viktoria asked. "Because you knew that Boris had escaped, and my brother sent you to me?"

Pav didn't lie.

She appreciated it.

"Partly," he replied, "but I also came because I wanted to be with you. My involvement with you has very little to do with what other people tell me to do, but rather, what *I* want to do, Viktoria."

That made it a little better.

Not much, though.

She swallowed hard and toyed with the phone in her hands. Putting the music on, she plugged in the earbuds, and put one of them into her ears. With music pumping into her brain as close as she could get it, it was easier to focus on not giving into her fear and anxiety.

It wasn't missed by Pav, either.

Of course.

His hand slid across the seats and, wordlessly, he squeezed her thigh. Just as quickly as his hand was there, it was gone. She didn't acknowledge the touch, although she appreciated it because it reminded her someone was there who might actually give a shit about her. He didn't seem to mind.

"They didn't give me a choice," she muttered. "About this flight and hiding away with my father in Russia, I mean."

Pav chuckled. "Me either, yeah?"

She gave him a good look, then. He wore his standard black ensemble—pants, shirt, and a leather jacket. He seemed calm on the outside. His hands stayed steady on his lap, and his body seemed relaxed, for the most part.

But it was in his gaze where she found it …

The nerves.

Irritation.

The way his stare darted from one person on the plane, to the next. When the flight attendant came into view behind the curtain at the front, his gaze was quick to dart to her, too. It was like he was an animal who had just been shoved into a very tiny cage, and he was watching every little thing that moved around him. His muscles were taut like springs when she reached over to place a hand on his wrist.

He was a coiled snake.

Ready to strike.

"Hey," she murmured.

Pav looked back to her. "Yes?"

"Did they take your knives?"

It was meant to be a joke.

He caught on.

Pav grinned. "They did. Apparently, I could not bring them with me."

"That's too bad."

"I know."

"Flying isn't bad, you know?" Viktoria shrugged. "It's one thing I don't mind that much."

He nodded. "It's not the plane."

"Then what?"

"Too many people."

Oh.

She hadn't thought of that.

He wouldn't be used to this.

Just like the party ...

"They're foolish," he murmured, dark gaze drifting to her again. "They think I need a knife to kill everyone on this plane." A dry laugh passed his lips, though he barely even moved at all. "I only need five minutes and some inspiration."

Well, damn.

"You still terrify me," she whispered.

Pav smiled a little. "Good. I should. I would be more worried if I didn't."

• • •

Pav stayed close to Viktoria's side as they headed out of the gate. He'd kept quiet for most of the trip to Russia, and she hadn't found she wanted to say very much, either. He had accepted one of her earbuds to listen to music with her. He'd made sure to keep a careful distance with his hands, never reaching out to touch her like he first did by squeezing her knee.

Now, though?

As they walked down the corridor toward arrivals, his hand rested at the small of her back with a light touch. Viktoria wasn't sure if that was more for her, to keep her close to him and away from the swarms of people, or if it was because he was looking to steady himself in a strange and new environment.

Either way, she liked it.

And she didn't want to deal with that right now.

Something else was on her mind.

"Pav?"

"Hmm?"

"Did you know who he was in the chambers?" she asked softly. "Did you know what he had done to me?"

Pav didn't take another step and he didn't ask her who she was talking about. It was like he just knew she meant Boris and was avoiding saying the name of the monster who had haunted her days and nights for two years.

In a blink, Viktoria was swung around. All it took was a quick press of his hand against her back before he had her backed into the wall of the airport's corridor. She was hyperaware of the people passing them by like nothing was wrong. They didn't even look their way.

Not that it mattered.

Now, all she could see was *him.*

Pav got close until it was only him clouding her vision. Her gaze caught his, and suddenly, she found that she didn't want to look away at all. Her heart raced like crazy, but as much as that feeling usually added to her fear, right then … she *enjoyed it.*

Maybe this man had a point.

Maybe fear was slightly better when one wasn't all that scared of it.

"I never know who they are," he murmured. "And I didn't know who he was, or why he was there. Just that he had earned his place in hell, and I was there to make sure he understood that. On my life—I promise it."

Viktoria nodded, and swallowed hard. "Okay."

"*Just* okay?"

"What would you have done had you known?"

Pav's cheek twitched, then. "Before I knew you or after?"

"Does it matter?"

"That's not an easy answer."

"Then, what?" she asked.

109

He leaned in closer and pressed a quick, soft kiss to her lips that felt feather-light before it was gone. As he spoke, his lips still brushed against hers. "I'd have killed him, and he'd have known every single second why he was dying."

Before she could respond, Pav had pulled her away from the wall, and the two of them were walking down the corridor again. Like nothing had happened, and his words weren't still echoing heavily in the back of her mind.

Yes, this man was something else.

A monster, for some.

Maybe heaven sent, for her.

That was yet to be determined.

Viktoria hadn't expected to find her father waiting for them at arrivals with a man standing behind him. Usually, a car was there to pick her up. The man would stand with a sign that had her name written on it and nothing more. He wouldn't even speak to her, which she preferred, considering she would panic the entire drive to her father's family estate.

Was Konstantin giving her father a bit of leash to move?

Was he allowed to leave the estate occasionally?

She didn't miss the way Vadim's gaze widened as he saw Pav walking in stride beside her. Quickly, his gaze darted back to his daughter and he smiled. "Viktoria, you're back soon ..."

She didn't reply to that. "Daddy."

Then, he looked to Pav. "And Zhatka, I didn't think there would ever be a day when I would see you outside of the chambers."

Pav was unmoved.

Cold, like ice.

Still, like a statue.

"I suspect," Pav replied, his tone dead, "that was exactly your intention for me, too, Vadim."

Her father only smiled.

10.

"OH, GOOD, you've learned how to use the cell phone."

Pav scowled at the wall in the bedroom he'd been using as he replied, "I don't appreciate your sarcasm, Konstantin."

He knew how to use a fucking phone. He'd regularly had one when he worked in the chambers, just in case he needed it for whatever reason. There were rules, and the phone wouldn't call anyone but the people in the contacts that had been inputted for him, but *still* ...

"I'm just saying, yes, that it has been a week since the two of you landed in Russia, and this is the first phone call you've afforded me out of your very busy days," Konstantin replied cheerfully. "That made me suspect you didn't know how to use the device."

"I know how to use it; I had nothing to call for."

"Mmm."

"I didn't have anything to call for, and I still don't, but I thought you might like an update anyway."

Pav shifted on his feet and scratched the back of his neck as he peeked over his shoulder at the closed door. There were *a lot* of men on this estate watching Vadim Boykov. The man was supposed to be in exile, but there were times when Pav stayed in the shadows and observed, that he thought this was more like a vacation for Vadim. The man simply seemed to be biding his time.

The point?

He didn't trust *any* of them.

There could be a man outside of the bedroom door right now, and he wouldn't even be surprised about it. Pav was terribly good at staying out of sight, if he didn't want to be seen, but the men on this estate made it their mission to sneak up on him at least once or twice a fucking day. He was starting to become uncomfortable.

"What is the update, then?" Konstantin asked.

"Nothing unusual. Viktoria is quiet and refuses to talk to most everyone here."

He didn't try to hide the bitterness.

Konstantin didn't miss it, either.

"Even you?"

Pav cleared his throat. "Even me."

Pretty regularly, too. Occasionally, she might say something to him in passing, but for the most part, the woman locked herself away, in a separate bedroom from him. She avoided her father *at all costs*, no excuses. He'd noticed that, too. She took her meals in her room, brought to her by a female maid, and that was basically the extent of her activity here.

Pav didn't know what to make of it.

"She's still angry, then?"

"And uncomfortable here," Pav replied.

"She is Vadim's favorite. He treated her like a princess for her entire life. Why would she—"

"She did learn some things involving her father before we came here. That could be why, don't you think?"

Konstantin made a harsh noise under his breath. "It could, yes. And how is he with you?"

Pav blinked. "I don't understand—"

"*Vadim*. How is he treating you? Does he speak to you? Does he … instigate you? These are things I had been concerned about with sending you there to watch over her."

"He barely speaks to me at all," Pav replied, "and when he does, he calls me Zhatka."

"I see."

"He's not asked about business, or my circumstance, if that's what you're trying to get at. He's …" *Mostly.* "… acting like a properly exiled man."

"He's still Vadim at the end of the day, which means I cannot trust him with even an inch. The spies I keep on his guard try to keep me informed, but when someone is not close to truly control the hands that feed them, one has to be worried they're not being entirely truthful."

"Is that what you believe?"

Konstantin made a noise on the other end of the call. "What I know is that Vadim is a secondary problem to me right now. He is *exiled*—far the fuck away from me where he can't really cause problems. His calls are monitored. His access to everything and anything is carefully supervised. No man is allowed on those grounds unless I know who they are and have given permission. Hell, even the whore he calls in to suck his cock is one I approved. He cannot *move* without me knowing it.

"The bigger problem that I have to handle right now is *here*," Konstantin snapped. "The man who attacked my sister is still on the loose, one of our warehouses was burned to the ground, and the gang activity in the Heights has picked up so badly that I even needed to put men down in there to try and get it under control. Vadim isn't even a blip on my radar right now."

"But you said it," Pav murmured. "There is a chance that you're not able to control each and every man in this house when you're so far away."

"And I will handle that when I can. There is nothing Vadim could possibly do to me, my brother, or the Bratva when he is where he is—a place I *put him*. He is a secondary problem and he will be treated as such."

Who was Pav to argue?

That didn't mean he had to trust Vadim.

Vadim taught him not to.

"So, the problems *there*," Pav started to say.

"Some may be related to Boris getting free. Others, probably not."

"Huh."

"It's not for you to concern yourself over," Konstantin replied. "You are where you need to be, Pav. Continue keeping an eye on her and try to make her slightly more comfortable. I don't want Viktoria coming back here unless I have no choice but to bring her back. We don't have any indication that Boris is going to attempt to come after her, but considering all the Boykovs have done to him over the last two years ..."

"It's unlikely that a part of him wouldn't blame her and want retribution."

"That," the man agreed, "and the fact he likely knows it would hurt us a great deal if he were able to do to her a second time what he did the first time."

He regretted more and more every day that he hadn't broken the rules of the chambers more often when he had been delegated to taking care of the men in the cells. Unless one died for other reasons—sometimes, their bodies just had enough—Pav wasn't allowed to kill a man except if he was given permission.

But how would they have known?

He could have said it was *anything*, burned the body, and been done with it. It would have been fucking easy. Yeah, he was really regretting that now.

Hindsight, and all.

"I will see what I can do," Pav said, "here, I mean."

"Do that."

Konstantin didn't waste any more time on the phone. He hung up without a goodbye, but Pav wasn't offended. He had other things to do—starting with finding Viktoria and trying to convince her to come out of her room for longer than five minutes.

· · ·

Pav was momentarily distracted from his task of going to Viktoria's room by the bright, blue sky outside. For the most part, the weather had been dreary since they'd arrived. Rainy or cloud-covered skies. Chicago hadn't been much better before they'd left.

It was strange.

He couldn't remember the last time he'd stood outside on a beautiful day and stared up at the sky. He wanted to do that.

Pav stood out on the back deck and looked over the rear side of the estate's large property as the sun beat down and soaked into his skin. A good acre of maintained, thick grass eventually melded into a line of trees that seemed to snake with trails. He wondered what those trails led to, but that was something for another day.

If he got the chance …

"Zhatka, a beautiful day, isn't it?"

Pav tensed at that nickname and the voice who said it. There was only one man in this large, lonely mansion who continued to use the name, even when he refused to answer to it because he knew that he no longer had to.

Vadim, that was.

Glancing up in the direction the voice had come from, Pav found Vadim standing at the railing of a smaller deck. Winding metal stairs led up to the second level—a private porch. The double French doors made Pav believe it likely connected to the man's master bedroom, not that it was important.

He would not have come outside had he known his private moment would be interrupted by Vadim. Never mind the fact that he didn't know how long Vadim had been standing there, watching him enjoy the bright sun.

"Well?" Vadim asked him.

Pav's gaze narrowed slightly. "Well, what?"

"The day. Beautiful, even."

"It's … nice."

He couldn't trust Vadim. He'd spent fourteen years of his life being controlled by this man; being told that he *belonged* to this man like a pet to be abused or otherwise, if he decided it was to be so. Vadim had taken away his entire life, and there wasn't a single part of Pav that believed the man intended to give it back to him at some point.

He was always meant to be a Boykov dog.

But that collar was gone now, wasn't it?

Mostly.

"Come up and join me," Vadim said, waving a hand and turning away from the railing. "I have coffee and food up here, yes?"

He didn't sound like he was giving Pav the option to choose. He could have refused and gone back inside the house without a word, but he decided not to. The entire point of him being here was to keep an eye on Viktoria and make sure she was okay. He didn't think making their situation *more* uncomfortable would be to their benefit for the remainder of their stay. So yes, even though he hated Vadim with a passion that burned him from the inside, he headed for those winding stairs to join the man on his upper deck.

Vadim was already sitting down at a two-person, glass table when Pav reached the top of the stairs. He carefully took the only free wicker chair and kept his gaze on the line of property at the horizon. It was better than the war that seemed to blow up inside his head every time he was forced to *make nice* with this man across from him.

"Coffee?" Vadim asked.

Pav shook his head once. "No, *spasibo.*"

"Food, then? I suspect you haven't eaten this morning."

Was it smart to eat food from the palm of the Devil?

Pav didn't think so.

"I'm not hungry."

Vadim made a noise under his breath, which drew in Pav's attention. He stared at the man while Vadim worked on stirring half a spoon of sugar into his black coffee. The man added nothing else—no milk or cream. Coffee would be good right now, but Pav still wasn't keen on taking anything from Vadim.

"You must feel … bitter toward me," Vadim murmured.

"For what?"

A slow, sly smile curved the edges of the man's lips, and instantly, Pav felt a strong fucking need to reach over and wipe it from Vadim's face. That cold grin … he'd seen it one too many times. He'd seen it out of the corner of his eye as Vadim ordered men to beat the hell out of a sixteen-year-old Pav when he hadn't done his job properly. He'd seen it when he was still a fucking *kid*, and Vadim had told him the monsters in his dreams were nothing compared to the monsters that he would find behind the walls of the Compound.

The bastard was right, too.

Pav was looking at the biggest monster of them all.

Vadim got a sick enjoyment out of seeing others suffer. Pav had not been immune to that simply because he took care of the people in the chambers. For those first few years, if anything, he had been an easy target for Vadim's sadistic games.

Just how far could he push?

When would Pav break?

It had all been a *game* to him.

Now, Pav didn't know how to be anything but the man that he was—this *thing* that Vadim had molded him into. Somedays, he wasn't sure that he felt human. Other days, he felt embarrassingly human and weak.

"So, you're saying you don't feel bitterness for me?" Vadim asked.

"I feel very little for you, Vadim."

The man did look up at that, and his gaze locked on Pav. "Shame, you would have died on those streets had I not taken you in."

"Maybe death would have been better—did you ever consider that?"

"Not even once. Ask your father how death suited him, boy. If he could talk, I doubt he would tell you that was the better option."

Pav's jaw tightened as he clenched his teeth in an effort to keep the sudden surge of anger at bay. He had no doubt that Vadim knew exactly what he was doing. *Purposely* poking at Pav and all his weaknesses. Things that he kept tight to his chest—things no one else knew and that he told *no one*. Oh, he was sure some knew that his father had been killed by Vadim, and that was how he'd come to the Boykov Compound, but he doubted they really understood all the details. Or what came for years afterward, either.

"Well, I don't know what my father would say, do I?" Pav smiled just as coldly as Vadim had moments earlier. "You never gave me the chance to hear him speak when it would have mattered to me the most."

Vadim scoffed. "*Boys.* Boys and their *fathers.* Fathers in this life forget all too often that the boys they bring into the world are nothing but little soldiers who need to be taught how to behave. They're not meant to be spoiled hellions running wild. That will do them no good when their time comes for the Bratva."

"I didn't know anything about the Bratva back then."

"Another error on your father's part."

Pav swallowed hard. "What did you do to him, anyway? Where did you bury him?"

If they even did …

Vadim shrugged as he slathered cream cheese on a bagel like they weren't having a conversation about the murder of Pav's father fourteen years earlier. He might have been bothered by that on another day, but frankly, he was accustomed to this. He found comfort in death more than anything else.

Something else caused by Vadim.

"Amusing," Vadim said under his breath.

"What is?"

"That you assume he was immediately killed that night."

Pav stiffened in the chair, all of his muscles and bones turning into ice at the simple suggestion Vadim had just made. "Excuse me?"

"Your father stole from me. Just a bit off the top, yes, but I couldn't let it go. He was a good soldier, and brought in decent money, but if I allowed him to take a bit off the top without some type of punishment, then every man working under me would assume they could do the same."

Pav refused to speak.

He knew how this worked.

Vadim didn't actually want a response; he wanted Pav to sit there, shut the fuck up, and listen to him as he laid every dirty, horrible detail on the table. And when it was all said and done, he wanted Pav to walk away because he knew there was nothing the man could do about the misdeeds he'd committed.

"What would I make *you* do with a thief when one was brought down?" Vadim asked. "If, of course, you were lucky enough to know I had brought you a thief to keep in the chambers for a while."

Pav didn't want to answer.

He knew.

Wasn't that bad enough?

"Well?" Vadim demanded, glancing up. "Speak, I know you can."

"He'd be kept alive, but throughout the weeks, he would lose pieces of himself—tips of fingers, then down to the knuckles. Strips of skin. His ears. Toes. Nose. Lips …" Pav swallowed the thickness in his throat, refusing to show how hard his heart was beating or the fact that it ached with each and every one. "Anything we could take without him dying, that's what we would do. And only once that was done would he die."

"And about how long would this process take, Pav?"

Fuck you.

Fuck you to hell.

"A month, give or take a week," Pav murmured.

Vadim nodded and smiled again as he peered up at him from his bagel. "Was he a good father to you?"

"Yes."

"Did he smack you around or shout a lot?"

"Never."

Not even once.

Vadim shrugged one shoulder, before biting his bagel. He chewed, swallowed, and then muttered, "Sometimes, I would have them record you in the chambers as you cried … when you were alone in the dark, asking for him … and we would let him watch it over and over before we took something else from—"

Pav was fast to get up from the table then, his hands already reaching out to grab Vadim and choke the fucking life right out of him. He would kill this man right there, with that bite of bagel still slipping down his fat throat, and he wouldn't regret even one second of it. To his credit, Vadim didn't look at all surprised when Pav came at him. If anything, the man looked *amused*.

The thing that stopped him?

The sound of a door slamming.

Pav looked over his shoulder in just enough time to see Viktoria crossing the grass. She wore a flimsy dress that danced around her legs with every step she took. She'd let her icy-blonde hair down, and it flowed over her shoulders and back. In her arms, it looked like she was carrying a blanket.

"She does this a lot," Vadim said. "Never sleeps at night, and then takes a blanket on a walk with her in the mornings. Have you noticed? I have. Same time every day."

Had the man planned this? Did he know what would happen? Pav couldn't think on it for long. He had other things to consider now.

Vadim.

Viktoria.

He had a choice to make.

It was an easy one.

Pointing a finger at Vadim, Pav uttered, "Another day, Vadim."

The man smiled back—unafraid and cold to his core.

Evil, really.

"Just because they've removed the collar and chain doesn't change what you are, Zhatka. You are, and will always be, a Boykov dog. Don't forget it."

11.

THE WATER of the creek bubbled over the shiny rocks that barely broke the surface. Viktoria couldn't remember how she'd found this creek that ran through the back of her father's estate the last time she'd been here, but it was a calm place. One had to go off the cut trails and hike a few minutes into the forest to find it and, as far as she knew, the men who watched the house didn't deviate from the pathways.

She never saw them do it, anyway.

Setting the blanket behind her in case it got a little chilly and she wanted to cover up, Viktoria rested along the edge of the creek. Leaning forward, she let her fingers drag through the surface of the water. A chill raced up her spine from the cold water, but she enjoyed that, too.

It was refreshing.

A reminder she was still *alive*.

Resting her arm over her bare knees where the skirt of her dress had ridden up, Viktoria set her chin on her hand and watched the water. It was memorizing. Almost, in a way, hypnotic. She could pretend like she hadn't tossed and turned all night in a room she didn't want to sleep in, while wishing she was somewhere else entirely. And when she wasn't tossing and turning, she was fighting the need to sleep in order to avoid an inevitable nightmare.

She didn't want to be here. Not near her father. Not in Russia. Not *here*.

She also couldn't go home.

It was the snap of a twig from somewhere behind Viktoria that had her flying up to her feet and spinning around fast enough that the forest was a blur. Not that it mattered—he was already standing less than a foot away from where she had been sitting, by the time she knew he was even there.

Pav looked her over and arched a brow when she glared. "What?"

"Do you just ... enjoy scaring the hell out of me?" she asked.

120

"I purposely stepped on a stick to let you know I was here. I've been standing here for five minutes, watching you."

Viktoria blinked. "Have you?"

"What?"

"Been watching me that long?"

Pav shrugged. "You seemed distracted. I didn't want to interrupt. I also thought it might bother you that you didn't know I was here, so I stepped on the twig."

Oh.

Why was this man so fucking complex?

"You were sitting before I came up," he said, gesturing at the spot on the ground. "So sit, and I will try not to interrupt you again."

Viktoria let out a little laugh as she retook her previous position on the ground after he had unfolded her blanket and set it out for them both to rest on. It was better than the hard, cold ground, she supposed. "I think just you being here is enough of a distraction."

"Is that why you've been avoiding me all week?"

She passed him a look as he came to sit by her, but Pav was looking over the water. He'd posed the question as though he didn't take issue with the fact that he felt like she was avoiding him, and she wasn't sure what to make of that.

"Not *you*," she muttered, picking at the grass.

"Then, who?"

"Vadim."

Pav let out a quiet grunt. "Hmm."

"What was that sound for?"

"I would avoid him, too."

Viktoria nodded. "Probably for different reasons, though."

"Probably."

"Knowing he made the choice to keep Boris alive and had everyone tell me he was dead ... I don't know what to think about that," she said, sighing heavily. "Konstantin said it was the sins of the father, and the guilt of a man, no?"

"He did say that."

"Vadim is not that complex."

Pav glanced over at her, then, but those dark eyes of his held an intensity she didn't think she had ever seen from him before. Like he was keeping secrets there and wasn't willing to share, but they glistened in his eyes at the same time.

"That man is more complex than you know," he murmured.

Viktoria swallowed hard. "Is he?"

"Not in a good way, babe."

The endearment left his lips so easily that it kind of shocked her. She was accustomed to the men in her life using Russian endearments for their wives or lovers. She'd been called one a time or two, as well.

But *babe* ...

Never.

And yet, she liked the sound of it coming out of Pav's mouth. Maybe too much.

"You're not sleeping well," he said.

"How do you know that?"

"Besides the fact that your eyes are dimmed and you *look* tired, someone has noticed your strange habits. They let me know."

She didn't ask who.

She didn't care.

"I have too much on my mind," she admitted.

"Because of what's happening back home?"

"What else?"

"I think your brother's intention in sending you here was so that you *wouldn't* have to think about what was happening in Chicago. You're far away—here, no one can touch you. Not that anyone would get close enough with me here, anyway."

She couldn't help it when a smile curved her lips. "Oh?"

"On my life."

"And just what is that worth, Pav?"

"Pardon?"

"Your life," she clarified. "What is it worth?"

He cleared his throat, drew his legs up to his chest to rest his arms over his knees, and then peered up at the sky through the canopy of trees. "I am coming to learn everything has worth, even if we're taught differently. I haven't settled on my worth ... I suspect it's different for each person who knows me and my view of my worth will never match theirs."

"Except they don't matter."

Pav smirked. "Some do."

He didn't say it directly, but when his gaze landed on her again, she knew that he meant her. That how *she* saw him mattered to him. That her opinion on his worth counted for something where he was concerned.

That felt like a lot to put on her shoulders. Sometimes, she was still terrified of this man, despite the fact he never gave her a reason to be. And sometimes, like now, just staring at him was enough to make her body hot and her mind high.

Funny how that worked …

"I think I can't sleep, either, because I don't know what's happening. When I call Konstantin, he won't tell me anything." Viktoria rolled her eyes and glanced away from Pav when she muttered, "Instead, he lets me stew and make up a hundred different horrible scenarios in my mind about that monster, and what might happen next."

"I'll tell you."

She peered back at him. "Would you?"

"Yes."

"What would you tell me?"

"Anything," he replied.

"*Anything at all?*"

"I said that."

"About him, too?"

Pav cocked his head to the side as he studied her. "Boris, you mean."

Why did her throat get tight, then?

Even saying that asshole's name was *hard*. Harder than it should be, knowing he didn't deserve anything from her now. He'd already taken too much from her. Her peace of mind and her body. Her trust and her self-worth. He'd taken all of it, and she was only now beginning to get it back, piece by tiny piece. So, why couldn't she just say his name without feeling like she was swallowing a rock at the same time?

"Boris," she whispered, forcing herself to say it. "About him. Would you tell me whatever I wanted to know?"

"I would."

"Even about his time there … with you at the Compound, I mean."

She didn't miss the way his jaw tightened ever so slightly, or how his gaze darkened. But he didn't look away from her, and she knew what his answer would be before it ever slipped past those lips of his.

"If you ask me, I won't lie," he replied, "but that doesn't mean I think you should know. I think you want to know because you assume it will help. It may not, it may only—"

"Did he suffer?"

"Often," Pav returned. "From various methods of torture and punishment."

"Give me an example."

"He was beaten every hour, on the hour, when he first arrived. He was left alone just long enough when that was over for him to believe things would get better."

"But they didn't," she whispered.

Pav shook his head subtly. "Of course, not. Nothing gets better in hell."

"Then, what happened?"

"You don't really want to know."

"I wouldn't have *asked*."

Pav cleared his throat, nodding. She knew that she had him, then. If she wanted anything from this man, all she needed to do was ask him. He'd told her that once, and she found that he wasn't the type to go back on his word.

Not if he could help it.

Pav's hand came to rest on her bare knee, just below the hem of her skirt. He squeezed gently, saying, "Punishment varied, and I wasn't the only one expected to deliver it. Kolya came in a few times—he greatly enjoyed those moments."

Viktoria blinked, but was unsurprised.

It was Kolya, after all.

"But what did *you* do to him?" she asked.

A part of her just wanted to know ... maybe if she did, then she could let some of the anger go about the fact her brothers and father lied to her about Boris still being alive after she'd believed he was dead. Like he should have been. If she'd known the bastard truly suffered for what he had done in the chambers, then the betrayal wouldn't sting nearly as bad.

Or maybe it would.

Who knew?

"A specific thing or all of them?" he asked back.

Viktoria shrugged. "Something that will make me smile."

Pav chuckled. "You're a dark soul, Viktoria."

"Maybe."

"I like it."

"At least someone does."

It must have been her words that shifted Pav's mood, because in the next breath, he'd rolled over to his knees, and was pressing in between her legs. His proximity, and the weight of his body, had her leaning back just a bit. She used her hands to keep herself steady as he hovered above her. There was something wild in his gaze as he watched her like that—something *dark*.

But like him, she liked it.

Only on him, though.

"There are a lot of things I like about you," he told her, his gaze drifting down to her mouth and then the column of her throat. It was his gaze alone that could get her heartbeat racing and her stomach clenching. She knew exactly what this man could do to her body if she let him, and it would be glorious. "A lot of things I would love to do to you, Viktoria. Things that would make you scream ..." He grinned, adding, "But in a good way."

"It's always good."

"With me."

"With you," she agreed.

His hand came up to rest against the low V on the neckline of her dress. His warm, calloused palm pressed against her chest overtop where her heart was thrumming hard. There was no hiding the fast beats, but she wasn't sure if it was from fear or lust.

Both, probably.

She still felt scared with him.

And yet, she trusted him, too.

It was complex and addicting.

"Tell me something you did to him," she murmured.

Pav wet his lips and his hand drifted higher. It came to rest at her throat, and his fingers curled tightly around the delicate column. It might have scared her any other time, but she couldn't look away from his eyes, or the way the watched her.

So heady and *wanting*.

His eyes, she thought. *They tell the truth*. His eyes told her everything she needed to know, even when she wasn't going to ask him to say it. There, she found what he wanted the most, and right then, he wanted her.

He wanted her *bad.*

And he was not going to hurt her to get it.

"I held him down with my hand just like *this*," Pav said, his fingers squeezing just long enough to make her suck in a breath before he released, "and then he learned pain, Viktoria. He learned what his skin looked like when it was cut from his chest to his ankles in little ribbons. He bled and he screamed … and he understood what it meant to be *hurt.*"

The only thing she could think to say to that was, "Good."

"Do you have what you wanted to know now?"

Viktoria nodded. "Yes."

"Can I have what I want, then?"

She didn't even need to ask what he wanted. She already knew. She could see it in the hungry way his gaze kept drinking her in, and how his hand at her throat kept tensing like he was holding himself back. His other hand was already slipping up the inside of her thigh, too. A tremor worked its way through her body—the promise of what was yet to come.

She *loved* the anticipation.

Only with him, though.

"You can take what you want," she said.

Pav grinned. "You won't regret that, babe."

She didn't doubt it.

Her heart thundered louder as he lowered down her body with the grace and slowness of a predator who had the prey in his sights. His hand left her throat, just to shove her skirt up around her thighs, exposing the thong she wore. Two of his fingers hooked around the gusset of her thong, brushing against her sex at the same time.

It was almost funny how her body reacted to just a *touch.* Or rather, his touch. Her stomach clenched, her eyes squeezed shut, and she felt like she couldn't breathe. That anticipation was back, too.

"*Watch.*"

That had her looking at him again.

Fucking instantly, too.

She found him between her thighs, grinning up at her. He shot her a quick wink and then his face was buried between her thighs. He kept her thong pushed aside with one hand, while two fingers slid deep into her pussy. His tongue flattened against her clit and then started slashing at it. His dark groan—so thick and loud—sounded like approval to her ears.

There was nothing sexier than watching a man eat at your pussy like it was the last meal he was ever going to be fed. Like he was fucking starved, and her pussy was the greatest thing he'd ever tasted in his life.

His fingers worked her G-spot.

His tongue ravaged her clit.

It took no time at all for Viktoria to be shaking, crying out his name to the empty forest, as the orgasm swept through her senses. The next few moments were a blur of her pulling at him—undoing his pants and tugging them down until she had his cock freed to her grasp. She stroked him with a firm grip as he rested along her side on the ground. His hands found her face again, dragging her in for another breathless kiss.

He hooked her leg around his hip while she got him between her thighs. On her side, with him at her back, they laid close together, bodies tight. His mouth found the side of her neck, teeth cutting into her skin while his hand tangled into her hair. It took one good thrust of his hips, and his cock was buried deep into her pussy.

That first thrust was always the best.

For a moment ...

The way he stretched her open and filled her full. Her hand slipped between her thighs to feel her arousal coating his cock as he slid in and out of her. So wet and *warm*. Every brush of her fingertips against his pulsing length had him whispering the *best* things into her ear.

"Show me what you want, Viktoria."

And ...

"Fuck, do you feel how wet you get, babe? *All over me*. Take that cock."

She felt wild like this.

Crazy like this.

And so free.

He kept her pinned to her side on the ground, and yet tucked safely into his side, too. Arms locked around her body. Kisses covered her throat, the line of her hair, and everywhere he could reach. She came again, faster the second time, and *harder*, too. It was only when she felt his body tense against hers and the way he growled her name against her throat that told her he was close, too.

He came deep in her pussy, fingers digging into her flesh hard enough to leave marks behind, but she didn't mind those. She'd wear them and be happy about them. She asked for these marks, after all.

It was only after he'd pulled out of her body and rolled to his back, did she let out a weightless laugh. Weightless, because that's how she felt, too. His dark chuckles echoed, too, but just as fast, she rolled over and hovered above him. She didn't miss the way his gaze traveled to the junction between her legs.

His eyes darkened as her hands dipped between her legs. She felt his cum slip from her sex to slide between her fingertips, coating her fingers with *them*.

"*Fuck*," he muttered thickly.

Viktoria grinned. "Want to do it again?"

"You don't even have to *ask*."

• • •

Viktoria edged closer to the window of the bedroom she was using at the estate and peered down over the backyard. There, she found Pav and a mean-looking Rottweiler making friends, if that were possible. It was almost amusing to see him shaking a stick only to make the dog crouch back on his hind legs like he was going to jump for the wood.

She didn't know who the dog belonged to—it was one of three that regularly walked around the property. They weren't nice dogs, either. More than once, one had pinned back their ears and growled at her when she'd passed them by. Usually, one of the guards on the property would whistle to the dog in question, and it would back off.

At the moment, though, one of the three Rottweilers looked like a giant puppy with Pav on the grass. Pav tossed the stick, and the dog went after it the second it left his hand. She caught sight of his grin just before he turned his back to the house, and watched the dog run after his new toy.

She smiled, too.

A lot of things about Pav seemed … strange, at times. He sometimes seemed out of his element, but especially around a lot of people. He was always more comfortable being still and quiet, and lingering behind a crowd. He never wanted to be the center of attention, and even a conversation could really test his lines, at times. And yet, he could make friends with a nasty dog like it was nothing for him.

A throat cleared behind Viktoria, and she spun around to find her father standing in the doorway of the bedroom. Usually, she would close it, but after her talk with Pav in the woods a couple of days earlier, she was *trying* to settle in here a little more. Who knew how long she was going to have to stay, right? She might as well get used to it.

Unlikely.

"What are you doing up here?" her father asked.

Viktoria peeked over her shoulder, and watched the dog run back to Pav with the stick hanging out of his mouth. "Nothing, really."

She turned back to her father in just enough time for Vadim to come stand beside her. There was no hiding the fact she had been spying on Pav as he played with the dog. For a long while, her father stayed quiet as he too watched the scene playing out on the grass below.

"Do they know about this? Your brothers, I mean?"

Viktoria's brow dipped. "Know about what—"

"*This.* You and this man. That he clearly has an interest in you, and you are returning it. That it's been physical."

"How do you know—"

"I know many things," Vadim muttered. "I did not ask you a question for you to reply in kind, Viktoria. Answer me, yes?"

God.

"They know," she said quietly.

Vadim tipped his head up as though he were looking at Pav down his nose. Looking *down* at him, even though Pav couldn't possibly know it. Her father stayed quiet for another minute, his gaze narrowing on the man as the seconds ticked by slowly.

Finally, Vadim asked, "Is that how Konstantin is controlling Pavel now, then? With *you.* Give the beast something he wants, and he'll do anything you want him to do, I suppose."

She blinked.

What?

Her father didn't give her the chance to ask the question before he continued on, saying, "That's what I used to do with him, too. For a period of time, whores would keep him in line. Although, he never hurt them or sent them back in any worse condition than they were sent to him. Other times, it was the promise of time away from the Compound. A night away, a taste of freedom … it was enough to sedate for months."

Vadim chuckled and turned away from the window. He gave her a look, raising his eyebrows as he did, like he was suggesting something she should already know. She didn't know a fucking thing, but especially not about her father.

"Maybe my boys learned more from me than I thought, if that's what they're doing by using you to keep him in line. Men are easily placated when something they want is dangling right in front of their grasp. Just because Pavel is a more complicated man doesn't mean he cannot be simplified down in the same way as any other man, Viktoria. Remember that."

She knew that wasn't what her brothers were doing. They wouldn't do that to her—they were *nothing* like their father. And she seriously doubted that Pav was as easy to control as her father liked to say. His life in the Compound's chambers had not been an easy one. She didn't need him to tell her the details for her to know. She had been around her father and his men more than enough for her to know he did not treat people with kindness and respect.

Everyone was just something to use to Vadim. If a person had a heartbeat, then he didn't mind finding their weakness, exploiting it, and using it to his benefit. Pav hadn't been anything different, and she didn't think he was controlled just because Vadim gave him things he wanted like they were treats.

It went deeper than that.

It was worse than that.

Her father had almost walked to the doorway when she spoke again. Another thought had floated through her mind—something Konstantin told her, and something her father just said mixed together, and things *clicked.*

Like a lightbulb going off in her head.

Vadim said it—*give a man what he wants; control him.*

Konstantin said it, too—*the sins of a father; the guilt of man.*

"Is that what you did to me, Daddy?" she whispered.

Vadim's shoulders tensed, but he didn't turn around as he stopped in the doorway. "I beg your pardon?"

"Boris." That time, the monster's name came out easier. "Is that what you did to him—used me to keep him in line? You had to know what he was like; that he was violent and he often hurt women. Everyone else knew, so there's no way you didn't know, too. Was that what you did with him? He wanted me, so you gave me to him to control him, like you thought it would *work*?"

Vadim stayed quiet, but she heard the grinding of his teeth from all the way across the room. His back was as straight as a board and his shoulders had tensed like something invisible had come to sit there.

Guilt of a man.

Sins of the father.

"You liked him, too," Vadim murmured quietly.

"But I was only willing to marry him because you told me I had to."

"I never thought he would cross the line, Viktoria. You were *my* daughter—not some female he'd picked up at a bar and taken home to break like a child might with a new toy. You were *mine*, he shouldn't have—"

"Except he did, and I was just a tool, right? I was something you could use to keep him in line because you liked him, and if you couldn't control him, then you would have to get rid of him."

Just like everything else in his life. Vadim was known for his viciousness, sure, but he was also famous for his ability to discard things that weren't useful to him. People included. Viktoria didn't know why she expected herself to be any different when it came to her father. Oh, sure, she was the favorite one, but not so much that Vadim wouldn't sacrifice her to a monster on the off chance he could keep the monster, too.

"I—"

"Are you going to lie?" she asked.

Vadim looked over his shoulder, then, and those dead eyes of his slammed into hers. "I took a risk. That's all."

Yeah, *a risk*.

"But it was me on the line, Daddy. Not some Bratva man—it was your child. *Me*."

"I never gamble anything I'm not already willing to lose, Viktoria. You, included."

Then, her father was gone. And she felt like her whole heart *shattered*.

Fuck her father.

Fuck *Russia.*

Fuck being safe.

She wouldn't stay here one more minute. She wouldn't share the same home—or the same air—as a man who was just as bad as the monster who'd held her captivate for days so that he could beat and rape her as often as he liked. Staying here was as bad for her mental health as her nightmares and flashbacks. It was a different kind of bad, but she was only now realizing just how much.

After all, Vadim handed her to the monster. She was the *gift*, wasn't she? Her father didn't even care.

No.

She wasn't staying here.

12.

VIKTORIA WALKED past the men waiting for them as they exited into O'Hare's arrivals. To his benefit, the man standing right at the front—Konstantin—didn't blink at his sister's cold attitude as she went by like he didn't even exist.

He did raise his brow to Pav.

"You couldn't convince her to stay there another week or so, then?" Konstantin asked.

Pav could have laughed at that idiotic statement, but he didn't think the other man would appreciate his dark humor. "Can anyone really change that woman's mind after she has decided something? If you know the secret, let me in on it, too."

Konstantin tipped his chin in Pav's direction; a silent agreement. "Point taken. Still—"

"Still nothing. She's a grown woman and she has access to everything and anything she might need right at her fingertips. Including credit cards to buy her own tickets home. Did you want me to let her come home alone? Because that was her plan."

"Fine," Konstantin muttered heavily.

"I did try," Pav replied. "I explained it would be safer. I told her what I knew of the situation back here, and that she should give it more time. I suggested a hotel or somewhere else other than Chicago."

"And what?"

Pav pointed a finger at the woman still walking away from them without as much as a glance over her shoulder. "You're looking at the result."

Konstantin scowled. "It's not safe for her here."

"As she told me, this is also *her* home."

"What?"

Pav shifted on his feet, avoiding Konstantin's gaze as he said, "Chicago is her home. This is all she knows, yes? Why should she have to leave it? I'm here. I'll be with her. Surely, you can spare another man or two that will watch her from afar. After all of that, I'm sure no one will be coming after her. It would be a death wish."

"We believe Boris is working with people. *How* or who, is the better question, and one we don't have any answers to. That's a *real* threat, Pav. And what, you're so caught up in *feelings* for my sister that you can't make a choice for her because—"

"Exactly that," Pav interjected sharply.

Konstantin straightened. "I beg your pardon?"

"I will not make choices for her. I will tell her if I think something is a bad choice, but it is hers to make. People have already taken enough from Viktoria—I won't be someone else who just adds to the list, Konstantin. Take that as you may."

"I sincerely hope she explained more to you than she did to me when she called and told me you were both coming back," Konstantin said. "About *why*, I mean."

"She did."

"*And?*"

The answer was simple.

"Vadim," Pav said.

Konstantin rocked back on his heels a bit and shoved his hands in the pockets of his suit jacket. "What happened? All I was told was that you were coming home, and she *didn't give a shit* if I liked it or not."

Pav eyed the woman in question. Viktoria hadn't gone far—to the luggage carousel where she was currently waiting with glaring eyes at the ready for anyone who thought to come to close to her. She had slept barely a wink the last two nights they'd remained in Russia, and she'd refused to speak to anyone but him. She only came out of her room when Pav asked her to, and only if he could assure, she wouldn't have to face her father. On the trip home, she slept for each flight. The whole way through.

"I don't know all the details," Pav said, "but she had a run-in with Vadim. He said some things about the incident with Boris, and that upset her a great deal."

"What *things*?"

"She only told me that Vadim was horrible, and she couldn't stay there any longer. That was it."

Konstantin's jaw worked hard, and he passed a quick look over his shoulder at Viktoria just thirty feet away. Pav didn't need the man to say the things he was thinking—they could both see what was right in front of their faces, neither of them were blind.

Viktoria was in a bad place; she was dealing with something inside her mind, and they couldn't see in there.

"He's always been horrible," Konstantin muttered.

"But did she know that?"

"She pretended like she didn't. I take it she can no longer do that."

"You would have to ask her."

Konstantin winced a bit, turning back to Pav. "Better to just let her … work through it on her own. Vik never reacts well when someone pushes her when she would much rather be left alone to deal with whatever it is."

Pav disagreed.

The only way to get Viktoria out of her head was to *make* her do it. Pav tended to be quite talented at getting Viktoria to react when he wanted her to, and given that he was able to handle all of her reactions—good or bad—he wasn't concerned.

"She has idolized a man who was not worthy of being an idol for a long time," Konstantin said quietly. "And so I imagine that's brought with it a whole host of issues." The man chuckled dryly. "*Daddy issues,* if you will."

Pav said nothing.

What was there to say?

"Also, I have these for you," Konstantin said.

He pulled the three knives they'd all but forced Pav to hand over before he'd left for Russia with Viktoria. That had been quite an argument, but Konstantin was *adamant.* No questions asked, Pav could not take the damn knives on the plane with him. If Konstantin didn't take them, then it was likely the security would confiscate them entirely. Was that a risk he wanted to take? That he might never get them back?

Not particularly.

There was a split second as he'd removed his knives and gave them to another man that he'd felt almost … naked.

Weak, even.

He'd had those knives for almost as long as he'd been at the Compound. He took as good of care of them as he did the men in the chambers. Each night, he pulled them out to carefully inspect them and clean the handles and blades. When nothing else could really be trusted around him, he felt comfort in knowing those blades were always waiting at his back. He didn't regularly use them, but he liked knowing that they were close by should he need to pull one out when the time called for it.

Except, they'd taken them.

No knives on a plane, apparently.

Fucking stupid.

Pav was quick to take the knives off Konstantin's hands and slip them into the pockets of his jacket. None of the people moving around them in the airport noticed the exchange, and once Pav had his knives back, he felt slightly better. Not that the knives made a true difference to his ability to kill someone or get a job done. He could do those things with or without the knives. He simply didn't like being without them.

"I told you I would get them back to you, didn't I?" Konstantin asked.

Pav's jaw clenched. "I'm not used to Boykovs keeping their words. Forgive me for my honesty, Konstantin."

The man smirked a bit. "But you're only really accustomed to one Boykov man, aren't you? I don't think Vadim is a good representation of the rest of us, all things considered."

That may be so.

He wouldn't deny it.

The facts still remained ...

"It was enough to teach me a lesson about the rest of you."

Konstantin's grin faded quick. "And what was that?"

"I don't hand you my trust. You earn it."

A simple nod answered him back. "Understood."

"Are we leaving now?"

At the impatient, cold voice slipping over the arrivals area, Pav sighed. He looked Viktoria's way to find she had gotten her luggage, and even his small bag that had gone under the plane, too. She arched a brow at him when his gaze met hers.

Difficult.

Sassy.

Cold.

Nasty.

He adored her for those things.

He also wished she didn't use them as a defense.

All in due time ...

Viktoria looked to Konstantin, then. "Well, is he coming with me now? You seem to think I always need a babysitter—I'd rather it be him. I want to go home."

"Have fun with that tonight," Konstantin told Pav. "She sounds like she's in a really winning mood at the moment."

"Understatement."

That was all he gave Konstantin as a reply before he headed after Viktoria. He figured nothing else really needed to be said.

Konstantin's voice trailed after him. "Oh, and there's a man guarding the house, Pav. Keep an eye out for him."

He tossed two fingers up high over his shoulder; the only acknowledgement he offered. Viktoria was waiting for him, after all. Pav had found lately that he really liked following after her, even if she was a little difficult to deal with at times.

It was worth it.

• • •

"Relax," Pav murmured against the shell of Viktoria's ear.

She shivered at the action, but at the same time, he felt the tension in her back melt away slightly. Not entirely, but it was enough to say she had listened to him. Outside the airport, they waited for the driver Konstantin had arranged for them to make his way up the arrivals. Another couple of minutes, likely, and they would be on the road.

"Another minute or so and we'll be away from all the people," he told her.

She nodded.

He was learning that he really didn't need her to voice what was going on in that broken mind of hers—sometimes, her cues were more than enough to go on. Like right now, and the way she tried to tuck herself in closer to him on the sidewalk. Or the way her gaze continued to dart from person to person who walked around or climbed into a waiting vehicle.

Too many people.

He understood that *well*.

Letting his hand slip around her trim waist, he coiled his fingers against her side and held on tight. That closed the small bit of distance that was between them and let him kiss the side of her head again. The smell of whatever sugary-scented shampoo she used soaked into his senses, and for a brief second, the rest of the world disappeared.

He didn't think she knew.

Not that she did that for him.

Pav didn't know how to explain it, either.

"Pav?"

"Hmm?"

"I'm terrified," Viktoria whispered. "Of being here, I mean."

He nodded, his lips still grazing her temple as he spoke. "I know."

Pav wasn't sure if her fears were unfounded or not. Could they really all keep her safe and away from the threat that was currently wild and on the loose? Were they capable of keeping their eyes on her twenty-four-seven?

He wanted to say yes, but he knew that would be a foolish pipe dream to do, and he didn't want to give her reassurances that he couldn't promise. He didn't make promises he couldn't keep. His word was the only thing he really had at the end of the day. Why would he want to break his word to this woman?

He was a pessimist and a realist, anyway. He looked at the facts first, and worked his way back from there. The facts said nothing good about this.

But she'd *decided*.

He said nothing about it.

"But this is my home," she said to him. The same thing she'd been telling him for the last couple of days; what she'd repeated to him on the flight each time she'd woken up from her naps. He believed that she said it so many times because she was intent on convincing herself it was a fact, and not him. If someone told themselves something enough, they started to believe it was the truth. "Chicago is *mine*."

"It is."

"I don't want to be afraid in my home. I don't want to be afraid at all. Not anymore. I hate that this is what it's done to me. That this is what *he* did to me. He made me afraid of my home—of my own shadow. Now, he sent me running away from the place that's mine. I don't want to run anymore, you know?"

Pav grinned a bit, the warmth of her skin brushing against his lips. "Learning to love it, are you?"

He saw the brief narrowing of her gaze before she asked, "Love what?"

"The fear. Remember what I told you?"

She let out a weak laugh. "I wouldn't say that, no."

"I would."

Her hand slipped up between them, and she grabbed onto the bit of his shirt just below the collar. Those deft fingers of hers wrapped tightly into the fabric, and she pulled just enough to bring him in close again. The silent action, to him, meant she wanted him to do what he had been doing just moments before.

Kissing her temple.

So, he did it again.

"Fear creates hate," he told her. "People take the things we fear, and then they amplify it so that it seems worse than it really is. All we see is this horrible idea that the thing we fear the most will take something from us, and we begin to hate it for that. We hate it because it makes us live in a constant state of fear."

She drew in a shaky breath. "Yeah, I guess."

"Hate and love is a *very* thin line, babe."

"I can say with absolute certainty that I don't love my rapist or what he's done to me, Pav."

"Perhaps not, but there are other things that have come from it that you may love. Parts of you would not be who you are without the things that have happened."

And him, too. Although he chose not to say that out loud, but it didn't make it any less true. If these horrible things never happened, he honestly believed that he would still be exactly where he had been not too long ago. Stuck in the deepest pits of hell, with cement walls and dying men to keep him company. He would never have known her, and wouldn't that just be a shame?

Pav couldn't imagine being without her.

How did he tell her that?

He didn't know where to start.

This was new.

Too new.

"I wouldn't know anything about that," Viktoria mumbled. "Love, I mean."

"Why's that?"

"I never had the chance to love something that strongly. I've only ever known how to hate something like my life depended on it because ... I think it did for a while."

"Taking control of fear is the same as learning to love it. When someone cannot use it against you anymore, then it's yours to do with as you want, if you understand."

"I do. I'm trying."

"That's all that matters."

Viktoria glanced up at him then, and when her sky-blue eyes met his, he swore the rest of the world drifted away again. All the noise of the airport stopped. The polluted air cleared. His world shifted back on a proper axis.

All because she looked at me.

When had this happened?

"Pav?"

"*Da?*"

"I don't know what I feel about you, either," she whispered.

"No?"

He didn't even think about it. He just leaned down and caught her soft lips with his own. There was something honest in her kiss. He could always feel that trepidation racing through her body when he kissed her, or the excitement. She never shied away from his kiss now, and if anything, she was the first to demand more. A hot strike of her tongue against the seam of his mouth or her fingers digging into his chest.

Her lips worked against his and every kiss took him higher. That taste of her wasn't nearly enough, but he wasn't going to complain about it, either. She was becoming a drug to him. A shot of heroin into his heart, making it blacken and beat for only her. She didn't know it, though. That was okay, too.

Now wasn't the right time to explain it.

She wouldn't mind waiting.

All too soon, she pulled away, but he let her. He could have pulled her in for another kiss, but there were too many people watching, and he never liked being the center of attention. Neither did she, really.

Viktoria swallowed hard. "There's a part of me that wants to keep you."

"I like that part."
Her laughter was sweet.
Her smile, beautiful.
She winked. "Yeah, me too."

13.

THE CAR pulled alongside the driveway to Viktoria's Melrose home, but she didn't immediately reach for the door handle to get out of the vehicle. She took a moment first to look over her house, the front walkway, and the windows with all the drapes pulled closed to keep anyone from looking inside.

Nothing had changed.

It all looked the same.

It was strange to her, though, how it all felt a little different. Like she was seeing the place with new eyes and different feelings. In a way, this house had felt like her prison for a long time. The home her father bought her after the attack—she would deal with that another time—and the place that kept her hidden away from the world. Here, she had felt safe, like nothing could hurt her and no one would ever know how broken she truly was when she closed the front door.

Like keeping the world out.

The thing was, she knew that in fact, all she had been doing was protecting herself in the only way she'd known how. She was building those walls up higher and higher because she couldn't afford for someone else to climb over them and hurt her again.

It was like a part of her knew ...

Some part of her just *knew* what her father had done even though she'd never asked, and he'd never told her until now. She'd been naive enough to believe for a long time that despite the fact her father was a horrible human being, he wouldn't be that person to her. In all truth, she hadn't wanted him to be that person to her, so she'd chosen to overlook a lot.

The way he treated others.

Things he did to his sons.

Everything.

Literally everything about her father was a constant reality check about who he actually was beneath his tailored suits and welcoming smiles. Sure, he reminded her of years gone past, and a childhood that was filled with a girl being spoiled and adored by her daddy ...

but she was just another pawn for Vadim at the end of the day. He'd let her think that his affection and adoration was because he truly felt those things, when, in fact, they were just another form of his manipulation.

She was not a special case.

She was not *the most* loved.

He didn't give a damn about her.

So yeah, despite the fact she knew for sure now, it was only because she couldn't pretend anymore. She was mad at the part of her that had to know but still went ahead and ignored it, anyway. Everything made so much more sense now, in a way.

Because wasn't she nastiest to those she loved? Wasn't she coldest to those who were supposed to care and protect her because the one she cared for and loved the most had been the same person who'd hurt her?

"Could you give us a moment?"

Pav's voice drew Viktoria from her thoughts, and she realized then that her hand was still on the door handle, but she hadn't actually made the attempt to open it. She was still sitting there in the back seat of a vehicle while she stared at her house, going over every moment of her life that passed her by in the last two years.

All her fears.

The mistakes she'd made.

Her pain.

The pain she'd caused.

"Now, if you wouldn't mind," Pav snapped at the driver when the man lingered in the front a little too long for his liking. "Move."

The driver finally got out of the car.

Viktoria still didn't move.

"I stopped looking into mirrors after it all happened," she said when it was just them alone in the back of the vehicle. "I told myself it was because I didn't recognize the person who was staring back at me."

Pav cleared his throat. "It's just a house, babe."

Viktoria made a noise in the back of her throat. "It's not ... it's a prison. One I made for myself after someone else handed me the keys. I didn't stop looking into mirrors because of that, I didn't like who was looking back at me. I didn't like who I had become, and the way I treated the people around me."

"Vik—"

"They wanted to help, but I just wanted to die. I couldn't have them get too close. They might hurt me, too, but if they didn't, then I wouldn't want them to be hurt when the inevitable finally happened. I didn't want them to feel pain when I died because I wasn't even worth that. Does that make sense?"

Pav's sigh echoed in the quiet car. "I suppose, in a warped way, yes."

"I don't know what I feel about this house anymore."

"We don't have to stay here."

His words were simple.

And true, she knew.

Everything seemed to be that way for Pav—things either were or they were not. He wasn't the type to add frills and nonsense to anything. He was very much black and white, and she appreciated that more than he could possibly know. Everyone else always wanted to get inside Viktoria's head and figure out all the nuances that attributed to her behavior.

It wasn't that deep.

She didn't want them that deep.

Pav managed to get exactly that deep, but he never even had to try to do it. He got under her skin, and there was no getting him out now. Every touch and moment with this man, even in passing, seemed to be wiping slates clean for her in different ways.

"We could get a hotel," she suggested.

Pav's hand came to rest just below the back of her neck. His fingertips drifted over the small patch of her exposed skin, causing shivers to race down her spine. She wasn't afraid of that feeling when he was the one causing it. She just wanted more of it.

Not here, though.

"I need to grab some things, but then we can leave," she said.

"Whatever you need."

She was scared a part of herself was starting to love this man; it terrified her even more that somehow, it had become a fear at all. She didn't want to be scared of love—of *him*. That was just the broken part of her that still had its claws dug into her mind.

Something for another time.

Right now, she had to deal with this damn house.

Viktoria pushed open the car door and stepped out onto the sidewalk. She dragged in a heavy breath of Chicago air—not quite fresh, but cool enough to chill her lungs and feel like it might be a new start for her in a way.

Pav followed, but he wasn't looking her way. Instead, he glanced at the driver of the car, who had pulled out his phone and had it pressed to his ear. The man seemed a hell of a lot more distraught than he had when he'd stepped out of the car.

"Stay here," Pav said to her.

"But—"

"I'll only be a minute."

She didn't understand what was wrong—if anything even was— but she didn't feel up to arguing with him, either. Today was emotional and difficult enough without her attitude adding to it. Even she knew that.

His fingertips drifted along her lower back as he left her side, to go to the driver around the side of the car. The two of them talked in low tones. She couldn't hear a thing either of them said, but the way Pav's face darkened and then blanked as he glanced back in her direction was enough to confirm her suspicions.

Something was wrong.

That growing ball of dread in her stomach seemed to get heavier with every passing second. She tightened her coat in an effort to keep away the chill that was suddenly running through her body. She wasn't going to panic—not yet.

Pav nodded at the man and then headed for the house. He gave her a nod and a half smile, but it didn't feel true. He hadn't asked her to follow him, so she didn't. But as he walked up the front steps of her house, and reached for the front door, her body moved forward on its own accord. Like a rope had come to knot itself around her middle, and was dragging her to him.

The door is locked, she wanted to say. *You'll need the keys, Pav.*

He didn't need the keys at all.

He just pushed the door open.

What was happening?

"Miss, you should wait out here a moment," called the driver behind her.

Viktoria ignored him altogether. "Pav, wait!"

He was already inside the house now. Who knew if he'd even heard her calling for him. Wasn't there supposed to be someone watching her house? She was sure that's what Konstantin had told Pav in the airport. Had they given the guard the keys to her house for him to *be inside*? Because she didn't like that at all.

The inside of the house seemed normal. Nothing was out of place, and everything was just as she had left it before going to Russia. Even the glass bowl on the stand near the door was still full of the bobby pins, hair ties, and a set of random keys. Her junk bowl, for all purposes. The coats still hung on the wall and her shoes were still lined underneath them. The floor didn't have a speck of dirt to be seen, and the place was quiet.

Eerily so.

Maybe *too* quiet.

"Pav?"

She heard the footsteps above her head instead of him answering her back. She didn't bother to call for him again, instead, heading down the hall and up the stairs to the second level on the home. She found him in her bedroom.

Along with a nightmare.

A *new* nightmare.

There was a dead man on her bed. He'd been gutted and his blood stained her white sheets.

On the mirror, heavy strokes of congealed crimson wrote out her greatest fear. It had her heart racing, and her head crackling with static as she went silent. Everything went quiet, then. The whole world just stopped turning.

Pav stood in front of the mirror, reading the message that had been written in what she suspected was the dead man's blood.

I miss you, Vik, the message read.

Pav's faint *Viktoria* calling out to her was the last thing she heard before she hit the floor, and everything went dark. The mind was such a funny thing … it was always there to drag her away from hell when she couldn't do it for herself. Except the bigger problem was it always delivered her to another hell.

There was no escape.

• • •

Pav stood in the doorway of the bedroom as Viktoria sipped on a hot cup of tea. He said nothing as the conversation continued in the sitting room, but his gaze didn't leave her, either. He'd been like this since she woke up—silent and stewing. She didn't have very much to say. What needed to be said?

The message was enough.

The hotel was one of the more expensive ones in Chicago. The Astoria was always known for its large rooms, and big-name guests. Honestly, she was just happy Konstantin had decided to pick a hotel for her that had better security.

But how much would that really do?

"We need to settle on a plan," she heard Kolya say. "For *everyone*."

"And we will, no? But we need to wait—"

"Zoya."

Maya's soft greeting had Viktoria glancing up from the cup of hot tea in her hands. She had been perfectly fine to stay in the bedroom while her brothers and their wives went over the plans. She didn't need to put in her opinion when in the end, Konstantin was going to decide what to do with her, and she would just follow his orders, anyway.

But at the sound of her sister-in-law greeting Zoya, her half-sister, Viktoria decided it was time to show her face. She didn't understand why her brothers would have the young woman come over to begin with—she wasn't involved in this and she didn't need to be. They were purposely dragging her into the danger zone, and she didn't deserve that.

Pav stepped out of the way when Viktoria passed him by in the doorway. He trailed close behind her, as she headed down the short hallway and came into view at the entryway to the sitting room. All eyes turned on her, including her half-sister's.

The two stared at one another.

Zoya, in a pretty dress.

Viktoria, in bloodstained skinny jeans.

Yeah, there'd been blood on the floor where she fell. She was trying to ignore it, but eventually, Pav would force her out of those clothes, and then she was going to see the remnants of the stains on her skin.

But not right now.

Staring at her half-sister, Viktoria could see the similarities between them. The few features they'd taken from their father, and that similar glint in their eyes that said they shared blood. She'd not made an effort with this girl—not to know her or to care. It wasn't that she didn't feel something for Zoya, because she did, but was this really the life she wanted to live? Did she want to be dragged into the mess of the Boykovs simply because she shared their blood?

Viktoria would tell her not to.

She'd tell her to run.

"Why is she here?" Viktoria asked, never looking away from Zoya.

She was quite aware how the question sounded. Rude and cold. Like everything else that came out of her mouth, probably. Usually, she would just let people assume her bitchiness was exactly what it was at face value, but this was not the same.

"*Vik*," Konstantin snapped. "Be nice."

She looked at her brother. "I am—why is she here? So whoever is watching us can report back that there's another Boykov target to use? At least when she's keeping her distance from us, nobody thinks we give a shit about her. It's selfish to have her here when she would be safer away from us, Konstantin."

Zoya cleared her throat, drawing in Viktoria's attention again. "I wanted to come. I wanted to make sure you were okay when I'd heard something happened at your house."

Viktoria softened in her stance a bit and nodded once. "I'm okay."

"Good."

This was probably the longest conversation she had ever had with the woman. She was hyperaware of her family, who had all turned into statues as they watched the exchange happening between her and Zoya. She didn't know what to tell them. The fact that they assumed they understood her complex feelings or opinions about this woman, or anything else for that matter, wasn't her problem.

"Someone will be watching Zoya as well," Konstantin said. "That was already decided a while ago."

"Even though she didn't want that," Amelia, Konstantin's wife, added. "He does account for others, Viktoria, even if you think he doesn't."

She passed Amelia a look.

"I'm aware," she replied dully.

It wasn't that she disliked Amelia, because she did like her, in a way. She simply found that when someone—but especially a woman—was similar to her own self in ways, they could easily rub her the wrong way.

"Come on," Pav murmured behind her, his hand coming to lock around her wrist. "Let's go sit back in the room and relax."

That sounded perfect.

"In a second," she told him.

He nodded but not before dragging her a little closer to him. She didn't mind that—being tucked into his chest, as one of his arms locked around her waist and his lips rested at the back of her head while he breathed in deep. It reminded her, for the moment, that she was safe.

What more could she want?

"Move her out of the city," Kolya said, gesturing at Viktoria. "We can move the others, too."

"I'm not leaving the city."

Konstantin looked her way, shaking his head. "That's dangerous. It would be better if you—"

"I'm not running anymore."

That was her hard line.

"I'll be with her," Pav murmured against her hair. "I'll keep her out of sight, and there'll be men posted here. If you think about it, someone could still find her outside of the city. At least here, we can control how difficult it is to get to her. Away from here, there are too many unknowns and variables that could cause issues should something happen."

Konstantin sighed. "He's right."

Viktoria was still staring at Zoya. She knew the girl had fucked up feelings about their father—the same way Viktoria did, but for entirely different reasons. Zoya felt like she'd missed out on a father because Vadim had always kept her and her mother a secret. He was around just long enough to toss money at them and keep them out of sight. He never gave a fuck.

"You didn't miss out on anything, you know," Viktoria said.

Zoya arched a brow. "I'm sorry?"

"Vadim." Viktoria shrugged and smirked a little. *Bitterly.* "You didn't miss out on anything where he was concerned. He didn't know how to be a father, Zoya, he only knew how to be the illusion of one.

And it's become painfully clear to me that no father at all would have been far better than the one I never really had."

The room quieted.

Truth might silence.

But truth was *power.*

Viktoria went back to the bedroom.

Pav followed behind.

14.

PAV ADMIRED the sway of Viktoria's hips as she paced from one side of the hotel room to the other. He could get up, distract her long enough to stop the pacing, and deal with it that way, but he figured this was more entertaining for him. He was able to watch all of her curves and the way that she moved in her frustration while he stayed shadowed on the chair in the corner near the heavy drapery.

It wasn't like she didn't know he was there. She watched him go sit down, of course. He wasn't attempting to sneak up on her again—he knew better than to do that; she didn't like it very much, even if he found it highly amusing. He was simply letting her work out this restlessness on her own.

And he got a good show with it.

Mostly.

"This is driving me *crazy*," Viktoria muttered, her pacing coming to an abrupt stop in front of his chair. He tipped his head back to stare up at her. "Doesn't it bother you to just … sit here and wait for something to happen?"

Pav smiled a bit. "Not particularly, no."

Viktoria gave him a look.

Pav only shrugged.

He wasn't lying.

"Besides, didn't you mostly just stay hidden in your house a good portion of the time?" he asked, arching a brow when she looked away from him. "And *now* when you actually need to stay hidden away, you want to be restless. Think about it."

Viktoria exhaled loudly. "It's because I'm *waiting* for something to happen, but it feels like nothing is happening."

He would have smirked, but she didn't exactly look like she was in the mood for his shit. Tense as hell, with a knot in her brow and a fire in her gaze, she was ready to *fight*. She was wrought tight with nerves and anxiety. That fear she was trying to suppress with every fiber of her being was more present than ever, and not because she wanted it to be; not because she was finding any sort of comfort in it.

Pav didn't need her to tell him what was going on in her mind. He only needed to watch this woman—*his* woman, if he thought about it—to know the war she was facing and trying to battle alone. He really didn't know what to tell her about this, though. She wasn't given a good choice about all of this.

The hotel.

Or out of the city.

That's what Konstantin had offered her, and Viktoria had refused to leave the city again. He'd like to say it was because she was stubborn as fuck, and that was a huge part of it. He also knew it had to do with the way she was trying to view her ... demons. If she continued to run from them, and never faced them, then they would always be one step away or ahead of her. Always ready to jump on her back when she wasn't paying attention.

She needed to *deal.*

She had to handle it.

Simple as that.

Pav scratched at the side of his neck with one finger and eyed her at the same time. "Do you want me to order you food from that place you like again?"

"No."

"Do you want to go down to the restaurant—"

"*Nyet.*"

"Hard no," he replied, amused.

Viktoria passed him a look that would have burned a weaker man, surely. He kind of adored that about her. Even if she was trying to soften her attitude and the delivery of her words when it would be easier for her to be sharp and cutting, she was still the same underneath it all.

The difference was where others couldn't handle this woman at her worst, Pav welcomed it. He *enjoyed* this side of her as much as he liked her soft, sweet, and kind. They were parts of the same woman, after all. He didn't think it was fair for him to like one part, but not the others.

"I want to go do something," Viktoria said. "Away from this hotel room. We've been in here for four days now. I can't leave this place and it's driving me insane."

Pav chuckled.

"Did you just *laugh* at me?"

"I did," he replied simply. "Because you're like a caged animal. You'd think you never had to sit and wait for something to happen before."

"Pav—"

"You remind me of the men when they first wake up in the chambers, yeah?"

Viktoria stilled, all that movement and jitteriness of hers coming to a stop at once. He wasn't looking at her then, instead he watched the clock on the wall tick down seconds. He could still feel the way her gaze landed on him in that moment.

It felt like curiosity. And *concern.*

"Do I?" she asked.

Pav nodded. "Most of them don't know where they are because they never knew the chambers even existed underneath the Compound. Those are probably the worst because they're waiting for something, but they don't know what. If I hadn't been ordered to go in on them right after they woke up, I would have to watch them pace, climb the walls, and drive themselves crazy in the darkness."

"And what about the ones who did know where they were when they woke up?"

Ah.

Smart woman.

Pav shrugged one shoulder. "Constantly on edge—*also* waiting, but they knew what they were waiting for. Some were violent and others tried to end their suffering before it could really get started. It was never a good experience."

"How long—"

"Since I was twelve," he murmured, looking back at her again. He didn't actually need her to finish her sentence to know what she was asking him. How old were you? How long were you down there doing that? "Although, at first, I had people who helped, if that's what you want to call it. Vadim called it training."

"That's … awful."

"I suppose."

Pav felt, in a way, that he didn't know any other way to live. He was learning now, and he'd had a period in his life where he'd been free of the chambers, broken men, and darkness. Then, he'd been just young Pavel, and now he was Pav who some still whispered *Zhatka* for when he walked past them. He'd forgotten a lot about who Pavel was, and he hadn't been given enough time as this person to know much about him, either.

But he wanted to learn.

Didn't that count for something?

The silence between the two of them stretched on, and Pav's own restlessness grew with each passing second. There'd been a part of him that had been itching to go back to a place he'd come from—a place his father had always cared for, and had looked after time and time again. He had been allowed to go back a couple of times as he'd grown older, but someone was always with him to make sure he never stepped out of line.

Where was home?

Was that what he was missing?

"It's harder to hit a moving target."

Viktoria glanced back at him. "What?"

"It feels like we're sitting ducks here, even with the people watching the place. Sitting ducks, nonetheless."

"A bit."

"What would it hurt to move around for the night?"

Viktoria grinned, catching on. "Do you have a place you'd like to go?"

"A couple," he admitted.

"What about the men watching the hotel?"

Pav shrugged. "One at the back, and the front. They're not watching every exit because one can only leave the exits, but they can't enter. They'll see us when we come back in the morning, but what will it matter, then? What's done is done."

Viktoria's laugh colored up the room, and he hadn't even blinked before she was in front of him again. Leaning in, she caught his lips with her own in a bruising, hard kiss. It took his breath away and made his lungs ache.

He kind of loved that.

And her.

Wasn't that what this feeling in his chest was? All tight, heavy, and yet warm and wonderful at the same time? Like he was going to hurt if she was gone, but he was okay while she was here? Like life really wouldn't matter if he wasn't looking at her every single day of it?

Love?

It felt like it.

He'd figure it out later.

· · ·

Pav kept his arm locked tight around Viktoria's waist as they maneuvered through the crowd of people getting closer to the cage in the middle of the warehouse with every passing second. He dragged her closer to his side, wanting to breathe in her vanilla and pear perfume, and feel her warmth soaking through his clothes.

At the same time, he murmured in her ear, "The first time they brought me to these fights, I was fourteen."

He didn't tell her the rest—that he'd found someone he'd recognized from his past who had lived in the large loft where he and his father stayed. That the person told him, no matter what, he could come back home, and they would always recognize him. He didn't mention how he had gotten the shit beat out of him that night in the cage, but this was one of the places where he'd learned to fight.

Here, he'd learned how to survive.

"Did you fight, too?" she asked.

Pav laughed low. "I did."

"And?"

"I lost—*terribly*."

Understatement. He'd suffered a broken nose, a cracked rib, and the guy who was at least a half of a decade older than him had been going in for the kill—pretty usual in these fights—when someone stepped in to pull Pav out of the ring before his opponent could end him. He'd had a concussion so bad from the fight that he only had brief memories of different things that happened throughout the night.

But he remembered that person.

That familiar face who'd said his father's name …

"And what about now?" Viktoria asked. "Do you think you would win now?"

"Guess we're going to see, aren't we?"

"*What?*"

Her question echoed, along with the call of the man who was judging the fights from the safety outside of the octagonal-shaped cage.

"Next fight—Gunner versus ..." The man climbed a little higher on the cage, causing the people around him to shout and move closer yet again. "Anyone who wants to challenge."

Pav didn't have a clue who *Gunner* was. The man in the cage waiting for his challenger didn't look particularly familiar, and he seemed to be the same size and height as Pav. He never found it to be very fair when they put a much smaller man up against a large man. But that was just how these fights worked—nobody gave a shit, honestly. It was all illegal, and far too many people lost their lives on that dirty, bloodstained mat.

Had they cleaned it in the last year?

Probably not.

"I challenge," Pav said, raising an arm high.

He felt the eyes in the warehouse turn on him as he moved close enough to the cage that he could reach up and curl his fingers along the chain-link. Viktoria was close at his back, her hands resting flat over his shoulders as her warm breath pulsed against his neck.

"What are you *doing*?"

She sounded horrified.

And *hot*.

"Relax," he murmured.

"*Zhatka*," the man hanging onto the cage said. "Been a minute since you've been around, yeah? Where's your handlers? They have to keep you in line, don't they?"

Pav nodded behind him. "She's looking out for me."

The man arched a brow as he studied Viktoria's face. If he recognized her, then he didn't say. "She's gonna pull you out of there when you cross the line, huh?"

"No crossing lines tonight—promise."

He even put his palms up to solidify it.

The guy still looked at the man inside the cage waiting. "Well, Gunner, you wanna fight or not?"

Pav grinned when Gunner's eyes lock on his. "Yeah, I'll fight him."

He was already climbing inside the cage and dropping his jacket and shoes over to Viktoria before the guy could call out the fight. He waited as the man across the cage got his knuckles taped up. *Nonsense.* The tape wasn't going to make anything feel better, but it might protect his hands from getting cut up if he landed a punch to Pav's mouth.

He wouldn't land one.

Not a single one.

He grew up in these fights, in a way. Twice a week for *years*, Vadim had Pav dragged to these warehouses. Best way to learn, he was told. He needed to know how to fight, but also how to kill. He figured it was also yet another way for Vadim to scare the hell out of Pav and show him just how far the Boykov name could reach.

One of many lessons.

"Pav!"

Viktoria's call of his name echoed above the shout of the man for the fight to start. He glanced over his shoulder to meet her gaze as his opponent made his way across the cage to him. She smiled at him, mouthing, *"Be safe."*

Right.

Safe.

He winked back at her.

She had nothing to worry about.

The sounds of the people roaring and banging on the cage deafened to a quiet murmur in the back of his mind as he turned his attention back to the man just a couple of feet away. Gunner was already throwing out a punch, and Pav had been expecting that. He ducked it, but barely, causing the man's fist to land right against the flexible chain of the cage. Just as fast, Pav hooked the man in his right kidney with a hit that he was sure would have taken his breath away. It definitely made the man take a couple of steps back.

It was enough.

Enough for Pav to move away and take a second to reevaluate what was going to happen in this cage. He played with the guy for a while, bouncing from one end of the cage to the other. He had fast feet and faster hands. That was before he counted in his keen eye, and ability to pick out anybody's weakness in less than thirty seconds. He let Gunner land a couple of easy hits—nothing to his face and nothing that even hurt.

And then, Pav got bored.

He tasted the blood in his mouth from that first fight—felt those bruises and broken bones again. He remembered the way the crowd had laughed when he'd lost, and how someone had shouted for his first opponent to kill him while he was almost passed out on the mat.

He thought about the damp, hard cement floor where he'd healed for days after, and the way he'd barely been better before they'd dragged him back for another round.

Those memories were scars now.

Like so many others.

Scars on his mind that he liked to pick at and irritate when he needed a reminder of just how far he could push his body before it would break. He never broke—not really.

Death was already dead.

One couldn't kill it.

Maybe his nickname was appropriate.

Gunner came for him when Pav put himself in the corner; the man should have recognized that was a bad idea. Nobody willingly put themselves into a corner if they didn't have a sure way out of it in a cage.

Well, Pav didn't, anyway.

Gunner reared back with a punch, while Pav kept his face covered and weaved back and forth just enough to make it seem like he cared if the man landed the hit. The punch came hard to his shoulder, sending Pav jerking back into the cage. But that was okay, too. It was where he'd already found the man's weakness.

It seemed whenever Gunner landed a good hit, he took a second to enjoy the sight of it before he went back in for a round of fast punches, one after another. The man moved back an inch, but Pav was already there grabbing his wrist before he could even pull his arm back from the punch he landed.

Pav punched down hard, right into Gunner's inner elbow—the popping crunch that answered the punch as he broke the man's elbow was a satisfying sound. Gunner shouted, already trying to pull away but it was too late. He was fucking *ruined*.

He went in again.

Pav aimed a punch to Gunner's mouth, a harder hit to his throat, and then he swung around with a roundhouse kick that landed right to the middle of the man's chest. One right after the other—*smack, smack, smack*. It sent the man flying, bleeding from the mouth with his eyes rolling back in his head.

He wasn't getting back up.

"*Zhatka!*"

He heard the guy calling for him when the man landed to the mat, done for. The guy probably thought Pav was going in for the kill as he loomed over Gunner's body. That's what he would do any other time he was brought here to fight.

They didn't know the truth.

That was the only way he could get out the anger and darkness in his head. He had no outlet inside the Compound—the chambers offered him nothing but loneliness and rage. He got it all out in these cages, when he was allowed.

Now, though ...

Pav turned away from the man on the mat and headed for the corner of the cage where Viktoria was waiting for him with his jacket and shoes. His knuckles ached like nothing else, but he was barely paying attention to them as he climbed over the cage. He slipped his shoes on and was shrugging on his jacket as she kissed him hard. Her smile forming against his lips had him chuckling.

"Told you," he murmured.

She shook her head, and those soft hands of hers cupped his face. "I pick the next spot."

Pav shrugged. "Yeah, all right."

• • •

"Stop glaring," Viktoria whispered.

Pav's gaze snapped away from the man who currently had his hands on Viktoria's inner thigh as the buzz of the tattoo machine started up again. He found her staring at him, amusement dancing in her eyes like she knew exactly what this was doing to him.

Someone was *touching* her.

A man.

Oh, sure ... for a tattoo, but right now, that didn't seem to make a difference to Pav. He had never quite known jealousy before. At least, not like this. It literally felt like it was eating away at his brain with every passing second. How he had managed to stay seated in the chair, in the corner of the room for the last hour was anyone's fucking guess.

The man—an old and trusted friend, according to Viktoria— chuckled. "Just about done here, actually."

Pav dragged in a burning breath. "Hmm."

Viktoria gave him another look. "You can step out, if you want."

"*Nyet.*"

Pav knew he was being ridiculous, but that didn't stop the way he was feeling, frankly. He was only calmed by the fact that Viktoria was actually letting this man put his hands on her, and while it wasn't intimate, it was close enough to an intimate spot. The trust she must have felt for this tattooist friend of hers ... it was a good enough reason for Pav to stay in his chair, and not rip the man's throat out with his bare hands like he'd been fantasizing about for the last hour.

Some people would never understand how close to death they came when Pav was near. This man was a good example.

"Done," the man muttered, moving his chair back a couple of inches as he straightened and eyed the work he'd done on Viktoria's inner thigh. "And no spelling errors."

Viktoria leaned up and gave the man a look. "Better not be, Dirk."

Dirk.

Right.

That was his name.

Pav hadn't cared.

"You wanna do the clean-up and wrap it?" Dirk asked.

Viktoria passed a look to Pav over her shoulder, and then nodded. "I think I better. He's about at his limit, I think."

Dirk snorted under his breath. "Don't bring him next time—don't think I ever felt that much pressure while working. Makes my fucking hands shake."

"Get out, asshole."

Pav scowled, knowing they were talking about him. He hated that his jealousy was *that* obvious, but what could he do? This was all new territory for him, and he didn't know how to handle it. He figured *not* killing the man doing the tattoo was a win for him, right?

And for them.

It was good for them, too.

"Nice to meet you, Pav," Dirk said before he headed for the door of the private room in the shop. "I suppose."

"You can say it wasn't," Pav muttered in reply, "everyone else does."

"*Yeah* ..."

Viktoria was giving him another one of *those* looks as the guy left the private room. She'd called her friend to see if he was working late and was up for doing a tattoo. Apparently, Dirk lived in the apartment above his studio—he owned the whole building. He didn't mind coming down and opening up to do a quick tattoo for her.

"You can stop glaring," she whispered to him, climbing off the bed and inching closer to him with every word. "He's an old friend—his father taught me how to tattoo, actually. He used to do work for my father."

Pav chewed on those words. "Oh?"

"Mmhmm."

Her hands came to land on his thighs, and those pretty fingernails of hers dug into his skin through his jeans as she leaned in close. Her nose grazed his, and those ice-blue eyes of hers locked with his. He couldn't help but let his hands trail up her outer thighs.

Smooth skin.

Satiny warmth.

"Do you want to see what I got now?" she asked.

Pav arched a brow. The tattooist had mentioned no spelling errors, even if it was jokingly, so he assumed the tattoo would be a word. "Maybe."

She hadn't told him what she was getting. Other than that small cursive B on her middle finger, and the eight-pointed stars under her breasts, she didn't have any other ink. He'd been a little surprised when she'd said that was what she wanted to go do tonight, especially considering those stars of hers had been ink forced upon her by her father after … the attack. It hadn't been a good experience for her, and thus, she'd not wanted more.

He figured this night meant more to her than she was saying. She was stepping way out of her comfort zone and doing things she wanted to do simply because she wanted to do them. It didn't matter that it terrified her, she still wanted to do it.

Learning to love the fear, he knew.

She was ruling it.

Not the other way around.

"Let me see, babe."

She pressed a fast, fleeting kiss to his lips that made him want to drag her in for more, but he restrained himself. It was a miracle. The second she stood back to let him get a peek at the black ink on her inner thigh, he felt the smile already growing on his lips.

He did that often with her.

Smiling.

It was a knife—maybe three inches long, and without a lot of details. A bit of shading made the blade look real and *sharp*. But what struck him the most was how much that knife looked like the ones he carried constantly. There was nothing else to the tattoo—just the knife, and the way it laid against her skin.

Like he'd done to her once.

He reached out and let his fingers drift around the ink, but not directly on it. He knew better than to touch it. It still made him feel some crazy kind of way—worse than the jealousy, but stronger than anything else he'd ever experienced.

In a way, staring at it, he felt like it was her way of saying ...

"Mine," he murmured.

Viktoria laughed. "Maybe."

"No maybe about it."

He knew it.

So did she.

She did *this*, after all.

If she didn't want to say it yet, then fine. He'd wait. He felt like he'd already waited his whole life for her, anyway. What was a little while longer?

"Mmm, are we going back to the hotel tonight or in the morning?"

"Morning," he replied.

She nodded. "Where are we staying, then?"

"I know a place."

"Do you?"

"I'll explain when we get there."

"Okay."

15.

"WHAT IS this place?" Viktoria asked as they climbed the stairs.

Pav's fingers tightened around hers as he replied, "A loft."

"Who lives here?"

He shrugged.

Viktoria laughed. "What was *that?*"

"What?"

"The shrug you just did. What, you don't know who lives here?"

He tipped his head to the side like he was considering her words but continued to pull her up the stairs with him, all at the same time. It seemed like he was familiar with the place, so much so that he knew the code to get into the stairwell for the loft, and he'd barely passed a glance to the stragglers sitting at the bottom of the stairs. They either didn't recognize him, or they did, and they didn't care that he was there. She never thought to ask.

"I know whose name is on the deed now, and he always stays here," Pav said, "but other people come and go, too. It changes."

"I don't understand."

Pav smiled back at her. "Yeah, I know."

He didn't offer more of an explanation, and Viktoria didn't press for more. He'd told her at the tattoo shop that he would explain when they got there, so she was putting her trust in him to do exactly that.

Was this a place he was allowed to come when they let him out of the Compound over the years? Did he know the people here?

At the top of the stairwell, a short, dark hallway led to a door. Like downstairs, there was an electronic pad on the door with keys to press in a code. Pav didn't let go of her hand as he used his other to punch in a six-digit code. A loud buzz echoed in the hallway, and then a click sounded, too. He grabbed the doorknob and twisted to open it up.

Darkness welcomed them, for the most part. Lights had been dimmed, and the loft was quiet. Immediately, she took in the space as best she could. The shoes lined up along the entrance, and the coats hanging on hooks that had been nailed to the wall. The place seemed clean, felt warm.

It was only the figure coming out from a back hallway in the loft that made Viktoria take a step behind Pav. He didn't tense or act like the person bothered him. In the shadows of the hallway, she couldn't see the unknown man's face, but the squeeze of Pav's hand against her side was enough to tell her everything was fine.

She still stayed behind him.

Just in case ...

"Pavel," a man's voice greeted. "Is that you?"

"Yeah, Grisha. It's me."

"Been a while."

Pav laughed. "A couple years or so. Thought you might have changed the code."

"I told you I wouldn't."

"*Spasibo.*"

She had so many questions in that moment. He spoke to this man—Grisha—like the two of them had known each other for years. The man came out of the hallway into the dim lighting, and she could see the gray at his temples, and the lines deepening his aging face. He had to be at least thirty years older than Pav, at least.

How would they know each other?

"The older you get," Grisha said, "the more you look like him, you know?"

Pav cleared his throat. "I can't remember his face most times."

"Trust me, Pavel. You look just like your father. The room is empty—as it always is. You and your ... friend there, keep it to a dull roar. You know the loft is always open to you, if you need to use it."

"Yeah, I know."

"If you're around in the morning, stay for breakfast. We have to catch up."

"Sure," Pav agreed.

Grisha leaned to the side a bit and his gaze landed on Viktoria where she was peeking out around Pav. "Have a good night, you two."

Then, the man grabbed a bottle of water sitting on the island in the kitchen area before he disappeared into the hallway again. He didn't make a sound as he left, but she heard the click of a door closing somewhere in the darkness.

"Who was that?" she asked. "How do you know him?"

Pav's hand squeezed her side again. "In a minute. Come on."

She didn't question him. He led her across the main area of the loft, and she took in the few scattered toys in a corner. Not to mention the gaming system sitting in front of the large flat-screen television, currently paused on some war game. She looked back at the shoes lining the wall next to the door, realizing there were every size, from men's boots to children's. Same with the coats lining the wall on hooks.

"How many people live here?"

"As many as he can keep, or as many that need help for a time," Pav replied quietly. "There's five bedrooms in the back. They built them in as they needed them."

"They?"

"Grisha and my father."

Her heart stopped for a second as she realized what he was telling her. This was where he lived … before the Compound and the chambers. Before hell had come for him, this was the place he called home.

"Is it like a shelter now?"

"No, it's just a home."

Viktoria blinked, unsure of what to say.

Soon, he had led them to the back hallway where Grisha had come from earlier. At the very end, past all the rooms that were closed tight, he turned the knob on a door and opened it to a quiet bedroom. Against one wall rested a queen-sized bed that was still made, and a dresser with a small mirror. A smaller bed—a twin— rested on the other side of the room. It too was made and looked untouched.

"He thought my father would come back," Pav said as he stepped into the room. She stayed in the doorway, taking in the space. On the dresser, there were framed photos. It wasn't hard, even from her position, once the light was turned on, to recognize the young face of the child holding onto the hand of a taller man. It was Pav. "He knew Dimitri was doing business he didn't approve of … dangerous business."

"With my father?"

"People around Vadim," Pav replied quietly.

Oh.

"But he said nothing because they needed money. They'd been friends since they were kids. He was there when my mother died; Grisha was there when I learned how to walk, or that's what he told me. So he didn't tell my father to stop—he just turned his cheek."

"You said he thought your father would come back?"

"He left the room empty; didn't touch anything. He never asked around because he knew what happened to people who asked about Boykov business. He just waited, yeah?"

She felt cold.

And warm, too.

It was strange.

"How did you come back here?"

Pav shrugged but didn't turn around to look at her as he neared the dresser with the pictures. "Someone recognized my face when they took me to the fights for the first time ... someone who was staying here at the time. He told me Grisha was still waiting for me, and if I knew how to get home, I was always welcome."

"You must have come back, then."

"I got away once. They took me out ... details don't matter. I came here. I was sixteen, I think."

He thought ...

He didn't even know.

That broke her heart.

"Grisha knew my face instantly and brought me in. I was here a day before they came looking for me. They already knew about this place—they knew where to find me because I didn't have a big world outside of my father. I went back because they left Grisha alone. They didn't touch this place."

"I'm sorry."

Pav shook his head. "There's nothing to apologize for. Vadim used this place as a reward, too. If I behaved, I could come back. He never told me when it would happen, they would just drop me off at the door, and let me go in. I would watch out the windows for when the black car would come back, and I would have to leave again. Grisha was always here; the room was always waiting just like it was when I left."

"Pav—"

"Come in, close the door."

She did and then crossed the room with quiet, quick steps until she was right behind him. This man ... he was always silent, lost in his mind and thoughts. When he spoke, he often said things that went deeper than just what he offered on the surface. This was something he'd never spoken about in all their time together, and she had to wonder if he even really allowed himself to think about it.

Was he scared they'd take it?

Would they?

Not anymore.

She knew that.

Viktoria wrapped her arms around Pav's middle and hugged him tight. She rested the side of her face right between his shoulder blades. The cool leather of his jacket smoothed against her cheek, but underneath it, she could feel the way his body vibrated.

It wasn't easy to be here.

She wished she could make it better.

"He changes the sheets and keeps everything dusted," Pav murmured, his fingers drifting over the framed photographs. "But he knows he's not doing it for my father anymore. He does it for me."

"Because he *cares.*"

"I forgot what that was."

"I don't think you did," she whispered.

He'd always known how to care with *her.*

Didn't that mean something?

"I used to think this was home. If I had one, then this had to be it."

"Isn't it?" she asked.

"Here ... *you* ... who knows?"

She did.

And so did he.

Viktoria just hugged him tighter.

Pav let her.

• • •

Naked under sheets that smelled like a floral detergent, Viktoria stared up at an unfamiliar ceiling. The room was warm, and her comfort was aided by the hot air blowing through the heater, and the hard body of the man tucked in beside hers. She knew he wasn't sleeping, a lot like her. Their silence coated the room heavily, and yet, neither of them closed their eyes to sleep.

His fingers trailed over the bare skin of her arm. With each stroke, goosebumps snaked over her skin and shivers raced down her body.

She loved it, though.

That's what scared her the most.

"Pav?"

"Hmm?"

His soft murmur made her smile.

Almost.

It was the racing of her heart and the tightness in her throat that kept the light happiness at bay. It was the way her anxiety thrummed deep and her fear danced over her nerves, that reminded her happiness was ever fleeting and easily taken.

She'd been happy once.

Someone ruined it.

She'd been *good* once.

Someone took it.

And somehow, she had found herself in this spot again. Happy, and *good*. She wasn't the same woman as she'd once been sure, but she was still there again. In a place she'd never thought she would be and feeling an emotion that she promised wouldn't *ever* make her weak, because that's all it could do.

Love.

"What is it?" Pav asked.

The huskiness of his tone said he was edging closer to sleep than she was, but she knew he'd wake up the moment she asked him to. Anything she wanted, he was there trying to give it. Sometimes, he didn't know how to do it.

But he tried.

That *mattered.*

He always tried.

"I'm terrified again," she whispered.

His fingers stilled on her skin. "Why?"

A lump was back in her throat. An impossible knot keeping her words at bay and forcing her to stay silent. She refused to let it, and somehow, managed to swallow it back so she could get this out.

So he could *know.*

Once she said it, that was it.

It'd be out there, then.

"Because I love you," she said, the words slipping out into darkness and warm air. "I love you, and I'm happy. I'm *good*, and you helped. I'm scared of being like this because I don't think I know how to do this anymore, and someone already took it from me once."

"But I *never* will."

"I—"

Pav rolled over in the bed fast, covering her naked body with his as those hands of his, that had never hurt her once, found her face in the darkness. He tipped her head back, and despite the lack of light, she could still see the way his eyes locked on hers. She found that truth staring back at her like she always did when she looked into his gaze.

His soul lived there.

Waiting for *her*.

"I will never take it from you—not happiness or love," he promised. "I only know how to give you those things. Don't you know that?"

"Forgive me for learning."

He let out a laugh, then, deep and rumbling. It echoed to the deepest parts of her soul and heart. Things she thought had been gone forever but came back alive by this man. She wasn't sure if he knew that he had done those things for her, but here they were.

And she was so grateful.

But *terrified*, too.

So was her life.

Pav leaned down and dropped the softest kiss to her lips. He lingered there, his words brushing against her mouth like a caress. "I only knew how to live in darkness, but with you, nothing is dark for me. Everything is bright and clear and *right*. Sometimes, it's still dark, but it's temporary. You're always waiting to pull me back out."

It seemed she did things for him, too.

Things she didn't know.

"I'm not sure what love *is*," he murmured, his mouth trailing over her chin as he spoke. "But this has to be it, doesn't it? It has to be it, because you're the only one who makes me feel it. I only want to keep it, not ruin it."

"Then, you should."

"I will."

His kisses burned hotter, then. His touches, frantic. It was made easier by the fact they were already naked and under the sheets warmed by them. His cock, already hard against her thigh, made her pussy ache and he wasn't even *inside* of her yet. His arms hooked around her thighs and widened her legs. She rolled her hips upward as her hand wrapped around his length, and she slid the blunt head of his cock along the seam of her sex.

He knew when he was *there* … one hard flex of his hips, and he was buried deep. The sound that crawled out of Viktoria's throat felt raw. It hurt like it, too. One of his hands came down to cover her mouth, but all she felt was him.

His words in her ear helped, too. "Let's not wake up the whole loft."

Fuck.

She wanted to laugh, but she couldn't.

Not when he was filling her full and fucking her deep. Every brutal snap of his hips against hers sent her flying a little higher. The slap of skin, and his harsh breaths pulsing against her throat were the only sounds in the room.

And yet, despite how hard he fucked her, the rest of it was oh, so soft. His hand gliding over her curves, and his kisses dotting her skin.

That was the best part of him, she decided.

The part she loved the most.

Even in his roughness, he was gentle.

And he was *hers.*

16.

IT WAS only the rhythmic, soft noise of Viktoria's breaths as she slept that kept Pav comfortable. In this room, he was far more likely to get lost inside his head. Memories that felt like punishments lived there. All too often, he didn't allow himself to think of his father or this place he'd once lived for the majority of his life.

He'd read a book once—one he'd found in the forgotten rooms of the Compound—that said everyone had moments in their lives that were considered pivotal. So much so, that after that point in time in their lives, people no longer saw life as a simple road that they had traveled. It changed to be something different. They saw their life as *before* and *after*.

Before the moment happened.

And after it occurred.

The night his father brought him to the Compound was that moment for him. Or one of those kinds of moments, anyway. His life before the Boykovs, and his life after them. He knew Grisha felt guilty and that was part of the reason why he allowed Pav to come and go when he was allowed off his chain and leash for a time.

Grisha would have been watching him that night for Pav's father, or another friend. Like he usually did every other night his father had to go out and work. But for whatever reason, on that night, things were different. Something came up last minute, the loft was empty when Dimitri got the call, and Pav had had to tag along with his father.

He was sure Grisha lived with a constant *what if* in the back of his mind. *What if* he had been home that night to watch him? What if he'd picked up Dimitri's call and hadn't let it go to voice mail? What if he never went to meet up with an old friend?

Pav didn't blame him—he'd told him that before, although Grisha never really listened. That what if was too strong, and Grisha was unwilling to let it go. He understood that all too well.

Despite the fact that the loft—and *this* bedroom, specifically—was a constant, aching reminder of his life before, and he knew it would put him in a bad place for a while mentally, he still came back here.

A part of him never left here.

It was made slightly easier tonight by the fact Viktoria was tucked into his side. Although he hadn't bothered to pull on any of his clothes except for the boxer-briefs, she'd pulled on her cotton panties and his T-shirt. With her arm slung over his middle and her head resting on his chest, she wasn't moving an inch.

He didn't mind.

Pav drifted the tips of his fingers with one hand through the soft waves of her hair, the rhythm calming him further, and dragging him out of his head. She was turned just enough that he could rest his chin at the top of her head and use his other hand to glide up and down her spine.

She slept better like this, but he didn't tell her that. He'd noticed she moved less in her sleep when he was holding her. She didn't whimper and her eyelids never flickered with nightmares she couldn't escape from.

He knew when it was a bad night for her in the morning—her eyes would be darker and dimmed. She talked less, and when the words did come out, they were dull and yet still sharp at the same time.

But not like this.

This way, she slept *well*.

He didn't mind staying awake for an extra couple of hours after she had fallen asleep to make sure she was in so deep of a good sleep that nothing was waking her up or interrupting those sweet dreams. There was something so primal in knowing that he was the only person who could really do this for her, or rather … the only person she allowed to do it.

She would be weak with him, but he saw it as a strength. She could be delicate with him in ways that no one else ever got to see, and he wanted to let her. She was his, and he found being hers was the easiest thing he'd ever done next to breathing.

It was terrifying, too. It had been a long while since Pav felt something akin to *actual* fear. It felt like they'd taken that ability from him, in a way. Or maybe they'd simply beaten the instinct out of him. Nonetheless, he felt it with her. A fear so visceral and raw, it felt *real*. An actual monster living under the bed.

A fear that, at any time, this thing he'd found with her could be taken away. Or she could leave, if she wanted. It wasn't that he chose to ignore it, but rather, it just wasn't as important as the rest of what he felt.

It was worth the risk, because it seemed he was the gambling type of man, anyway. Not that he'd been one of those before, but he was more than willing to be one now if it meant he was with her. If he got to keep her for a while, then that would make whatever came after far more than just worth it to him.

That was trust.

Love.

Right?

If this feeling in his chest that constantly felt like it was wrapping around his heart to squeeze it to death wasn't love, then what was? If the deep, thrumming need to keep this woman close and safe and *with him always* wasn't love, then what was it?

He didn't mind it.

Pav was close to sleep, too, knowing Viktoria was already there and safe in dreams where she didn't need him to scare the darkness away. He was just beginning to drift into his own slumber when a noise had his eyes flying wide open as he tensed on the bed. It wasn't something … *bad.* A normal sound, usually.

A car engine revving.

All normal, considering the loft was situated in the art district of Chicago, a massive urban center. Noise was common. It was everywhere. And yet, something about that sound was quick to drag him away from the sleep he craved.

He listened for more sounds—the walls of the loft were thin, which was why he knew Grisha brought in extra heaters during the colder months to keep anyone who was living there for a time warm while they needed it.

A horn honked.

Then, another.

Although he wanted to stay right where he was with Viktoria in the bed, Pav rolled over slowly as to not wake her up, as he reached for the jeans he'd discarded to the floor earlier. His jacket with his knives were all the way across the room, thrown over the back of a wooden rocking chair.

He never even got the chance to get to his jacket. He only managed to get his pants yanked up around his waist when the noise got a hell of a lot louder. First it was boots against wood—kicking the front door of the loft in, and then beating against hardwood floors as someone, *many*, someones stormed the loft. Their shouts came next.

Pav was stuck between turning to calm Viktoria as she woke up in a sleepy daze, and darting across the room to where his jacket and knives were waiting for him. He had one arm reaching out for her, and another going for his jacket when the screams started.

The people using the loft as a temporary safe haven were woken from their beds as their bedroom doors were kicked open—a baby cried, and a slightly older child called out for their mother.

"Pav?"

"Don't move," he told Viktoria.

He darted for his jacket, but he didn't get to it in nearly enough time. He'd just grabbed the leather to yank it off the back of the chair when the door to their room was kicked open, too. He didn't recognize the masked men who stormed the bedroom, but one must have known who they were when they found them inside.

"*Found 'em*," one of them growled.

Pav slipped a hand into the pocket of the jacket, his fingers slipping around the cool, firm handle of a knife but it was too late. The butt of an assault rifle cracked him right in the face and sent him sprawling to the floor.

Blood bloomed in his mouth. A ringing echoed in his ears, but even over the sound, he heard Viktoria cry out for him.

Pav blinked when his back hit the floor with enough force to take his breath away. He didn't waste time down there, or rather, he tried not to. He was already attempting to get back up, that knife still firm in his grip, when a boot landed right in the middle of his chest. The next kick hit his kidneys.

The third?

His *face*.

"*Pav!*"

He cursed under his breath in Russian, thick blood slipping from his lips as he spat to the floor and another kick landed to his back at the same time someone else kicked him in the stomach. If they were intent on kicking him to death like a bunch of cowards, then they were doing a damn good job of it.

"*Leave him alone—hey, let go of me, you fucking piece of shit!*"

Viktoria's words quickly turned from English to Russian. In the darkness, because no one had yet to turn on a light, and they'd stormed the bedroom—how many were there again?—without any kind of flashlights, he fucking panicked.

He couldn't see her.

Couldn't *help* her.

Wasn't he most terrifying in the dark? Wasn't the nighttime and shadows his safe haven? He did his best work where no one could see his face, and he couldn't see theirs. And yet, in that moment, he could do nothing.

They took his greatest strength and turned it into a weakness. They made him useless, and he felt it in every part of his body. It hurt far worse than the pain they were causing him with this beating.

Far worse.

"Don't ... touch ... *her*," he snarled between kicks to his body.

It was pointless.

The last thing he heard before a particularly hard kick left his vision and mind black?

"*A waiting king never sleeps. Do let the Boykov brothers know.*"

• • •

Pav's vision was blurred—blackened at the edges, and fuzzy directly in the middle. And still, even with shaking hands, he tried dialing the number on his phone again. He knew he fucked up the numbers when the call failed and continued to not go through.

"*Fuck*," he mumbled.

"Pav, what in the hell happened?"

Grisha's voice was too close, and right then, he didn't want the man near him at all. For Grisha's safety, but also for Pav's own selfish reasons. He continued walking past the huddled people in the loft, his face bruised and bleeding, his lips stained with cracking blood. He could feel the aching in his jaw and bones. If something wasn't broken, he was going to be a lucky man, honestly.

But he could ignore it.

Right now, he *could*.

Surely.

"*Pav!*"

"Don't," Pav snapped over his shoulder. "Just … *don't.*"

That was the best warning he could give Grisha. He knew the man had questions. Although no one in the loft had been touched except him and Viktoria—which should have been a clue that this was about them to Grisha—the man still had questions.

It wasn't that simple for Pav.

He was in a bad fucking place.

His mind, *so dark.*

His heart, tearing itself apart.

His soul?

Entirely gone.

He hadn't even realized he had a soul until Viktoria came around. All the vicious parts of her had clawed their way under his skin and burrowed deep into his body. She kept digging until she found the parts of him that he thought were long gone.

She took them, too.

Took them for herself.

And now she was *gone.*

That meant he was gone, too.

Pav could not be trusted in these moments. Not to care about someone else, even if it was Grisha or the people he was trying to help. He certainly couldn't be trusted to show them care or concern if they got too close to him, when all he wanted to do was cause the worst kind of violence to make himself feel even a little bit better.

Yeah.

A bad fucking place.

Pav was almost to the front door—almost gone, but not at all better. Walking was difficult when he felt like his legs were unsteady. His head pounded hard enough to make him think it might explode at any moment. The constant taste of blood in his mouth had him worried.

Oh, he'd gotten worse beatings.

He'd been in far worse places.

It didn't matter.

Pav didn't quite make it to the door—trying yet again to dial the correct fucking number on the stupid cell phone—when Grisha got ahold of him. The man grabbed the back of Pav's jacket … a mistake, if there ever was one, and yanked hard.

It was enough to stop Pav.

He turned fast, his lips already pulled back to showcase bloody teeth as a sound left his mouth that was entirely inhuman. And yet, Grisha didn't even blink at the sight. As tall and as wide as a brick shithouse, he wasn't easily intimidated.

He should be scared of Pav.

Terrified.

And he just stood there.

"Are they coming back?" Grisha asked.

Pav blinked. "No."

"You're sure?"

"They got what they wanted. I … have to go."

He turned, but Grisha was still there, blocking his path as he scooted past him in the hallway. A part of Pav was warring with himself on the inside. He didn't want to hurt this man—he didn't want to ruin a part of his past. The one connection to his father that he had left. But he was going to do it if Grisha didn't get the fuck out of his way, and *fast.*

"Get out of the *way,*" Pav said, his voice pained.

"Let me help."

"*Help?*"

"That's what I said. Give me the phone—I will call. You're not in any kind of state right now, Pavel. Give me the phone, dammit."

Grisha didn't give him the opportunity to argue when the man simply yanked the phone out of Pav's hand. To his credit, Pav was starting to think he was three seconds away from vomiting all over the floor from the intense pounding in his head.

Concussion?

Probably.

"What is the number you want to call?" Grisha asked.

Why wouldn't his heart calm?

Why did his *hands* hurt?

Maybe because he'd balled them into tight fists at his sides to keep them still and hide their shaking. Now, his fingernails were cutting into his skin, causing him more pain, but he didn't even care.

She was gone.

"Pavel!"

Pav rattled off the number he needed to call, and when Grisha had the call ringing through, he handed the phone back. Phone at his ear, Pav turned his back to his father's old friend, listening to the call ring and fucking *ring*.

Pick up. Fucking pick up.

On the fifth ring, just before the voice mail, Konstantin finally picked up the goddamn phone call. Pav wasn't sure what he expected the man to say. A hello, maybe, because there would be no possible way Konstantin could know what happened here tonight.

Pav fucked up.

They weren't supposed to leave the hotel.

This was *his fault*.

He would pay for this.

He already was.

Instead of hello, Konstantin said, "Every man to the Compound, *now*."

He didn't even ask who it was—not that he would have needed to if he looked at the caller ID and saw Pav's number. Did he even do that?

"Konstantin—"

"No time to talk," Konstantin barked back. "We've had two attacks tonight. Every man to the Compound before the hour is out."

Pav swallowed hard. "They took Vik."

Silence echoed.

And then, "*What?*"

"Viktoria. They took her."

• • •

It was pandemonium.

Chaos mixed with *rage*.

Pav stood silent in the corner as words were hurled, and anger spilled between men. He watched them all, their faces unimportant to him as he went over each and every mistake he had made in his lifetime. Every second that led up to this moment right here. He didn't need others throwing his errors in his face, when he was quite aware of how and why this happened.

He was sorry.

They didn't care.

He got it.

He *understood.*

"We *decided,*" Kolya hurled at him. "The hotel was the safest place as long as she *stayed there!*"

'Kolya," the man's wife whispered. "Calm down for a second and—"

"No, he fucked up."

"But did he?" Konstantin asked. "The attacks—the ones on our homes and the one on the loft—seemed very deliberate, didn't they? As though someone knew she would be in one place, or the other. It would have needed to be someone who knew she left the hotel because they would *check.*"

"Are you saying …"

"A man of ours, yes," Konstantin said.

"It still wouldn't have happened, had he just kept her there, then," Kolya said harshly.

"Or they would have made a bigger mess when they went in on the hotel, Kolya. *Think about it.* It was made very clear during our attacks that this came from Boris, so he clearly has access to something or someone that is helping him. If not tonight, then it would have been another night."

"Konstantin is right," Amelia said from her position on a couch in Konstantin's office. "And it won't help for the rest of us to fight with one another like a hoard of snapping turtles. All that does is take away more time we could be out there looking for—"

"You will not be going *anywhere,*" Konstantin barked at his wife.

Amelia's burning gaze met her husband's. "I didn't ask, did I?"

"I decided."

"That's nice."

Pav almost smiled.

Viktoria would have enjoyed the scene. Then, he just got pissed all over again.

Fuck.

"How did this happen?" Kolya asked, his tone losing that rough edge from before. He didn't pose the question to anyone in particular, and though for the moment there was only them in the office, the hallway outside was filled with men waiting for orders. "We had it all planned, Konstantin. We had everything set up just as it needed to be, yeah?"

"I … don't know," Konstantin replied.

Rather lamely.

Pav knew that feeling.

This whole thing left him feeling useless.

"We missed something," Konstantin replied, "or someone inside the Bratva who had contact with Boris before he escaped. This plan was … on going for a while."

All eyes turned on Pav again. He was *Zhatka*, after all. He should have the answers.

"Well?" Kolya barked.

"Well, what?"

Kolya gave Konstantin a look, but the other man ignored it. Konstantin, to his benefit, turned to Pav and asked, "Is there anything you might not have told us about Boris' time in the chambers? Someone who visited him often, or would have had enough time with him to figure out a way to make this plan of his work?"

"No."

"Pav—"

"Other than Kolya, who regularly came around once a week to use him as a punching bag," Pav said, giving Kolya a look—"then for the most part, he was left for me to handle, yes?"

Konstantin quieted for a second before asking, "What does for the most part mean, exactly?"

"Vadim visited him often before he was exiled. A couple of times a week for anywhere from a half hour to an hour. I thought … after what you told me about Viktoria, that it was to remind Boris why he was there. Before I knew about that, I didn't have a reason to question Vadim on what he wanted to do with people *he put there*. I learned not to ask for details, Konstantin."

As soon as the words came out of his mouth, Pav saw the dawning understanding in Kolya's eyes where he stood beside his brother. Pav, too, understood what he had missed in those moments.

Was it possible?

Was it … *Vadim?*

"A waiting king never sleeps," Pav muttered.

Konstantin's jaw tightened when he asked, "What did you just say?"

"My mind is fuzzy—they kicked me in the head a lot."

"*So what?*"

Pav wet his lips. "One of them told me to tell you that a waiting king never sleeps. There's only one man who thinks of himself as a king, and would have the ability to do this, isn't there?"

"Goddammit," Kolya growled. "I told you ... I told you to fucking *kill him*. Didn't I tell you, *brat?*"

"Not possible," Konstantin snapped. "I put him in exile. I have people watching him. I monitor his calls, his people ... I know when he goes to fucking sleep at night! I know everything about Vadim, Kolya."

"Kon—"

"I know more about him than I want to know about him!"

"But he has people who are loyal to him ... he didn't waste the years he spent controlling the Bratva. We know personally how manipulative he is. We dealt with several men who were loyalists for him, but that didn't mean some didn't *learn*, Konstantin. They could have learned to sit down and shut up unless they wanted to *die*. Who's to say they weren't working with him? He knew what was going to happen."

"Men like Vadim always know," Pav murmured.

Konstantin let out a harsh noise. "I would have *known*. If he were planning something, I would have known about it."

"Not if he found a way around us, and you."

"Viktoria has always been his favorite. He's not going to sacrifice her a second time when—"

Kolya's gaze slid to his brother, silencing him instantly. "So was I, for a time."

Konstantin's stare dropped to his brother's chest, and then quickly snapped back up to Kolya's face. Pav didn't need to know what Konstantin was remembering. Zhatka had been there that night in true form when Vadim literally had the flesh burned from his oldest son's chest to remove tattoos he no longer felt Kolya was worthy to wear.

If he could do that to his heir ... and they already knew what Vadim had been willing to do to Viktoria before, then what would stop him now?

Nothing.

"Can we find her now?" Pav asked quietly. "I think we've talked enough."

All eyes turned on him again. He wished he wasn't so quiet. He didn't know any other way to be.

Not now.

17.

DARKNESS.

That's what Viktoria woke up to first. Complete and utter darkness surrounding her. It was too close, and it felt too fucking tight. Her first thought was to roll over and seek Pav out in the bed next to her. That was the last thing she remembered immediately. That they'd been in bed together, her in his shirt and tucked in close to his side, and his fingers gliding over her body as she drifted off to sleep.

But she couldn't turn.

Her hands wouldn't move.

Why were they at her back?

Attempting to straighten out her legs did nothing for her, either. The harder she tried to kick, the more it pulled on her arms. That was when she realized her ankles were tied to her fucking wrists at her back.

Like a hog.

She'd been *hogtied.*

Holy fucking shit.

Don't freak out. Just breathe. Relax, Viktoria.

Her inner thoughts really didn't do much to calm the situation. Maybe because a part of her knew something was very wrong here, or it could have been because the memories were starting to flood into her hazy mind.

Loud noises—boots against the floor. People yelling, and mask-covered faces looming over the bed. The sound of Pav's pain and his last threat before he'd stopped talking altogether, and everything else went dark around her, too.

Had they hit her?

Given her something to knock her out?

She didn't know.

Despite remembering that someone—several people—had taken her, a part of Viktoria's mind was not actually willing to believe it. That part of her still wanted to pretend like she was in the bed with Pav, and nothing was wrong.

No, she'd just woken up to a little bit of darkness. The bed wasn't as soft or as warm as it used to be, and he was too far away from her. That's all that was happening, surely. She even tried to call out for him … to wake him up because Pav would make this better.

Didn't he always make it better?

"*Pav.*"

Instead of her call of his name coming out clear and loud, it was muffled and quiet. Far too quiet for anyone to hear. That's how she realized she was gagged as well as hogtied because wasn't that just her fucking luck?

Of course, it was.

Viktoria had done her best not to panic in those immediate seconds after opening her eyes and realizing she couldn't actually move. She'd tried to pretend like nothing was wrong even when her body was screaming at her that literally *nothing* was right about this, but she couldn't do it anymore.

The panic came.

The fear rushed in.

It coated her whole body with a cold grip and squeezed tight. It took all of the air right out of her lungs and made her chest ache. The tears fell from her shut eyes, slipping past her eyelids and wetting her lashes despite the way she tried to hold them back.

The sob that fell into the gag was muffled, too. Like her scream for help. Like her choking when she gagged on whatever was stuffed in her mouth.

One part of her whispered, *this is not good.*

Another part screamed, *get me the fuck out of here.*

It didn't matter that she was gagged and tied like an animal. She still tried to fight in the small, cramped space. She couldn't see through the darkness, but that didn't stop her from trying *anything.* She flipped back and forth and attempted to kick her legs free, even though her shoulders burned from the actions. She did her very best to get the gag out of her mouth, but the damn thing wouldn't budge.

Fuck.

By the time she was done trying to fight her way free, Viktoria's entire face was a mess of tears, and she felt like she couldn't breathe again. It was as though she had used up all of the air that was left in the dark, tiny space and now she was going to die of suffocation.

More panic, she knew.

That was all.

Despite knowing that, it really didn't help. It was yet another panic attack that she had to ride out because what else could she do at this point?

Nothing.

She was *fucked*.

It was then that whatever she had been put in seemed to move, or *jump*, rather. The swell of her panic calmed just long enough for her to realize she was actually rocking slightly. Not enough that it was noticeable, but every so often her confines would jump, and she would be rocked harder to one side than the other.

That's when she knew.

A trunk.

She had been put in a trunk.

The panic was back.

The fear silenced her again.

Thick.

Visceral.

Raw.

Her body was tired from the last round, not to mention her attempt to escape, as fruitless as that had been. It didn't seem to matter to her mind when it went through yet another war. She was ready to fight again—ready to try anything again.

Her fight renewed, and so did the tears.

Her shouts increased, and so did the pain.

Was it pointless?

Probably.

She still had to try.

Especially when every single time she closed her eyes in the darkness of that trunk, she continued to see bloody words written on the mirror in her bedroom. Words of a man who had clearly not had enough of her yet.

Who else would have done this?

No one.

Just the monster.

Only Boris.

She wasn't going down without a fight.

Not for that piece of shit.

Never.

• • •

They'd shoved a goddamn hood over her head, and that more than anything else probably pissed Viktoria off the most. Wasn't it bad enough that they'd tied and gagged her, but they had to cover her fucking head, too?

She cursed and fought against the people carrying her, not that it made much of a difference. Other than the occasional threat a man threw at her, and the mutter of someone else, they didn't say anything to her.

Not even *stop*.

Not a *quit it*.

Nothing.

It was scary in the way that it felt like they had been prepping for this. It was as though they already knew what their job was with her, and how they were supposed to act once they had her in their possession.

Viktoria kept her struggle up as doors were opened, and more voices filtered to her through the thick, black hood they'd shoved over her head. She didn't even get to see their faces when they did it—they opened the trunk, still wearing those ski-style masks, and in seconds, had her hooded and pulled out of the trunk.

Bastards.

Then, all at once, without any warning, Viktoria was dropped. She hit the ground hard, landing on her wrists and back. Her head cracked against the floor, too, but that was the least of her fucking worries. She could feel hands at her back—*touching her.*

Someone was touching her!

She screamed and tried to jerk away from the stranger's hands, but it didn't do her any good. Her words and threats fell into the gag, and more tears spilled. Soon enough, those hands were gone, and it was over.

She could move, then.

Her ankles had been cut from the ties at her wrists. Someone grunted under their breath, before a hand landed on the top of her head. Fingers curled into the hood and her hair underneath it before she was dragged upward and forced to sit on her knees with her hands still tied firmly at her back.

Oh, God.

"Sit there and shut up," came a familiar voice.

Vomit found the back of her tongue.

She never wanted to hear that voice again.

Ever.

Boris.

"I see you haven't learned very much in our time apart," her captor taunted.

It was made worse by the fact she couldn't actually see him or where he was. If he got behind her, what might he do? What could he do *in front of her*? That was the thing ... Viktoria didn't need to wonder at all. She knew exactly how this man could hurt her. She knew all the ways he could rape her, tied or not. She'd lived it once.

"That's fine," he told her in a murmur.

She wasn't expecting his touch again, but when his knuckles reached out to stroke her cheek behind the hood, she did all she could do not to jerk away. That wouldn't work well for her, it would only piss him off more.

That meant bad things.

Bad things would happen quicker.

She didn't realize until right then how fast her mind had dropped the panicked state from earlier and gone into a whole other mode. She remembered this—she knew exactly what this was, and what her mind was trying to do.

Survive.

It was trying to *survive.*

Again.

"You'll learn, Viktoria," Boris said, his voice closer now as the sound of shoes squeaked against the floor. Had he kneeled down to be at eye level with her? *God.* "And I did miss you. I didn't lie about that. I have waited so long, *suka.*"

She sucked in a breath that tasted like her own blood and tears.

"You deserve this," he added. "After everything, he owes me. Vadim *owes me*, and so, I get to have fun with you for a while before he comes and we have to get back to business. Are you excited? I am."

Fuck her father to hell.

May he burn there.

Viktoria supposed when Boris wasn't getting the reactions from her that he wanted with the hood still on her head, that's when he decided to rip the damn thing off. The tie around the neck choked her as he yanked it off her head, but he didn't seem to care.

Not surprising.

This man felt nothing.

For the first time in two years, Viktoria came face to face with the man she hated more than anything else in the world. She stared him in the eyes—the same eyes she'd watched light up with glee as she'd begged him to stop and when he'd made her bleed. She sneered at the sight of his cold, evil grin; a smile that he'd used to lure her into a house that was supposed to be the start of their marriage, but was actually a prison where he'd hurt her worse than anyone else ever had.

This man was her monster.

She knew the scars on his face. The slit in his lip from a fight he'd said happened when he was a teenager. The slice through his left eyebrow from a wayward knife at a bar. Where his hands rested on his jean-covered knees, his knuckles were full of white, crisscrossed scars from fights he'd gotten in over the years, and men he'd beaten to death.

Those hands he'd used to hold her down. Those hands he'd beat her with. Fingers that had touched her *bad*. Touched her *wrong*.

Boris reached up to touch her face again now that it was visible, but Viktoria wasn't having that. Not this time around, not when she could see the bastard coming for her. She snapped back away from his touch, but never once looked away from his face.

She wanted to see those eyes. Then, maybe he would know. Yes, she was scared. Yes, he did this.

But *yes*, she hated him. Yes, she was going to fight.

He could take from her again and hurt her. But no … she was never going to be his. He could take but if she didn't give, then it wasn't his.

He was evil.

He was a monster.

That didn't mean much to her anymore. She was frightened of the things he might do to her, but she was not scared of him. Those were different things.

She knew what he could do to her. He'd already done it. She knew how he could hurt her. She'd lived through it once. Was he going to do it again? Would it be worse?

"Fuck you," Viktoria spat.

Boris smiled and leaned in close so that his mouth grazed her ear as he spoke. She shuddered as his warm words drifted over her skin like the way his teeth had left their marks on her throat once. "Soon, Viktoria. Very fucking soon."

"Boris, we need to go over the plan!"

The call from the other room was the only thing that pulled the monster away from her. His cold gaze never left hers as he straightened. It was the first time she took the chance to glance around and see where she was.

In a room.

Obviously.

A house, maybe?

She couldn't be sure.

Boris winked when she looked back at him. "Don't go anywhere or make plans, yes? I'll be back soon."

Yeah, she bet.

The prick.

18.

"*STOP.*"

The dark, irritated order drew Pav's gaze away from the tip of his knife that he'd been spinning against the pad of his fingertip. He'd been so focused on his task that the rest of the passengers on the private jet—compliments of Konstantin, apparently, because who didn't want to be rich enough to own a fucking *jet?*—simply drifted away from his immediate thoughts. He had other things to handle, now.

Across the aisle from him, Kolya sat like a brickhouse in another seat. The man's cold gaze continued surveying him like he was trying to understand what Pav was thinking about. He had news for him— *don't bother, you'll never know*. He'd never tell them, anyway.

It was better for *everyone* if Pav just stayed tucked away in his mind while they handled this business. They didn't know the dangerous, horrible things he was considering doing to everyone in his path right now, and they didn't *want* to know.

Kolya included.

That, he could promise.

"You're dripping blood on the seat," Kolya said. "Konstantin will have a pissy fit. None of us want to listen to him bitch, yeah?"

It was only then that a panging pain began in the tip of Pav's finger that he'd been using to spin the knife. Looking at the digit, he found several thin cuts crisscrossing along the skin, and the blood that oozed from the cuts quickly turned into a droplet that fell to his pants. Sticking the tip of his finger between his lips, he sucked the rest of the blood off. The tangy, metallic taste of the blood barely registered, but at least it was gone.

It really didn't hurt.

Had he been pressing that hard?

"Poor Konstantin," Pav murmured dryly.

Kolya arched a brow, but Pav only shrugged in reply. He *did not* want to be here, and he was not going to pretend like he did. This jet, the flight, and what would happen when they finally landed in Russia was all on Konstantin. The man made orders, and the rest of them were just expected to follow them, whether they wanted to or not.

Apparently, that was how the Bratva worked.

Pav had the stars now, as he had been so *nicely* informed when he pointed out that there was no way in hell they were removing him from Chicago when they had absolutely no proof that Viktoria was gone, too. It didn't matter, he was told, because he had the stars. His job was to listen to his boss—the man who allowed him the privilege of the stars.

Right.

That was fucking hilarious.

A *privilege.*

Like he wanted them or something.

Pav remembered that going down far differently than they did, clearly. He'd been *told* he was going to be given the stars, and that was the end of it. This wasn't something he had been given a choice in. Just like this fucking *flight.*

"You're still sour, no?"

Pav scowled at the port window. "I should be looking for *her.* Not going after your fucking useless father. You don't need me for that."

"Wrong."

"Oh, you think?"

"I like to think I know, actually."

"Do tell, Kolya."

The other man sighed and gave Pav a look that said he was just about done with his shit. He very well could be, but Pav simply didn't have the fuck to give him at the moment. His mind was in too dark of a place to care what someone else thought or wanted.

Unless their name was Viktoria, he didn't want to know.

Seemed easy enough.

Apparently, not.

"We very well could use you in Russia," Kolya said.

"So you keep saying. I've yet to figure out why."

"You're the only person who has a different understanding of Vadim, in a way. A part of me thinks he might even be afraid of you—he created the whole idea and image of *Zhatka*, didn't he? He knows what you can do with a little inspiration. It might even … inspire him to behave and tell us what we need to know?"

Yeah, sure.

Pav didn't care.

He wanted to find Viktoria.

They could handle Vadim at literally any other point in time. It didn't have to be right now, but because Konstantin panicked after a few hours of Viktoria being missing, his first decision was to put a small army of men—Pav and Kolya included—on a private jet and send them all the fucking way to *Russia*.

But who was he to say?

Clearly, *no one*.

"For reference—" Kolya started to say.

"You continue to think I care or want to have a conversation with you, or that I give a damn about why I'm on this plane because someone else told me to be, but surprise, I do not give a fuck, and I don't want to talk."

Kolya cleared his throat, and then chuckled. "I didn't think I would like you … but I'm beginning to, and that's interesting."

"Fascinating, really."

"The attitude is a little much sometimes."

Pav rolled his eyes and went back to staring out the window. "Just say what you want to say, Kolya, and let me stew in peace."

"Fine." The man shifted in his seat, saying, "For reference, he's not always going to make choices you agree with—Konstantin, I mean. He often does and orders things that make me want to choke the fucking life out of him, but he is the Pakhan. The *boss*, Pav. That means you shut up, and you do what he wants you to do because he is not the same kind of man our father was as a boss. He is *better*."

"How so?"

Because sometimes with Konstantin, it was hard to tell where the line began and ended when it came to the similarities between him and his father. Pav was not so stupid that he didn't see how Konstantin was also very different, but there were enough similarities at the same time to actually make him take pause.

"Because Vadim never gave a shit—it was always about him. In the end, that was all that ever mattered to him. He would do whatever it took as long as he was the one who came out on top. Konstantin may seem just as selfish when he makes choices that offend you, but the fact remains … Vadim would have never done *this* to begin with; he would have never looked for Viktoria or tried to save her. He didn't the first time around, we had to go in for her. Vadim simply gave the okay, and we had to chase him for it."

Pav sucked in a hard breath, and the air of the plane ached in his lungs. He knew he was being a bit of a shit, sure, but that was only because he felt he would be better if he was just looking for her. Not … going farther away from Viktoria.

"I know he's not the same man as your father," Pav eventually replied.

Kolya nodded. "Keep reminding yourself as you need it."

"This trip is still a waste of time."

He wasn't budging on that.

"Look at it like this," Kolya said, his tone turning uncharacteristically cheerful. That in itself was enough to make Pav give the man his attention. Kolya didn't get *cheery*. He was perpetually pissed off and quick to be violent. Cheerful? *Never.* "At least for this flight, you were allowed to keep your knives. Konstantin made sure of that—wouldn't want our Reaper having a meltdown over some pieces of metal, would we?"

Kolya wouldn't be so quick to make fun if Pav decided to toss one of those knifes at him, just to see if he could stick it in his throat from five feet away. Then again, it didn't seem like a good idea for him to get violent when he might need Kolya later on in this trip.

Pav weighed the pros and cons of tossing the knife that he was dangling between his fingertips at Kolya. The cons won out, eventually. Surprise, surprise; he never got to do the things he wanted anymore.

He let the comment slide.

Barely.

"Mmm, yes," Pav said. "I do like my knives."

It was the little things.

Kolya grinned coldly, all the cheeriness gone in a blink as his ice-blue gaze turned on Pav once more. A weaker man might have looked away from Kolya then, but Pav was far from weak, and he didn't scare easily. "And if *I'm* lucky, maybe we'll get to use them on Vadim."

Pav didn't reply.

What could he say?

• • •

"Ready?"

The comm buzzed in Pav's ear. He instantly wanted to rip the fucking thing out and toss it to the ground. Listening to the mutterings of the other men in their ambush party as they surrounded the estate property where Vadim was hidden away from the rest of the world was enough to drive any man insane.

Pav was already crazy.

He didn't need to add to it.

It was only the look Kolya shot him from the side—a silent order of, *don't you fucking dare or I will beat you into the ground right here and now; test me, you stupid fuck*. Pav greatly disliked that he had spent so much time with Kolya that he was basically able to know what the man was saying to him without him saying anything at all.

"All right, let's—"

"*Go*," Pav snarled into his own comm.

Kolya nodded at him. "Yeah, let's go."

It seemed like even Kolya was done with waiting. *Good*. Pav couldn't take this shit for one more second. They were either ready, or they were never going to be able to go in on this asshole. It wasn't so much Vadim in the mansion at the middle of the estate property that they were worried about, but more like the loyalists he might have surrounded himself with.

None of them could trust the men Konstantin put here to watch Vadim. How many had been turned to Vadim's side of things? How many were feeding the prick information, or helping him in some other way?

No.

They couldn't assume anything.

Certainly not *trust*.

"Oh," Pav said, tossing the statement to Kolya as they broke through the tree line, "and there's dogs, yeah?"

"*Fuck*," Kolya grunted.

"Watch for them. I liked them."

"Right."

Pav shrugged.

He had other things to do now.

Thankfully, they didn't have to deal with the dogs. Or rather, if the dogs did come out, they attacked the others who came in from different directions. Kolya and Pav, on the other hand, came in from the back of the property with four extra men. They had no problems crossing the property, not even when they entered the house by kicking in the back door.

Pav knew that was *strange* ...

To say the least.

Why wasn't *anyone* fighting back? They were storming the fucking property, fifteen men coming in from every direction. One man for every man they knew should be in the house or on the property with Vadim, and yet, no one fought back. Not a single one of those men came out of the shadows to defend the property like they should have.

Yeah, strange.

Pav tried not to think on it for too long. He had other things that he needed to focus his attention on and be done with it.

Kolya entered the house first, but Pav was right behind him. The back hallway, darkened with dimmed lighting, also didn't have anyone waiting to answer their attack. The men who came with them to storm the back of the house slipped in behind them, guns ready just in case.

It wasn't until they neared the middle of the house that they finally found *someone* waiting for them. Or rather, three men. Pav recognized the older men as three that had been delegated to watching Vadim, like the others who had been here when he visited with Viktoria a while ago.

They hadn't said much then.

They didn't say much now.

Kolya and Pav already had their guns aimed, and he pulled back the trigger on the weapon easily. He wasn't as good of a shot with a gun as Kolya was, though. Where Pav missed his first two shots, Kolya nailed each and every one of the men with clean head shots.

Pav decided he needed to learn that skill ...

Another time.

They rounded the corner quickly, stepping over the dead bodies of the three men, and coming to the entryway of the grand sitting room. And there, in the middle of the room like a fucking king on his throne, sat a bored looking Vadim with a glass of vodka in his hand.

Just the sight alone was enough to make Pav want to kill the asshole. Vadim looked so smug—a grin tilting his lips upward as he offered his glass to Pav and Kolya like he was asking them for another drink.

"Boys," Vadim greeted.

Kolya stiffened beside Pav. "Vadim, seems we have some business to handle here."

"Do we?"

"Pav?" Kolya asked.

Pav's gaze narrowed in on Vadim across the room. "You visited Boris often before your exile while he was in the chambers. *Several* visits, actually. And now he's freed himself, has taken Viktoria hostage, and we have reason to believe it connects back to you."

Vadim's eyes widened. "Me, but *why?*"

Oh, he was going to kill this man, and he would enjoy it, too.

"Cut the shit," Kolya uttered.

His father smirked. "I'm having fun—let me enjoy myself. I've waited a while for this."

"You are—"

"Still very much five steps ahead of you and Konstantin, son," Vadim countered easily. "As for Boris ... well, I cannot help if I spoke to him during his time in the chambers, and that he took it a certain way. I never deliberately told the man to do *anything*. I never gave him orders, or anything of the sort. I certainly didn't help him find his way out of there. I simply *talked*, and he may have learned from it, that was all."

Vadim scrubbed his hand over his unshaven jaw and his gaze drifted to Pav when he added, "People often remember those who showed them mercy during their darkest hours. Isn't that right, *Zhatka?*"

Pav said nothing.

But the man wasn't wrong.

Unfortunately.

Kolya decided it was his turn to begin speaking again. "Where are the others who Konstantin put here to watch the house and you?"

Vadim lifted his glass up for a drink and winked. "Dead, of course."

"Dead?"

"They were in the way, Kolya. I didn't need very many to work. Just a couple that I could trust, and even then ... I knew they would have to go in the end. I didn't tell them that, you know. It wouldn't have been good for this thing. But you took care of them."

At that, Vadim glanced at the dead bodies just beyond the entryway. He smiled again.

Something was broken in this man.

Pav *knew it*.

Vadim chuckled as he set the glass down on the table beside his large, red leather chair. "Konstantin allowed too many of my loyalists to remain, hmm?"

Pav had every strong urge in the world to lift his gun so he could shoot Vadim right in the mouth to shut the man up, but he managed to hold it back. That probably wouldn't do them any good right now.

Kolya eyed his father. "Your plan is pointless, and you know it. We're here ... we *will* get the information about Viktoria, and then where will that leave you?"

"Oh, *will you?*" Vadim scoffed, and glanced away from his son. "You must think I am stupid. After all these years, I assumed you might have learned something about me. Who is your brother going to ask to handle Boris, hmm? Can Konstanin really trust *any* man of ours back in Chicago to take care of business? How many of them do you think I have been able to turn to my side of things since he put me in exile? All those loyalists who remained ... I didn't have to do much, did I?"

"I—"

"It is a death sentence for Konstantin and the rest of them back in Chicago, Kolya," Vadim continued, refusing to let his son get a word in edgewise. "The Boykov men cannot be trusted, and even if he does use one who can be, there are still many others waiting in the wings to step in when needed to put him down. He never should have turned against me. It was only a matter of time."

Yeah, Pav had enough.

He dropped the gun, and in an instant, had two of his three knives in his hands as he crossed the room with steady, long strides. Vadim didn't even have the chance to move or fight back before Pav had the tip of one knife digging into the man's throat, and the other pressing into his gut. He put so much pressure on the blades that, already, a trickle of blood from the one at Vadim's throat started to dribble down the blade. A small red stain began to appear on Vadim's silk shirt from the other knife, too.

Pav didn't lighten up, either.

"The one at your throat," Pav said, "it will go in *slowly*, Vadim. You will feel every fucking inch of it as I cut your vocal cords and slit your esophagus in two. I will see what the inside of your throat looks like by the time I am done with you. You will choke on the blood—you will *drown* in it, and I will watch you do it."

Vadim swallowed against the blade. "And the other knife?"

"Just for fun. You know how I like having a bit of fun."

"Not a good move, *Zhatka*," Vadim said.

"I think it's just fine, actually."

"*No*. Kolya, who will call off a man who believes he's answering to me, hmm? Consider that while this knife gets deeper in my throat, son. If Boris truly believes he is working for me and I am the only one who can give him orders he will follow before I can return to my position in Chicago … who will call him off? Think about what I am telling you."

Pav already knew.

He said it before Kolya could.

"He's talking about Konstantin."

"Boris is going after Konstantin," Kolya said.

Vadim smiled again. "Good job, boys." Then, his gaze drifted back to Pav's as he relaxed a bit under the knives digging into his body. "In case you don't know what that means, *Zhatka*, she wasn't the goal for me. Viktoria is something I can use—something to dangle in front of a man who has little to no control over his baser urges. If I could give her back to him, he would do almost anything for me."

"I'll fucking kill you," Pav hissed.

"Not yet," Kolya muttered from behind him.

"But—"

He pressed those fucking knives harder.

Kolya snapped, "*Nyet*, Pav. Not yet. We have to wait—let Konstantin take care of Chicago."

Vadim laughed darkly. "You keep saying that, son, but I already told you. He has no one he can trust in Chicago. I made sure of that."

"How little faith you have in him," Kolya returned. "I guess now is the time we wait and see, hmm? Grab a chair, Pav, and we'll sit while we wait. I'll call Konstantin, and we'll go from there."

Pav didn't move, but he did remove those knives from Vadim's body. He crouched down a bit, enough to be eye to eye with the man. He used the tip of the bloody knife to point between his own eyes, and Vadim's.

On the other side of the room, Kolya's cell phone rang and rang on speaker but no one picked up. Konstantin wasn't answering his calls.

"Come on, *brat*," Kolya muttered. "Pick up the phone."

Pav didn't look away from Vadim.

The man kept grinning.

The phone continued ringing.

"Pick up, Konstantin," Kolya growled.

He didn't.

The voicemail picked up instead.

Kolya called again.

And *again*.

No one answered the calls.

Vadim looked all too happy.

Pav would fix that soon enough, telling Vadim, "What happens in the next few hours will determine what happens to *you*. What happens to her will determine how I will kill you, Vadim. Whether I get her back, or not, will determine how much you suffer. And believe me … either way, you *will* suffer."

19.

"YOU LOOK lonely in here all by yourself," Boris said as he darkened the doorway of the sitting room, his large figure filling up the entire space. *Looming* would be an apt description, but Viktoria didn't want to get stuck in her head when this man was around. "Care for some company?"

"Not highly."

His gaze flashed with violence.

Viktoria regretted nothing.

"Still mouthy, I see," he murmured.

Viktoria raised a brow but said nothing.

Mouthy was the least of her problems.

And certainly not a flaw.

For the time she had been stuck in this house with Boris and the men helping him—too long, but she was trying *not* to pay attention to the passing time—he'd mostly left her alone. *Mostly*. Sometimes, like now, he would come in and taunt her, but it was almost like something was holding the asshole back from really doing what he wanted with her.

She had to wonder …

Was that because he'd been told to wait?

By who?

Her father, likely.

Fucking Vadim.

Her lack of responses didn't seem to be what Boris wanted. In a flash, the man had crossed the room to come and stand right in front of her position on the worn-down couch. He'd finally untied her, but not before slapping her for good measure and warning her to behave.

She was allowed to move from this room to the bathroom, but someone was always watching her. She couldn't even piss without a companion standing next to the toilet. And they would watch her the entire damn time, too.

Dignity.

What was that?

Viktoria was barely able to suck in a sharp breath before Boris reached out and grabbed her face in his hands. His fingers dug into her flesh, probably leaving his disgusting marks behind, like he hadn't already left enough scars on her body for her to relive time and time again. Not that he cared about those, either.

He cared about *nothing*.

Just causing pain.

He shook her face a bit, and she sneered right back at him the tighter his hold became on her jaw. She refused to give this man a single fucking inch now. He'd not ever shown her mercy in the past, and she highly doubted that he was going to start now.

So yeah.

Fuck him.

She would fight this time.

Boris bent down. The ache in her jaw increased from the pressure of his hold, but she didn't show it. She looked him right in the eyes, unafraid, and wanting him to know it, too.

"I'm going to enjoy breaking you," he said, a sadistic smile curving his lips upward. "And I will enjoy it even more to watch you cry and beg while I do it, Viktoria."

"You can't break something that's already broken."

His teeth clenched.

She spat on him.

All things considered, that probably wasn't the best thing to do, but it was too late now. Viktoria couldn't find it in herself to regret doing it, either. Not even when Boris reared back, lifted his hand, and slapped her with enough force to send her sprawling over the couch.

Blood bloomed on her tongue.

Her jaw *ached*.

In her chest, her heart raced.

For a brief second, a part of her wanted to tuck herself into a tiny ball in the corner of the couch and cower away. If only because she knew the more she fought back against this man, the worse it would be for her in the end. The past had proven that to her, and she knew it without a doubt that he would make her pay for each and every mark she left on him.

Still, she had to try.

She would not hide.

Not from him.

Monsters were only scary when one didn't face them. Well, here she was. Staring hers right in the face. *Broad daylight, too.* She couldn't be scared.

Not anymore.

And still, Viktoria pushed up from the couch to sit straight again, sneered at Boris, and struck out at him. She used her hands to claw down his face, and got at least one good, hard slap in before he finally snapped out of his surprised daze just long enough to catch both of her wrists in his beefy hands.

He shoved her back to the couch. She kicked and bucked, spat and screamed, for all she was worth. She refused to let his man take anything from her willingly—he was going to have to force every fucking thing he wanted from her, because she wasn't giving it.

Fuck you.

Fuck all of you.

Her angry, hateful words only seemed to spur and encourage Boris on more, but she didn't give a shit. He forced her back to the couch, his heavy, disgusting body pushing her into the rough cushions as he worked his way between her thighs. He pulled at her jeans—too-big clothes she have been given by her captor—as his other hand came to wrap around her throat.

She spat at him again, using her fingernails to dig even more red lines down his face while he continued his attempted assault. He didn't seem to be the slightest bit bothered by her fight, or thwarted from her efforts to stop him, either.

If anything, he *liked* it.

The pig.

In the background, Viktoria could hear a phone ringing. She knew there were other men in the house, but they certainly weren't coming to her rescue. They could hear her shouts—they had to, given they were just one room over, but it didn't matter to them.

She was a pawn.

She didn't make a difference.

Boris had just ripped the zipper of her jeans down when someone in the next room called out, "Boris, we've got confirmation the bastard is back at his place with the wife. It's time to act. Let's go."

It took Boris a second.

Then, two.

He pushed away from Viktoria like it was the last thing he wanted to do. At the same time, he pointed a finger at her, his gaze nailing her to the couch as he muttered, "We're not finished here, I promise you that."

She wanted to let out a sigh of relief but didn't.

What would be the point?

Without warning, Boris reached for her and dragged her off the couch to force her to stand beside him. "Let's go. Yes, we have business."

"What—where am I going?"

"You're my guarantee."

His ... *what?*

• • •

Boris's hand clamped around Viktoria's mouth to keep her quiet while his other one wrapped tight around her throat. He effectively took away any ability she had to speak and breathe, all at the same time. Somehow, he still managed to have a gun in his hand, which he pointed at the men they came face to face with when they stormed Konstantin's home.

"Shoot, I *dare you*," Boris taunted the men with their guns pointed at him. "You're willing to risk the fact that you might shoot her, too? What will happen to you then, when Konstantin finds out you risked her life for *mine?*"

Finally, Viktoria understood.

She knew what he meant by a guarantee.

Boris was using her to get him through Konstantin's home, while the rest of his men took on the people outside. It was like a goddamn war happening behind the walls of her brother's house. She tried to bite Boris's hand, but the bastard didn't even react.

"Step out of the way," he demanded.

The men never lowered their guns.

Unquestioningly, he took his own weapon, aimed it at the side of Viktoria's temple, and laughed. He pushed the cold gun metal so hard against her head that she sucked in a shaky breath from the chill that passed through her body.

Memories flashed behind her eyes. Her whole life. She focused mostly on Pav.

They hadn't gotten enough time together. She wanted to tell him more that she loved him, even if it was crazy and she didn't understand how to be the best she could be for him. She wanted the time to learn, though.

She wanted *so much* with him.

"I will kill her right here and now if you don't *move*," Boris taunted the men in the entryway. "Now get out of my fucking way."

Slowly, one by one, each of the three men lowered their weapons and stepped back to allow Boris and Viktoria to pass. He practically had to drag her along with him because she still refused to give him anything, even something as simple as her walking for him.

"Konstantin!"

Boris' shouts echoed through the darkened, quiet house. His voice bounced off the walls and came back to them time and time again the longer they walked through the house. They were on the second floor, maybe ten feet away from Konstantin's office when finally, her brother answered Boris' calls back.

"I've been waiting for you, Boris," her brother said. "Come in, and we'll chat."

She didn't understand why her brother seemed so calm when inside, she felt like she was dying. This was not a good situation—she could hear the violence happening outside the house, and Konstantin's men? *Nowhere to be seen.*

Boris jerked Viktoria forward, not seeming to be the slightest bit concerned about what might be waiting for him in the office. Maybe it was because he still had the gun pointed to her head and he figured Konstantin would be like his men. He wouldn't be willing to risk his sister's life when push came to shove.

But would he?

She always thought—or a part of her did—that her brother was just enough like their father to scare her. That at the end of the day, Konstantin was the one who would make the difficult choices. Maybe in a different way than Vadim would, but he would still make them, nonetheless.

Did that include sacrificing her, too?

She didn't know.

God.

She hoped not.

Boris dragged her to the doorway of the office, and Viktoria quickly found her brother sitting behind his large desk. Calm and collected in a three-piece suit, as though nothing in the world were bothering him. Konstantin sat with his hands folded on the desk and his cold gaze on them. Amelia was nowhere to be seen, and that was a clue to Viktoria.

Hadn't they said Konstantin's wife was here?

Where was she?

Did he ... *know*?

Had he known they were coming, and put Amelia out of the danger zone because—

"Viktoria," Konstantin murmured.

Her gaze snapped to her brother.

He didn't smile.

Didn't blink.

Nothing.

"*Don't talk to her*," Boris snarled.

He pushed the gun harder against Viktoria's head. She swallowed hard but didn't look away from her brother. There was something in Konstantin's eyes—a glimmer of calm that she had never seen from him before. A resolute understanding that he was in control here, even if it didn't look like it.

Maybe that was what calmed her the most.

She couldn't be sure.

"I never forgot," her brother said. "How standing next to Boris, you seemed so small. I would think ... *he's not a good match*. He would swallow you whole, and there you would be, shadowed against him. You were far too brilliant to be hidden by *any* man, Viktoria. Do you understand me?"

She nodded.

Boris' arm tightened around her throat. "I said don't talk to her."

"Or what?" Konstantin asked, his gaze snapping to the man. "*Or what?*"

Boris jerked forward.

Konstantin smiled.

It was just enough—just beyond the doorway a little. A few inches, maybe a foot, if that. But the gunshot that echoed, shattered through the glass of the window behind Konstantin's desk, and then plugged into the side of Boris' shoulder had Viktoria freezing in place.

All the air left her lungs.

Her body stiffened.

She felt the blood splatter the side of her face. She knew she could finally breathe when his arm loosened around her neck. Her entire body screamed for her to move away from him as he fell to the floor with a shout, and the gun in his hand clattered across the floor.

She didn't move, though. She didn't know what to do. Konstantin moved, instead.

He was quick to come around the desk after grabbing his own weapon, which he apparently had hidden somewhere. Pointing the weapon at Boris, he looked to her.

"You okay?"

She shook her head.

His blood was on her.

She wanted it *off*.

"Sniper shot—courtesy of the Albanians," Konstantin explained when Viktoria looked at the ruined window. "We were owed a favor … or two. I knew I couldn't trust this bastard if he was working with Vadim. How many other men of mine would be working with them, too? I had to go outside the organization for help."

She dragged in a raged breath.

It literally hurt to breathe.

"You had to think like Vadim," she whispered.

Konstantin nodded. "But just enough … I can't be him, too."

"I know, Konstantin."

"I'm sorry."

Viktoria shook her head. "It's okay."

It really wasn't.

But it would be.

"I should fucking let him suffer," Konstantin said, digging in his pocket to pull out a ringing phone. "He should *suffer*, Vik."

She couldn't let that happen.

The gun at her feet—Boris'—gained her attention. Her brother was too busy looking at the screen of his phone while still pointing his gun at the man groaning on the floor. She didn't even think about it before she bent down, plucked up the gun, aimed, and fired.

The last thing Boris saw before the bullet plugged into his forehead?

Viktoria.

It was what he deserved.

It's what *she* deserved.

Konstantin said nothing, but he did nod before offering the phone to her. She didn't understand what he was doing, and the only thing she really wanted right then was to ask where in the hell Pavel was and why he wasn't here.

With her.

Where she needed him.

Konstantin nodded at the phone. "Take it and call Kolya back. Pav will be there to take the phone, too. I couldn't have them here. Not when I needed people I trusted to be with Vadim, too. I couldn't trust anyone, remember? I needed people there, too. So, they had to go, yes? But I couldn't explain that to them. And what if he had a backup? What if he had something else that he could use against me that I hadn't planned for? At least they would be there … if we all died here, they would be there to end him, too."

So yeah, he was just like their father.

Just *enough*.

Enough to make the hard choices.

She didn't tell him that, though.

Viktoria took the phone.

20.

"IT SHOULD be done by now."

Vadim's gaze finally drifted away from Pav, but only long enough to check the clock. He could see the wheels turning in the man's head—working out the time difference between here, and Chicago, before he nodded.

"Yes, I believe it should be done," Vadim said.

The smile that turned on Pav could only be described as fucking sadistic. This asshole was ridiculously proud of the fact he was about to—if he hadn't already—arrange the murder of his second son and hand his daughter to a monster like she was a gift for him to devour.

There was rage, sure.

But there was hatred, too.

Hatred was a whole different kind of beast for Pav. He could subdue his rage—he could feed it with something other than violence to keep it in its cage until he was ready to act upon it. Hatred, though?

He couldn't control that at all.

Right then, it's all he felt, too.

At some point during their time with Vadim, Kolya had pulled a chair across the room, and forced Pav to sit in it whether he wanted to or not. That was fine—he continued to sit right in front of Vadim, regardless of the man's opinion of his proximity. He wanted a constant reminder on Vadim's mind of what was coming for him soon.

Very fucking soon.

Like right now.

Pav jumped out of that chair like he was a bullet coming through a gun. He'd never been so focused on one thing before—never zoned in on just *one* thing that nothing else existed. Except for Viktoria, maybe.

It wasn't the same thing.

He never wanted to kill her.

Pav *greatly* wanted to kill Vadim.

Those knives he'd been playing with all evening, another constant reminder for Vadim to see while the two sat only inches apart, were back in his grip and ready to be used again. He never felt more comfortable and more at peace than when he was holding a knife— or fucking Viktoria. Two entirely different things, sure, and yet they both brought him a calm like nothing else ever could.

Vadim couldn't even prepare for the man coming at him. He leaned back a bit, but where the hell was he going to go? The high-back, leather chair stopped him from being able to get away, and given that Pav was already sitting so close to him, it wasn't like the asshole could come forward without ramming right into him.

He was fucked.

Pav liked that.

The tip of one of his blades caught Vadim right on his lower, right eyelid. The other came to the right side of his mouth to catch him on the very corner of his mouth. He started with the eyelid first, pulling the blade down through the skin so that when it tried to heal, the scar would be horrible, and the pain would be made worse by the fact every blink would pull on the wound.

He kept the blade at the corner of Vadim's mouth pulled taut to keep him in place while he worked on the other side of his face. Vadim let out a shout, and his hands came up in an attempt to fight back against Pav, but it was useless.

"Try me right now, and that knife is slicing through your fucking cheek," Pav said. "The blade is so sharp ... it won't take very much at all for it to do the job. Never took you for a Glasgow kind of man, Vadim, but if you want one, keep it up."

The *grin*.

A scarred grin.

Vadim knew exactly what Pav was talking about, and the man was quick to stop his fight. That didn't mean it stopped hurting him, because it didn't. At all. He could feel Vadim's trembling, and the way the blood from his cut mouth pooled down his chin onto his shirt. The other side of his face? Even worse.

"*This*," Pav said, his voice deathly dark and yet calm at the same time as he stared into Vadim's eyes. "... this is a fucking taste of what will happen to you if I don't get her back in the same perfect condition she was in before this happened. Do you understand me, Vadim? This is going to get so much worse for you ... it doesn't matter what happens in Chicago because you're never leaving this house. Not with a heartbeat in your chest, anyway."

Pav laughed, the sound surprising even himself with how cold it came out. He leaned in a little closer to Vadim, enough that the two of them were only a breath away from each other as his gaze locked on Vadim's. He could smell the liquor on the man's breath that he'd seen sipping on, but it didn't bother him nearly as much as the deadness in Vadim's gaze did. It was as though he couldn't feel anything at all.

Funny.

Pav often felt the same way.

Just not right now.

He finally pulled the knife away from the man's face, but he kept the one at his mouth just in case he needed a fucking reminder about who exactly was in charge here.

"And I will personally make sure that your heart is no longer beating." Pav told the man, tapping the tip of his knife against Vadim's chest all the while, "Because I will fucking cut this organ out of your chest and burn it."

"*Pavel.*"

Kolya's sharp warning echoed in the back of Pav's senses, but it took the man calling his name another three times before he finally backed away from Vadim. And even then, he continued pointing that knife at Vadim like a silent warning.

He needed to *know.*

Pav liked it when people saw him coming.

"We've got a call," Kolya said.

At that statement, Pav did glance over his shoulder. When had the phone rang? Because he hadn't heard anything. Then again, he had just been two seconds away from slicing Vadim into the smallest of pieces that he could manage. He was still in that headspace, if he were being honest.

Instead of sitting in the chair like he'd been before, Kolya was now standing in the doorway to the room. Pav didn't even know when the man had left—his attention for the last several hours had been hyper-focused on Vadim only. Everything else, including Kolya, was nothing more than a background noise.

"What was it?" Pav asked.

His heart ached from pumping so hard. His nerves were pulled as tight as they were going to go. At any second, he might blow.

That's how it felt, anyway.

He just needed something.

A reason to hurt Vadim.

One more second with Viktoria.

Anything.

"It's Vik," Kolya said, holding the phone out like he intended for Pav to cross the room and take the device from him. "She's calling from Konstantin's phone."

Pav stilled in place.

The air slipped past his lips—*relief.*

Kolya passed a look to the man in the chair behind Pav, still bleeding and waiting for the second round with a knife. "They're fine, and Konstantin asked us to leave Vadim alive until they arrive here."

Pav didn't move.

Not to take the phone.

Not to acknowledge the order.

He just didn't move.

He couldn't.

"She's coming?"

Kolya shook the phone a bit. "She wants to talk to you, yeah."

Pav didn't know why he hesitated to cross the room and take the phone. Maybe because everything that was great and good in his life had been taken from him so many times that he was scared this was just another sick joke.

It wouldn't be her on the phone.

His life would be pointless.

He'd *just found her.*

"Pav." Kolya said quietly, "come get the phone, yes?"

He nodded, shaking off the odd feeling in his gut and closed the space between him and Kolya. Taking the phone, he glanced at the name on the screen—Konstantin's contact—and then put it to his ear.

"Viktoria," he murmured.

"Pav?"

Relief never felt so sweet.

"*Da, krasotka.*" He swallowed thickly, easier words slipping out then when he added, "*Ya lyublyu tebya.*"

Viktoria laughed lightly. "I love you, too."

He wanted to say he was sorry. This shouldn't have happened again—she deserved to be loved and protected every day of her life. God knew she had suffered enough already, and he felt strangely guilty that here she was, yet again in this position.

But now was not the time.

"I will see you soon."

"Soon, Pav," she promised.

Good enough.

Surely that would keep him from killing Vadim until they got there. Wouldn't it? Pav passed a look over his shoulder at the bleeding man in the chair who was currently glaring at him like he was ready to get out of his seat.

The asshole could try it. And no, he couldn't guarantee that he wouldn't kill him.

That was promising too much.

• • •

Pav was a caged animal.

He paced like one, back and forth in the hotel room alone. He wouldn't even allow Kolya to come in and sit with him as they waited. He stared out the windows, looking for any sign of movement, as though they were bars that he was peering through and he was waiting for his captor to come back.

The slightest noise outside of the door would make him jump. He'd never been *this* jittery or restless. He'd been on his feet for hours—days, actually, if he thought about it. Trying to remember how much he had slept the last several days was pointless because it wasn't anything worth knowing. An hour, maybe, if he totaled it all together.

Nothing good.

Earlier, Kolya had thought to point out that it might be smarter if Pav allowed someone in his room to give him company. *Someone to talk to, no,* Kolya said. Pav was damn close to throwing one of his knives at the man for that because *no,* he did not want anyone near him right now unless their fucking name was Viktoria Boykov.

End. Of.

Kolya left him alone after that.

Thankfully.

He assumed that Kolya, like the rest of the people who knew him, was so accustomed to Pav being the silent figure in the corner. The one who never spoke, or rarely, and when he did it was always quiet and with few words. They weren't used to seeing him anxious and pacing like a fucking animal. They didn't know how to handle or deal with him when he was ready to bring a hell of a lot of pain to anyone who got too close.

So, Kolya left him alone.

Smart, really.

The sound of a car door slamming sent Pav flying across the room to the window. He was too late to see whoever it was that the car had dropped off, though, because by the time he got the curtains moved aside so he could look down at the street below, the car was pulling away and no one was standing on the sidewalk.

Fuck.

They should be here soon. Their flight should have landed already. It was driving him absolutely *crazy*.

Pav could not remember a time when he felt more out of control than he did in those moments. Backing away from the window, he tipped his head back and stared hard at the ceiling up above. He scrubbed his hands down his jaw, the feeling of his thick facial hair scraping against his palms reminding him that he needed a shave.

He needed a lot of fucking things.

None of them were here right now, though.

Not a single one—

"I didn't take you for a praying man, Pavel."

That thing in his chest?

That thing that *beat?*

That kept him alive?

It stopped.

Altogether quit.

All it took was the sound of Viktoria's sweet voice behind and his heart jumped in his chest like someone had fucking shocked it. It stopped beating for a split second, and then it restarted, beating twice as hard as it ever had before.

He spun on his heels, and *there she was.*

Standing just beyond the door of the hotel where Kolya had set them up until Konstantin and Viktoria could arrive in Russia, there she was.

She smiled a little, like she could read his mind and all the craziness that was happening up there. Without looking away from him, she reached back and shut the hotel door. It was only then, right before the door closed, that he could hear the familiar voices of her brothers filtering out in the hallway.

He didn't care about them.

Not right now.

Viktoria pulled off the leather gloves keeping her pretty hands hidden and worked on undoing the buttons of her tweed jacket. Pav took that moment to check her over, his gaze drifting over the column of her neck, and the lines of her face. She was bruised—makeup did wonders, but he could see the odd yellowish and blue tints where she hadn't been able to cover the color entirely.

His rage danced again.

His hatred flared.

Still, he swallowed it back.

"He hurt you," Pav murmured.

Viktoria looked up from the buttons on her jacket, whispering, "Only a little."

"Not *only a little*. Too much, babe."

"I'm okay."

Was she?

He would soon find out.

"Did he—"

"No," she said quickly, like she already knew what he was going to ask. "No, not again."

Pav was back to feeling like a fucking animal again. Like the one thing he wanted was just beyond the bars of his cage. He could *smell her*—that vanilla and pear perfume she wore that made him think of innocence and sin at the same time. Perfect for her.

He was able to wait just long enough for her to remove her jacket, but then his control snapped. He'd already waited too long as it was to get her back in his arms again. He'd been stuck in his head for days, thinking constantly about every horrible thing that might be happening to her because he hadn't been able to help her.

The second Pav had Viktoria in his arms, the world felt *slightly* better. Like the axis titled just a bit, and the world was starting to turn again. It wasn't completely right, but it was getting there, which was better than nothing.

It was made perfect when she kissed him.

So fucking perfect.

"I felt crazy," he muttered against her lips. "An *animal*."

Even with that admission, she kissed him again, and her fingers came up to drift over the tense muscles of his face. With every swipe of her fingers, his clenching jaw relaxed, and he breathed a bit easier.

She helped with everything.

Did she even know that?

"It's okay," she whispered. "I'm okay."

"Was it okay that I wanted to rip your brothers' throats out with my bare hands because they made me come *here*, and I just wanted to be there?"

Viktoria let out a little laugh and her thumb caressed the spot under his eye. "I love you, Pav."

"Good thing."

Nobody else would.

She smiled, then, bright and sweet. A smile that she didn't give to anyone else. He knew because he saw the way she smiled at other people, when she very rarely did. And it did not look like the smile she reserved just for him.

"I just ..."

"What?" she asked.

"It's been a bad ... time," he said lamely.

His head was dark.

His mood, too.

All of it.

She seemed to understand without him saying it. Thankfully.

"What do you need?"

"Shouldn't I be asking you that?" he replied.

Viktoria kissed him again, harder than before and he *loved* it. Her lips still grazed his when she pulled away just enough to say, "We're not a *me* thing. We're an *us*, right?"

"Are we?"

"That's what I want to be."

Pav nodded. "Then, that's what we are."

Whatever she wanted.

He was going to say that for the rest of his life.

"I'm *fine*," she said, stressing the word hard. "But you're not. So, what do you need?"

"You. I need you."

"Whatever way you want me, I'm here."

That was easy for her to say.

"I'm not in the right headspace," he told her, trying to be honest. "I'm worried I'll be too rough, or that I won't know if—"

"I'm not scared of you."

Pav gave her a look, then. "You should be."

He didn't miss the shiver that wracked her shoulders, or the way her lips curved into a sinful grin. That was the thing about this woman—she liked the darker parts of him as much as she enjoyed everything else.

"Never, not anymore," she swore.

Maybe that was what he needed the most. Maybe he just needed her to say it, confirm that together, she knew that she was safe with him and always would be. Because the moment those words left her lips, the careful control he had over his darker urges was gone in an instant. Like the chains broke and the monster was free.

He was her monster.

Just not one that hurt her.

Pav dragged Viktoria as close as he could get her, his body pinning hers to the wall when he backed her into it, and then he kissed her. A bruising kiss, but she didn't shy away from the force or the desperation behind it. If anything, she answered him back just as hard. Her tongue found his, and warred.

A battle he loved.

He needed that.

Needed her.

Viktoria didn't shy away from the harshness of his hands driving over her body. Her sexy little moans when he yanked the clothes away from her body to get her naked as fast as he possibly could only urged him on further.

It was only once she was naked but for her black cotton panties and standing in front of him that he took a moment. Just a moment to lean back and let his gaze drink her in. He didn't miss the marks on her body—the fingerprints on her throat, and the bruises on her sides. His fingertips drifted over those same spots, rage festering and burning like never before.

"He's dead," she said, reading his expression again. "And I did it."

He was *angry*.

So fucking angry.

It should have been him.

It was lucky for the bastard that it was *her*.

"They'll fade," she said when he kept touching the bruises with a light touch.

"Not soon enough."

"Yeah, I know."

"I'm sorry," he murmured.

A subtle shake of her head was all that she answered him back with, but he heard her silent words loud and clear. *He doesn't matter here.*

And she was right.

"This is unfair." She told him, "Because I am the only one without clothes."

Pav chuckled. "I don't need to be undressed yet."

"Why—"

He was down on his knees before she could even finish her question. His hands wrapped into the waistband of her black panties, and he yanked them down her legs. Once she'd stepped out of the item, he pushed her legs open. A primal sound fell from his lips at the sight of her pussy laid out in front of him. Just a sliver of silky, wet flesh. All pink, and ready for him. He adored the sight of it, and he *loved* the taste of it.

In the next breath, he had his smirking face buried between her thighs, getting what he wanted the most. Her taste coating his tongue, and her moans filling his ears. Her fingers threaded into his hair to pull hard as he fucked her pussy with his mouth. His tongue tunneled into her slit while his thumb toyed with her clit.

The hotter she got, the creamier her sex became.

Fucking beautiful.

He was all too aware that he was grabbing onto her thigh *hard*. Likely leaving his own marks behind, but it was her sounds and the way she kept rolling her hips into his mouth and hands that said she was *fine*.

And so was he.

Now.

This was what he needed.

She was what he needed.

As her shaking started to make her whole body shudder, and his name started to echo in the quiet room with every breath she released, he increased the pressure on her clit with his thumb just enough to push her over the edge. And when she finally came, he licked every fucking drop of her arousal that he could, loving the way she got hotter when she came. All the while, he watched her up above, shattering into a thousand tiny little pieces in her mind before she came back up for air again.

For a second, Pav grabbed onto Viktoria's hips tightly and rested his forehead against her stomach. He really was like a fucking animal—he wanted to get close to her warmth, feel the softness of her skin, and *smell* her. All things that calmed him like nothing else, and once again, he found that he was just doing it to remind himself that she was fine.

She was *here*.

Everything was good.

Her fingers drifted through his hair softly, and he looked up at her then to find she was smiling a bit. "You're still *very* dressed, all things considered."

He laughed.

Yeah, he got it.

She was quick to tug on his hair, then, drawing him up from his knees. She didn't mind helping him out of his clothes, and once all that fabric was discarded to the floor, she was kissing him again. Her legs were already lifting to wrap around his waist as he backed her into the wall, using it to help him keep her steady as he thrust into her body.

So fucking wet.

Warm.

And tight.

God.

That first thrust took his breath away. The second felt like a punch right to his chest, too. He couldn't kiss her hard enough. Couldn't fuck her deep enough. He couldn't get his hands on all the spots he wanted to touch on her body at once. But fuck him if he didn't at least *try*. She was his heroin, and the needle was right in his fucking heart. Every thrust of his body against hers was yet another shot of her drug directly into his bloodstream.

Those marks on her body were replaced with his own.

She bit his lip until he fucking *bled*.

And damn, that's what he wanted.

All of it.

"*Please, please*," Viktoria mumbled into his throat. "*Almost …*"

He didn't let her come like she wanted. Not then, anyway. Instead, he dragged her away from the wall, backed up until they were at the arm of the couch, and set her back down. Pulling away from her body just far enough that he could flip her over, he was thrusting back inside her cunt before he could even *think*.

It was heaven.

All around him.

"Fuck, *yeah*," Viktoria mumbled into the couch. "*Harder.*"

He gave her exactly what she wanted, fingers winding into her hair to yank her head back while his other clamped down on her hip. He pulled her back into every brutal thrust, loving the way her pussy clamped down around him, tighter with every beat of his hips against her ass.

Her cries were loud.

The whole hallway knew his name now.

"Give it to me," he demanded.

She did.

Beautifully.

She was still trembling and panting his name into the couch, the orgasm slipping through her body, as his started to build. It came on fast, tightening his spine and balls, heat shooting up through his gut into his chest.

So fucking intense.

He held her tight to his cock, as deep as he could get, and emptied into her. The long, satisfied sigh she released echoed in the quiet room, but all Pav could do was stare down at his cock and where it was still filling her up. He pulled out just to watch their mingled fluids slip from her slit, falling over the head of his cock before he smeared it between her thighs.

It was primal, that need.

To see *him* mixed with *her*.

Fuck, he loved that.

"I think…" Viktoria said, her words still light and breathless. "That my brothers want to talk sometime tonight."

Nope.

Pav barked out a laugh, and in a blink, had Viktoria cradled in his arms before he headed for the hotel bedroom. "They can fucking wait."

She grinned up at him, pleased and sly. "Okay."

• • •

Pav stayed close to Viktoria's back as she drifted farther into the damp, dark room. Walls made of cement, and a floor with cracks deep enough for a rat to live inside, this was not a comfortable cell.

It never would be.

And yet, it was where Vadim found himself. Back at the Compound—a place he'd always called home and made sure everyone knew it belonged to him. Here he was, in the very same chambers that Pav had once stayed in, to care for the men Vadim had put here for various reasons.

Chained, like they had been.

Broken, like they had been.

Terrified … like they had been, too.

Finally, Pav figured Vadim was starting to understand the hell he had put everyone else through in his life. Viktoria edged closer to where her father rested in the corner of the cell, and though she tried to hide it, he could see the way her hands trembled before she stuffed them into her jacket.

He stayed close and yet gave her space.

It's what she needed.

"Konstantin says the Compound is temporary, Vadim," Viktoria whispered.

If he heard her, he didn't acknowledge it. His head didn't move, and his opened, wide eyes staring blankly at the wall didn't flicker with movement, either. Pav was able to get regular updates about Vadim and his time here—what of it was left, anyway—and from what he knew, Vadim rarely spoke or stepped out of line.

He just … was.

Dead man walking.

"I chose this for you, if you didn't know," Viktoria continued, her fingers coming up to flick a few strands of her blonde hair over her shoulder. "I didn't want him to kill you, although that's what *he* wanted. That's what everyone wanted for you."

She wasn't lying.

It had been a battle.

Somehow, this woman won.

He hoped she kept winning, and that she let him come along for the ride, too. She was amazing. Vicious and strong and *beautiful.* He was going to spend the rest of his life chasing after her, as long as she let him do it.

"I didn't want them to kill you because that would have been *easy,*" Viktoria told her unmoving father, but there was no way he wasn't hearing her. "Death would have been a gift, and what I really needed was for you to understand and *know* the pain and fear you caused me, and everyone else."

Viktoria inched closer, and then crouched down. For the first time, Vadim's gaze drifted her way. Those dead eyes of his locked on her, and the two of them stared at one another for a long time. Pav might have gone closer just to … be there and make sure the man didn't try anything.

He didn't need to.

Vadim couldn't move far from the wall, and Viktoria had enough space between the two of them. Besides, this was about her, not him. She needed to do this, and he was just here to let her do exactly that.

Nothing else.

"I showed you mercy by asking Konstantin to spare your life," Viktoria said, brushing her fingers over her jacket to remove any dust that might have been clinging to the fabric from their walk down the dirty hallways. "But you'll live the rest of your life cold, alone, and *without.* They won't beat you—they won't even *look* at you. Because you don't deserve that either, Vadim. You don't deserve anything, and that's exactly what I've given you now."

"Poetic, really," Pav said, more to himself than her.

Because she was *right.* Everyone had been so quick to deny Viktoria when she'd asked that she be the one to decide Vadim's punishment. Death was the one thing everyone else wanted, but no, she had something … *better.*

The vicious ones always did.

She still laughed a bit.

Yeah.

Damn.

He loved her.

So much.

"You deserve to die," Viktoria said, standing straight but never looking away from her father. "And you *will* die, eventually, but I get to decide that. You will live the rest of your days wondering when I will decide your time is up. You'll never know, and you will be so alone and broken and isolated in this dark, cold place—or wherever Konstantin sends you next—that the only thing you'll wish for is death. Except you'll have to beg me, *Daddy*, you'll have to beg *me* to let them kill you. Until you gain the courage to do that … well, you can wait while you wonder if today is finally the day I decided you should die."

She laughed again. "It's kind of appropriate, if you think about it. You were so quick to teach us that we would have to wait for pain. You taught us that we should *love* the fear because you were fear … we all correlated fear to a man we were supposed to love. So, it's your turn, now. Learn to love your fear, Vadim. It's what you deserve."

Viktoria stopped at the doorway as she left, tossing a laugh over her shoulder as she added a line to her father that burned even Pavel. "And I was lying, Daddy. You thought we would let you live after *everything*? Never. Enjoy your place in hell."

Vadim jerked away from the wall at that statement. They had all known the truth—this would be nothing more than *hope* to Vadim. This place, and permanent seclusion, to pay for his sins like the monster he was. It would never have worked. It only would have given him hope, and eventually, they would pay for giving it to him.

They had learned their lesson.

Viktoria had truly only asked for *one* thing—that she be allowed to make her father feel like he had done to her. To put hope and trust in his hands, and then rip them away from him. It was what she had been owed, after all.

"I'll be upstairs, Pav," Viktoria said.

He nodded her way, and then she was gone.

Pav still found comfort in this place.

He hated it.

But he knew it well.

Vadim's gaze drifted to him, but the man still stayed silent even as he tugged against his chains like he thought that might save him from *Zhatka*. It wouldn't.

"Nothing to say now?" he asked the man on the floor.

Vadim trembled, but said nothing. Pav didn't really mind. He didn't need Vadim to speak for him to have the last word, honestly.

"Do you remember what you told me that first night I spent in the Compound?" Pav chuckled a bit and stuffed his hands in his pockets as he rocked back on his heels. "After you dragged me from the car that I was hiding in ... before you decided my life was no longer my own, do you remember what you said?"

The man kept quiet.

Pav understood why.

"You don't have to speak because it feels *most* appropriate tonight for me to remind you of those words," Pav said, grinning just a bit. These walls were no longer his home, but he might come to visit occasionally. Why not? "Beware of those who show you mercy, for those are the people who know the essence of your fear."

Pav kneeled down, three knives already in hand. He knew without a doubt as he put the knife to Vadim's throat, and the man's eyes widened back as huffs of air left his body from fear, that Viktoria was still close enough to hear her father's death.

That's what she'd wanted.

Pav smiled at the man.

Death always smiled.

"Say hello to the Devil, and tell him the Reaper sends another one, Vadim."

The knives slid in.

21.

One month later …

KOLYA LET out a harsh hiss when Viktoria started the shading on the left side of his chest where he wanted one of the cupolas on top of the church to be black and white. The rest were in color, but with all the shading work that came along with a portion of a black and white piece … well, it wasn't comfortable.

Especially on top of scar tissue.

At first, when her brother had tugged off his shirt to begin this session, it'd taken Viktoria more than a couple of seconds to look away from the scarring covering the majority of his chest. He still had his eight-pointed stars, and his Latin script under his throat, as well as the epaulettes on his shoulders to signify his rank in the Bratva.

A long time ago, he'd used to have a cross, too. A thieves' cross. It was put there, not by his own choice, but because Vadim decided Kolya would be the man to take over once their father was done with his position.

And then, when Kolya had chosen to go against their father, Vadim decided to have the tattoo removed. She hadn't known very much about the incident. Her brothers never talked about the night that event happened, or how it was done.

Now, she figured out why.

She *understood.*

They didn't want to tell her about the horrors that caused his knotted, puckered pink skin that covered a good portion of her brother's chest. It would not have been an easy punishment to have his tattoos burned off, not by any means.

"It still hurts, no?"

She glanced up at her brother, away from where her black-gloved hands were pulling the skin taut as she tried to work fast over a particularly rough edge of a scar that was bothering him. She could always fill anything in later, but the most important part today was just laying down as much ink over the bad scarring as she could.

"Sorry," she whispered, glancing back down at her work.

"Not you," Kolya muttered. "Well, yes, you too right now. You're not as heavy-handed as some tattooists I've sat in front of, mind you, but yes it hurts quite a bit. I just meant in general. I wake up, and it's tender, or I shower, and it burns for a while."

God.

No one deserved this kind of punishment.

"Take a minute," Kolya said when Viktoria didn't put her machine back to work right away. "And then we'll get back to it, Vik."

She nodded, grateful for the second to think.

"You were lucky this didn't kill you," she said.

Kola grunted under his breath, a mixture of disgust and a laugh. "It almost did. Infection was terrible, and Maya about finished the job when she realized it got infected *again.*"

Viktoria didn't even try to hide her smile. "She's good for you, Kolya."

"She is. We don't tell people that, however."

"Never," she promised.

He gestured at his chest, and the scarring. "I know it looks bad to you, but I've become accustomed to seeing it, now. And it is *just* a moment in time, you know? Something that happened before but is over now. That's how I see it, and that's how you should see it. Don't feel guilty or bad over something that is over and won't happen again."

How simple that sounded.

She didn't think it was.

"I idolized him for a long time," she said quietly.

Their father, she meant.

Kolya sighed. "That doesn't change anything."

He always saw things as black or white ... a lot like Pav, too. Their minds were either made that way or broken that way. She couldn't say quite the same about hers, but she would try to look at her brother's pain in the same way he did, if only for *him.*

It wasn't about her, after all.

"Do you want me to start again?" she asked, hitting the trigger on the machine and making it buzz.

Kolya chuckled. "Might as well."

Viktoria went back to work. She'd taken a chair and room in her friend's shop so that she could get out of the apartment more often.

She never went back to her house—put it on the market, and watched it sell faster than she'd thought was possible.

Tattooing felt like home, though.

It was familiar.

An *outlet*.

She was halfway through the black and white cupola when Kolya cleared his throat and drew her attention to him again. She'd never known her brother to be very chatty—he simply wasn't the type—but he seemed to have a lot to say today.

Or maybe he was like her ...

Making an effort to be better.

Trying to do better.

Who fucking knew?

They were still Boykovs, right?

"What?" she asked.

"I heard, from a little bird—"

"Maya," Viktoria said instantly.

Kolya scowled. "I did not say it was my wife."

"Your wife is the only one who gossips to you because she is the only one you allow to gossip around you. You would never tell her to shut the hole in her face like you tell everyone else because then she might *cry*."

His cheek twitched. "Maya never cries."

"Because you have killed people for making her sad, Kolya."

"But was I wrong, though?"

Oh, my God.

She had to send up a prayer in that moment to give her the strength not to laugh at her brother. She might have done exactly that if Kolya hadn't looked entirely serious staring at her while he waited for a response. He literally thought it was a perfectly acceptable thing for him to kill someone simply because they upset his wife.

In fact, he'd do it for less.

He *had* done it for less.

"It was Maya who told you whatever you're about to say," Viktoria said, refusing to argue further with her brother or listen to him justify his violent streak. "So, what did she tell you?"

"Fine," he grumbled, glancing away. "It was Maya."

"As I said ..."

"Shut the hole in your face."

Viktoria grinned.

See?

Just like she said.

Kolya was predictable.

"*Anyway*," he muttered, giving her a look to quiet her. "She mentioned that you and Pav had moved into a new apartment a couple of weeks ago. Did the hotel not suit your needs, or what?"

"The hotel was not a home. And I already sold the house."

"I know I've been busy with Maya, and the baby coming ..."

"Just say what you want to say, Kolya."

"Okay."

She glanced at him, raising her brow. "Okay?"

He nodded. "I'll just say it, yeah? If you want me to kill Pavel because he steps out of line on you, you let me know and I will do it whenever you ask."

Viktoria pressed her lips together to keep from smiling. Oh, sure, her brother's promise was typical Kolya wrapped up in his taste for violence. She would expect nothing less from her brother, of course. At least, not *this* brother.

But it was also something else ... It was his way of saying *I love you, Vik, and I'll always look out for you if you need me to.* She loved him for that, but she was a lot like Kolya, too. She didn't put her emotions on her sleeve, and she never outright said what she was feeling unless it was to the person she loved the very most in her life.

Pav.

Viktoria nodded, and leaned in to give her brother a quick, one-armed hug. "I know you would, Kolya."

He laughed under his breath as she straightened on the stool again. "I don't think I'll have to worry about hurting the bastard, anyway. He's not very good at being away from you, and he gets a little stir crazy when he thinks you're out of reach."

That he did.

Pav just liked her close.

She understood that, too.

So many things he cared about in his life had been taken away. He was finally given a second chance to do or be whatever he wanted to be in this life of theirs, but there was still a part of him that felt like that boy hiding in a car.

He didn't want to be without her.

She wouldn't let him ever be alone again.

"And he did go speak to Konstantin today, so I think that says good things for him," Kolya added.

Viktoria's hand froze as she reached for her tattoo machine again. "What did you just say?"

It wasn't the fact that Pav went to see Konstantin that made her pause. He worked for her brothers, so that made sense. It was the way Kolya offered the information, like there was something he knew that she didn't.

Kolya glanced up at her, calm and unaffected. "Oh, I don't gossip. Shut the hole in your face, and let's get back to the tattooing, Vik."

"You're such an asshole."

"I really am," Kolya replied, smirking.

• • •

Viktoria paced the length of the living room in the new apartment. Part of her mind continued to drift to Pav, and what Kolya had told her earlier. Another part of her mind kept glaring at the hardwood floor and thinking she needed to go out and buy a rug to make it look less ... boring.

The brain was a funny thing.

"Why do you look like a little mouse hiding from the cat?"

Viktoria spun around so fast that the rest of the room was nothing more than a blur. She wasn't the least bit surprised to see Pav leaning in the entryway of the living room with his arms crossed over his chest like he'd been standing there for a while.

He probably had been.

The man could move without making a sound. If he didn't want her to know he was around, then she wouldn't know. It was as simple as that. She had become accustomed to it now, or as much as she ever would be, anyway.

It was his thing.

What could she do?

"A scared *mouse*?" she asked, arching a brow and giving him a look. She even bared her teeth in a bit of a smirking sneer just for good measure. She was so far from a frightened little mouse now. "Is that really how you see me, Pavel?"

He grinned right back. "See, *now* you look like the cat waiting for the mouse."

"Who do you think the mouse is?"

"Is it me?"

"It might be if you keep calling me the mouse."

His laughter colored up the apartment, and Viktoria relaxed a bit. She knew things were difficult for him sometimes.

He'd spent so much time hidden away from the rest of the world that he didn't always know what to do ... or what he should do, rather. He was still getting accustomed to being free, in a sense.

He was learning the world.

With her.

"You went to see Konstantin today, huh?" she asked.

Pav's expression melded into calm nothingness. "I did."

"Why?"

"I work for him, Vik."

"Is that the *only* reason?"

Pav shifted on his feet and tipped his head down so that she couldn't see his eyes. She didn't like that—all of his truths always shined back in his gaze, and like this, she couldn't tell if he was trying to hide something from her, or not.

"And what if it wasn't the only reason I went to speak with him?"

"Care to tell me what or why?" she returned.

Pav chuckled. "You won't drop this?"

"Nope."

He stuffed his hands in his pockets, straightened up against the entryway, and met her gaze again. *Finally*, she felt like she could see the truth staring back at her.

It spelled out *love.*

Like it always did.

"It wasn't about work," he said.

"No?"

Pav shook his head. "No."

"Was it about me?"

"Perhaps." Pav grinned a bit and shrugged. "I'm not very good at this thing, you know?"

"At what?"

He pulled a hand from his pocket to gesture between the two of them, saying, "*This.*"

She disagreed.

Entirely.

"You're very good at this, Pav."

"I don't always know what's the right thing to do."

"That's okay. I didn't ask you for perfect. I asked for you."

Pav cleared this throat, and his tongue peeked out to wet his lips. "I thought … maybe I had to make sure you were going to be mine. Forever, yes? I thought I had to *ask*."

Viktoria blinked. "You asked Konstantin that?"

He tipped his head to the side, muttering, "He said I didn't have to ask him."

"Because you should already know the answer, Pavel."

Or, that's how she felt.

Pav's gaze lifted again and nailed into hers. "I should, shouldn't I?"

She didn't even think about it before she crossed the room, reached up to catch his face in her palms, and then she pulled him in for a kiss. He didn't hesitate to answer her back—his lips worked hard against hers while he took her breath away all at the same time.

Yeah, he was still figuring things out.

About the world.

About life.

About *himself.*

But her?

Them?

She didn't ever want him to wonder.

Never.

Viktoria pulled away from the kiss, but still stayed close enough that their lips grazed as she spoke. "You don't have to ask anyone anything—I am always going to be yours. And you're *mine.* I decided."

Pav smirked. "That's how it is, then?"

"That's how it is."

"I like that."

She winked. "You better."

ABOUT THE AUTHOR

Bethany-Kris is a Canadian author, lover of much, and mother to four young sons, three cats, and four dogs. A small town in Eastern Canada where she was born and raised is where she has always called home. With her boys under her feet, a snuggling cat, barking dogs, and a spouse calling over his shoulder, she is nearly always writing something ... when she can find the time.

Find Bethany-Kris at:

www.bethanykris.com

OTHER BOOKS

Boykov Bratva

Fractured Ties
Essence of Fear

The Guzzi Legacy

Corrado
Alessio
Chris
Beni
Bene
Marcus

Renzo + Lucia

Privilege
Harbor
Contempt
Forever

Andino + Haven

Duty
Vow
Andino + Haven: The Complete Duet
One Last Time

John + Siena

Loyalty
Disgrace
John + Siena: The Complete Duet
John + Siena: Extended

Cross + Catherine

Always
Revere
Unruly
The Companion
Naz & Roz

Guzzi Duet

Unraveled, Book One
Entangled, Book Two
Cara & Gian: The Complete Duet

DeLuca Duet

Waste of Worth: Part One
Worth of Waste: Part Two

Standalone Titles

Pink
Pretty Lies
Dirty Pool
Effortless
Inflict
Cozen
Captivated
Dishonored

Donati Bloodlines

Thin Lies
Thin Lines
Thin Lives
Behind the Bloodlines
The Complete Trilogy

Filthy Marcellos

Antony
Lucian
Giovanni
Dante
Legacy
A Very Marcello Christmas
The Complete Collection

Seasons of Betrayal

Where the Sun Hides
Where the Snow Falls
Where the Wind Whispers
Seasons: The Complete Seasons of Betrayal Series

Gun Moll Trilogy

Gun Moll
Gangster Moll
Madame Moll

The Chicago War

Deathless & Divided
Reckless & Ruined
Scarless & Sacred
Breathless & Bloodstained
The Complete Series
Maldives & Mistletoe

The Russian Guns

The Arrangement
The Life
The Score
Demyan & Ana
Shattered
The Jersey Vignettes

FANTASY ROMANCE BY BETHANY-KRIS

The Hunted: A 9INE REALMS Novel

Find more on Bethany-Kris's website at www.bethanykris.com.

www.ingramcontent.com/pod-product-compliance
Lightning Source LLC
Chambersburg PA
CBHW051340020726
47501CB00007B/2186